EAST BAY GREASE

ALSO BY ERIC MILES WILLIAMSON

Novels

East Bay Grease
Two-Up
Welcome to Oakland

Short Fiction

14 Fictional Positions

Nonfiction / Criticism

Oakland, Jack London, and Me
Say It Hot: Essays on American Writers Living, Dying, and Dead
Say It Hot Volume II: Industrial Strength: Essays, Reviews and Interviews

Praise for *East Bay Grease*

"Williamson's writing becomes transcendent. His prose cuts loose in torrid rhythms that evoke the peril and exuberance of jazz."

—*The New York Times Book Review*

"A confident debut, an arresting, often harrowing read."

—*The London Times*

Praise for *Two-Up*

"...a little like falling face-first against a concrete slab. It puts you in close touch with cold reality and could even change you forever."

—*The San Francisco Chronicle Book Review*

"Some novelists enter readers' brains subtly. Not Eric Miles Williamson. He enters noisily, with a jackhammer. Williamson, the bard of the blue-collar laborer."

—*The Kansas City Star*

"*Two-Up* is rare work of fiction whose sharp realism and dark center recall the sagas of an earlier, more authentic sort. Williamson's triumph is to open up one of the great currents of American literature, the saga of the American worker, a bloody battered, disabused hero. Two-up is an effort where words never fail."

—*The Bloomsbury Review*

Praise for *Oakland, Jack London, And Me*

"Williamson's white-hot scorn for literary fashion lights up nearly every sentence here. One of the least politically correct texts of our time."

—*The Atlantic Monthly*

"Fans of *White Fang* and *The Iron Heel* will rejoice. The deconstructionists on the other hand...As if Norman Mailer had devoured Derrida and spit out the bones."

—*Kirkus Reviews*

"Williamson is the most effective in blasting the pretentious, theory-ridden, politically (if not ethically) correct academic Establishment. And his aim hits the target dead center in a tough but honest, often brilliant indictment of current literary critics with their supercilious and jargonish posturing."

—Earle Labor, editor of *The Portable Jack London*

Praise for *Welcome To Oakland*

"This powerful slice of greasy, grimy life is highly recommended."

—*Library Journal*

"Eric Miles Williamson is the mystic on the street corner."

—*East Bay Literary Examiner*

"Most readers will veer away the way they would from a street gang descending on their car with the iron and handguns... Williamson gives a contemporary turn on a literary genre pioneered by Hugo, Dostoyevsky and Celine and in the American canon by Kerouac, Burroughs and Bukowski...Ignoring Williamson would be a mistake."

—*The Washington Post*

ERIC MILES WILLIAMSON

EAST BAY GREASE

Down & Out Books Edition: June 2018

Down & Out Books
3959 Van Dyke Rd, Ste. 265
Lutz, FL 33558
www.DownAndOutBooks.com

Cover design by Lance Wright

ISBN: 1-948235-48-X
ISBN-13: 978-1-948235-48-8

For my sons,
Guthrie Mitchell Williamson
and
Turner Miles Anthony Williamson

CHAPTER ONE

Starting from Oakland

I smelled dope. My mother had a ten-hosed hookah in the front room, and every night she and the Angels sat around getting stoned and drinking Oly's.

"T-Bird, get your little ass out here," she said. "I know you're awake."

I opened the door. The front room looked like the school's yearly haunted house, the black light purpling the fluorescent posters. About eight or nine dudes sat around the hookah, hoses in their mouths and hands.

"I want you to meet someone," she said.

She was sitting next to an old guy. He didn't have a beard like the other men, just stubble. The top of his head was bald.

"This is your Uncle Ray," she said.

She gave him a look like she was going to slap him.

"So what," I said.

"Watch your mouth," she said.

She looked at Uncle Ray. "This is my son, T-Bird," she said.

He rolled the brass end of his hose slow between his thumb and index finger, looking at me while my mother stared at him.

His eyes were silvery and pale, like mine, shining even in the dark room. I couldn't watch them. I looked around at the other bikers, at the black light, at the candles, at my mother, then back to Uncle Ray. He kept staring at me.

"Come stand next to your Uncle Ray," my mother said.

The floor was sticky, and when I walked across the room my feet smacked each time I peeled up a foot. Everyone was watching me.

"Now what?" I said.

"Shut up and stand there," she said. She wet her hand and wiped it across my forehead, pulling my hair out of my eyes. "Stand up straight like a gentleman."

I stood there a long time. Everyone was looking at me except her—she was looking at everyone else, sweeping her eyes across their faces as if she was waiting for one of them to confess to a crime. Finally she looked at me. "Go back to bed," she said.

I went to my room and made like I was going to bed, but instead pressed my ear against the door.

"Well?" my mother said.

"Not a chance," Jimmy Flynn said.

"Nope," said Fat Fred. "No resemblance at all."

"Satisfied?" Uncle Ray said.

"Someone hand me a fucking beer," my mother said.

The front room the next morning was filled up bright light. My mother loved burning candles, and little candle stubs were stuck in beer bottles, in Spanada jugs, in a hollowed-out turtle shell, in teacup saucers, a hubcap, an abalone shell, in the woodwork of our grandfather clock, in the mouth of a human skull someone had given my mother as a present. About fifteen bikers lay passed out on the floor, on the Chesterfield, one with his face in a bowl of something, some kind of green crap in his hair. The doorway was blocked by Domer.

I nudged Domer with my foot. He didn't move. I nudged him again.

He jolted awake and went for his hunting knife.

"It's me," I said. "T-Bird."

Domer wrapped his hands around my chest, picked me up, and pitched me.

Everything went slow-motion. It was like being in an airplane, sailing over everything, the hookah, the bikers, the coffee table. I smashed into the wall by the fake fireplace.

Uncle Ray woke up.

"What the fuck's going on?" he said.

"Domer threw me. It's not my fault."

Uncle Ray stood up and walked over to Domer and kicked him in the stomach. Domer went for his knife, and Uncle Ray kicked his neck. Then Uncle Ray lifted Domer up by the armpits and slapped him twice. The backhand slap tore Domer's cheek.

"Don't you ever let me catch you fucking with the kid," Uncle Ray said.

He turned to me. "Come on," he said.

He put his hand out. His huge silver ring was bloody from Domer's face. That suited me fine. Fuck him.

I asked Uncle Ray to drop me off where the school bus was unloading the other kids. I climbed down from the bike and glanced over toward the bus. All the kids were looking at me. Stephano and Andrew got off the bus together.

"You're not my uncle," I said.

"Nope."

"Who are you, then?"

He didn't say anything.

"Who are you?" I said.

He looked at the kids staring at us. He pulled a cigarette from the pocket of his leather jacket and lit it and took a deep drag. He blew smoke from his nose. He said, "Stay out of Domer's way."

I nodded. "No shit," I said.

The bell rang and all the kids started inside the school.

"Thanks for the ride," I said.

Uncle Ray cranked on the throttle and let out the clutch and pulled away, shifting through the gears. Teachers looked out of the classroom windows.

In class, Stephano said, "Boss bike."

I nodded.

"Who is he?" Stephano said.

"That's my uncle," I said. "My Uncle Ray."

After school, Andrew said, "I want to see your house."

Andrew was my best friend, but no one at school knew it. I never talked to him at school because no one else liked him. Every day after school, the bus driver would stop the bus, step out, and hold up his STOP sign in the intersection, and when he did, my other friend, Stephano Kliranomos, and three or four other kids would beat up Andrew in the back of the bus. While they kicked and punched him, I always sat in my seat and tried not to listen, hoping they wouldn't come after me.

"Why don't you hit them back?" I said.

"I can't," Andrew said. "Do unto others as you would have them do unto you."

"They do unto you every day," I said. "And they're going to keep on doing it until you hit them back."

"My parents said that if they find out I've hit someone they'll beat me until I can't ever hit anyone again. Why don't you help me?"

I noticed my shoes were untied.

"Why don't you ever help?"

I didn't say anything. We both sat there quiet a long time.

"I don't want to go home," I told Andrew. "You really don't want to see my house. It's not that great an idea. Let's go to the fort instead."

It had taken us a year to dig the fort. After we dug the hole, we made a roof with corrugated tin, camouflaged it with dirt and leaves, and fitted rain gutters from U-shaped brick shingles, channeling the water away. We had plans to seal the dirt walls with plaster, then panel them. We had plans to run an extension cord from the house into the fort so we could have a lamp and a radio. We had plans to someday dig so many rooms that our fort would be the size of a house. Inside the fort it was quiet, and we couldn't hear the cars on the Nimitz Freeway backed up and trying to get out of Oakland and into San Francisco. We couldn't hear people screaming at each other out their apartment windows. If someone was getting beat up on the street, we couldn't hear it. When it rained we listened to the water slide along the tin, and when it wasn't raining sometimes we heard birds. It was as if we weren't even in Oakland.

"I want to see the motorcycles," Andrew said.

"Your parents forbid you to come to my house," I said. "You'll be in trouble if you get caught."

"They'll never find out," Andrew said.

"No."

"If you don't let me come to your house, I won't let you come to mine. No motorcycles, no fort."

I tried everything I could to talk Andrew out of it, but he wouldn't give in.

"If you don't take me to your house," Andrew said, "I'll let out Moses every time I think you're in the yard."

Moses was Andrew's parents' big black dog. Moses killed anything that moved—mice, cats, and one time a junkie who'd hopped the fence.

"My place is yours," I said.

On the way to my house we stopped at Jack London Park, a concrete slab with a slimy green pond in the middle. Before he got thrown in jail for punching my mother, Pop used to bring my brothers and me to this park, and we'd feed popcorn to the pigeons. He beat up my mother because he found out that while he was at work, she was hopping the fence to the neighbors' yard. The neighbors were the Hell's Angels—their headquarters was in the house behind ours. She was humping the Oakland chapter. My brothers had both been farmed out to foster homes, and I had to live with my mother. The last time I'd seen Pop was the night the astronauts landed on the moon. I missed the moon landing because my mother said I couldn't leave the table until I ate my liver. Every time I took a bite I gagged, so I sat there staring at my food. But I didn't have to finish my liver, because Pop and my mother started yelling at each other, and my mother picked up a knife.

Pop slugged my mother three times.

"You can go to hell," he said. "And you can take your goddamn kid with you."

The only people in Jack London Park were old ladies and old men and some winos. One of the winos pulled a handful of crumbs from his pocket and sprinkled them around his feet. A pigeon fluttered down and began pecking at the pile of crumbs. The rest dropped off the telephone wires and surrounded the food, jabbing at each other's necks with their beaks, acting like no one had fed them in a long time.

We took the shortcut to my house instead of crossing the bridge over the railroad tracks. We hopped the Cyclone fence that surrounded the graveyard. KEEP OUT signs dangled lame from the fence. It was an old Indian graveyard, and no one had been buried there in a hundred years. Most of the markers were chunks of splintered wood sticking up out of the ground. Cellophane wrappers blew around in little twisters, and the ground sparkled with broken glass like thousands of wrinkled stars.

One time, Stephano and his gang dragged Andrew into the graveyard and tied him up to a tombstone. It was a white tombstone, and it didn't have a name, just an etched cross and the dates 1888-1898. Andrew was ten years old like the dead person. Andrew screamed and screamed, but no one could hear him.

"Tell God to save you," Stephano said. "If he's so studly, tell him to untie the ropes."

"I'll forgive you," Andrew said. "And so will Jesus. Please untie me."

"Admit God's a phony," Stephano said.

Stephano kept trying to get Andrew to do it, but he wouldn't. So Stephano left him there. Andrew was lucky that I saw the whole thing from across the railroad tracks, or he might have been tied up to that tombstone all night.

When we turned the corner, we saw the motorcycles lining the street, handlebars all tipped in the same direction. Some of the guys were working on their bikes in the yard. Beer bottles stood in rows on the railings of the porch, and cigarette and dope smoke chugged out the windows as if the house was on fire. The house we rented had a long gravel driveway and plum trees in the back yard. The yard was big enough to build a fort as good as Andrew's if I'd wanted to. Flies buzzed over the plums that rotted in the dirt.

Then bottles started breaking in the house and everyone was yelling. A man crashed through the screen and tumbled down the steps of the porch and lay in the gravel bleeding from his ear. A peg-legged biker stood in the doorway and pointed his cane at the guy on the ground.

"Don't touch the peg," he said. "I told you not to touch the peg. You *know* not to touch the peg."

Andrew started backpedaling.

"No problem," I said. "Uncle Ray will take care of us."

When we got into the house, Fat Fred blocked us off and said, "T-Bird brought me a little boy for dinner!" He grabbed Andrew under the shoulders and lifted him up and pushed Andrew's head against the ceiling. Andrew was about to start crying when Fat Fred let him down, and Andrew bolted out the door.

"I was only playing," Fat Fred said.

Of all the Angels, I liked Fat Fred best. He was so fat his butt went all the way back to his Harley's sissy-bar. Fat Fred always rode alone. His stringy blond beard looked like a straw broom. One time, my mother made a meatloaf and Fat Fred ate the whole thing. I used to poke him in the belly when he wasn't expecting it, and then he'd try to chase me down. He usually didn't catch me, but when he did, he always thought of some way of getting me back. One time, he tied me up alongside the hanging motorcycle frames in the garage and tickled me until I cried.

I ran down the street after Andrew, and a bike came up and rode onto the sidewalk and cut me off. It was Domer. He knocked down his kickstand.

"You see this?" he said. He put a finger against his gashed cheek. "I said you see this, you little fuck?"

He left his bike there on the sidewalk and dragged me back to the house, down the gravel driveway into the back yard.

He cupped his hands, and then he popped my ears and threw me down. I landed in the rotten plums. Domer was saying something to me, but I couldn't hear him. He stood me up and popped my ears again, and again he popped them. I got dizzy and fell down.

Domer turned me around, and he kicked my ass so hard I fell on my face. I got right on out of there.

I ran down the railroad tracks behind the house toward the old Indian graveyard, heading toward Andrew's. When I got to the graveyard, I saw Stephano and an older kid, a sixth grader who always had detention for getting in fights. I couldn't hear them, but I saw them laughing. The ground began to rumble and I felt a train coming, but I couldn't hear a whistle or the clacking of its wheels. The spiraling light of the train whipped across the graveyard and then into my eyes and then across the tracks and against the warehouses on the other side, rippling across the bent-up and banged metal. I jumped the fence and tore my jacket on the barbed wire, and when I came down on the other side I started running toward Stephano and the sixth grader. Andrew was on the ground twisted into a knot, his legs pulled tight against his chest.

Stephano and the other kid opened their mouths and raised

their fists into the air and I think they were cheering for me to help them beat on Andrew. I saw their mouths move but I couldn't hear them for the dull ache in my ears and the rumble of the train, and I wanted to rescue Andrew and not rescue Andrew, I wanted to pound Andrew and to save him, I wanted to beat his brains out on a tombstone and at the same time cut Stephano into pieces and feed him to Andrew's dog, Moses.

I stopped running when I got to Andrew, and the train was still passing and it was a very long train and Andrew was begging for me to help, his eyes watery and pleading for me to admit I was his friend. But instead of saving him I screamed, and I couldn't hear my scream but my ears popped and my throat went sore with pain, and I kicked Andrew and I kicked him again, and Stephano and the other kid laughed and kept laughing, and then I turned around to them and still I was screaming, and then I boiled over and swung my arm and smashed Stephano in the nose. He dropped to his knees, and when the old kid leaned down to help, I kicked his face. Andrew got up and started running, and then I started running too. I tried to catch up to Andrew, but he was scared of me and he ran faster than anyone has ever run.

I walked to Andrew's house and knocked. Andrew answered. He only opened the door enough to get his eyeball in the crack. The door was chained.

He said something to me, but I couldn't hear him.

"Let's go out to the fort," I said.

He shook his head.

"The fort," I said.

He said something and softly shut the door. I went to the side of the house and started over the fence. When I got my head over the top, I saw Moses. He was tearing apart a bird, feathers hanging out of his mouth, pitching his head back and forth like he was going to twist his own head off. Moses ripped his head back and forth, feathers flying, parts of the bird dropping onto the dirt. Then Moses looked at me.

The windows of the apartments and houses were dark, and I knew it was late. I hoped my mother wasn't home when I got there.

A FOR RENT sign was stuck in the lawn. A dozen Harleys lined the driveway. I walked around back of the house and tried the bathroom window, but it was locked. In the back yard, I looked at the plum trees without plums, without leaves, networks of branches like giant cobwebs. Fog reflected streetlights down into Oakland.

The light came on in my mother's bedroom. Shadows of her and a man undressed each other through the curtains. They started hugging, kneeling on the bed.

I ducked down and started toward the window so they wouldn't see me. I knew if I got caught, I'd have hell to pay. My mother really knew how to punish, how to teach you about what to do and what not to do. If she punished you for doing something wrong, you never got caught doing it again. One time she found a bunch of candles I'd stolen from the Bel-Air market. She made me bring them back to the store and make a full confession to the manager, then when we got home she poured boiling water on my hands so I'd remember not to steal. One time she caught me eating a peanut butter and jelly sandwich between mealtimes, and to show her friends she knew how to discipline me, she made me put my hand on the ironing board and she ironed it. "Think about this the next time you put your hand where it doesn't belong, you little bastard," she said. She heard me cussing once and made me eat two bars of Lava soap, and I wasn't allowed to spit any out. Another time, she caught me having a spit-fight with Stephano, and she put me in a corner with a tin pot and made me spit and spit until the pot was full, then made me drink the spit while all her boyfriends watched. Fat Fred said, "Aren't you being a little harsh?" and my mother told him, "If I don't teach the boy some manners he'll end up like all of you."

I slowly stood, until my eyes rose above the sill. I could see between the curtains. Their legs were knotted together. They lay on their sides, wiggling. The man stroked my mother's hair. It was Uncle Ray. His legs were thin and hairy. His shorts had holes in them.

He pushed my mother on her back and got on top of her. He bucked and bucked. My mother's legs were stiff, feet pointed at the ceiling.

I sank down to the ground and sat there for a while, and then I stood up and went to the garage and got the shovel.

I walked into the back yard and stood by the fence. The wind blew and the branches of the plum trees shook. The light went off in my mother's room.

The smell of the wet, rotting plums beneath my feet was sweet.

I jabbed the shovel at the ground. And man, I started digging.

CHAPTER TWO

The Girl Haters Club

It wasn't long after I saw Uncle Ray humping my mother that Mr. Nasimiento, the principal of our school, held "Boys' Assembly." He told us that if we had intercourse with girls, we would get VD. VD made you go crazy, get sores, go blind, and sometimes it killed you. I thought you had to screw girls to get them pregnant and to catch VD, but the principal said all it took was intercourse. I looked up *intercourse* in the dictionary, and the first definition in the dictionary said *intercourse* meant contact with another person or another group, communication. The second definition said "coitus." I looked up *coitus*, and it said "intercourse." I figured if intercourse wasn't fucking it had something to do with eating a girl out, and if it was so nasty down there that you could get diseases and die just from going near it, I wasn't going to have anything to do with that shit. I decided to start the Girl Haters Club.

By unanimous vote I was elected the president, because no one hated those bitches more than me. Lunchtimes, on the thin brown tablet paper that tore if you wrote too hard with your pencil, I drew customized tanks designed especially to exterminate girls. The tanks featured lures like toilets, since girls went to the bathroom so much, bear traps, gigantic hammers, iron safes that fell from tow-truck winches, catapults that threw anvils, girl-size meat grinders with nothing but their legs and feet showing while they got ground into burger. In the library I made photocopies of the Girl Killer tanks and I passed out the copies to the other members of the Girl Haters Club.

We wrote out a set of rules.

Rule Number One: Never touch a girl.

Rule Number Two: If a girl touches you, wash the infected part of your body with soap and hot water three times.

Rule Number Three: Never play with girls, at recess or any other time.

Rule Number Four: When warball is played at PE, it is the duty of Girl Haters Club members to demolish all girls before trying to kill boys.

Rule Number Five: The Girl Haters Club is secret.

Rule Number Six: If any member of the Girl Haters Club breaks any of the rules, he will be killed.

Laureen Miranda was the worst girl of all. She followed me around wanting to do whatever I did, play tetherball, football, kickball. Sometimes when I'd be riding my bike home, she'd ride up behind and follow me. She left things in my lift-top desk, love notes, sugar-candy hearts with gross little sayings burned in red, a wooden *T* for my name, T-Bird, she'd carved out of a piece of plywood, candy canes at Christmas. In class she stared at me and her friends giggled and acted stupid. The other members of the Girl Haters Club made fun of me. Laureen Miranda was about a foot taller than I was. I hated her.

For a class project, we took care of pet rats. Each day a different kid got to feed Lester and Lucy and play with them and clean their cage.

It was Laureen Miranda's turn to take care of Lester and Lucy, and after lunchtime, when we were working on our state capitals, Laureen dropped the lid of her desk, and then she started screaming and crying. Mrs. Woodhouse rushed to Laureen's desk and we all watched. Laureen's dress was spotted with bright red blood. Lester the Rat's head hung from the lip of the desk. Mrs. Woodhouse opened the desk and picked Lester up by the tail.

"It was not rat time, Laureen," Mrs. Woodhouse said. "You were not supposed to have Lester in your desk."

She held Lester up for all of us to see.

"Responsibility," she said, "begins with obeying rules."

Mrs. Woodhouse looked at Laureen and told her not to cry, that everything would be fine and that she should obey rules and that we could get another rat to replace Lester. Laureen stopped crying and sat sniffling at her desk.

When Mrs. Woodhouse walked outside to get rid of Lester, I leaned over to Laureen.

"Murderer," I whispered.

She started crying hard again.

"Murderer."

For Stephano's birthday, Mr. and Mrs. Kliranomos gave him an Erector Set, complete with a battery-operated motor and wheels and pulleys and lights and a buzzer.

As a Girl Haters project, we built a car from the Erector Set and stole one of his sister's Barbie dolls. We swiped some M-80s and cherry bombs and firecrackers from his father, and before school one day we put everything together. We tied the Barbie, naked and pussyless, to the car, and lined the car with a network of M-80s and cherry bombs, linked together with timed firecracker fuses. We timed the fuses by unraveling them and scraping the gunpowder out, then twisting them together into a long fuse that would burn slow.

When the recess bell rang and everyone went running back to their classrooms, we set the car in the hallway, taped the motor-wire to the battery, and lit the fuse.

Two or three minutes later, after Mrs. Woodhouse started the daily history lesson (we were learning about how Cortes brought civilized ways to the Indians) the explosions started.

All the kids got under the desks like in an air-raid drill, and Mrs. Woodhouse pulled the heavy green curtain across the windows in case they shattered.

Stephano and I looked at each other and tried not to laugh. The explosions kept going off. They sounded like gunshots.

When the blasts stopped, Mrs. Woodhouse went out into the hallway and I heard the teachers yelling at each other.

Mrs. Woodhouse came back into the room.

"All clear," she said. She pulled the curtain open, and we got back into our desks.

She was holding some tin strips of Erector Set and a scorched Barbie leg.

"Anyone who knows the responsible party gets an A for the day," she said.

But no one except us in the Girl Haters Club knew, and the teachers never found us out.

One day Mrs. Woodhouse found the pile of photocopies in my desk.

"What are these?"

"Drawings," I said.

"Girl Exterminator Number One," she read. She flipped the pages. "Girl Exterminator Number Two, Girl Exterminator Number Three. The Girl Haters Club Rules. Girl Exterminator Number Four."

She looked at me. All the kids in the class stared at their desks.

"T-Bird, you will stay after class."

After class, Mrs. Woodhouse sat behind her desk and looked at me.

"Well," she said. "What do you have to say for yourself?"

"Nothing."

"Do you really hate girls?"

"Yes."

"I can understand you not *liking* girls at this age," she said. "But you shouldn't *hate* them."

I didn't say anything.

"Do you hate me?"

"You're not a girl."

"What am I?"

"A teacher," I said.

"Do you hate your mother?"

I didn't say anything.

"What would your mother have to say if I called her about this?"

I didn't say anything. I wasn't afraid of her telling my mother. My mother had been gone for five days already, off on a motorcycle trip with her fuck-buddies, and she probably wouldn't be back for a while, not until she was all fucked out.

"Why do you hate girls?"

"They give you VD," I said. "They're not good for anything. They're lousy at sports. They can't play tetherball, or football, or hardball, or basketball, or warball, or soccer. They can't keep up if you ride bikes with them. They can't even play chess. If they smack you upside the face you can't hit them back. If they kick you in the balls you have to smile and act like a gentleman and pretend you don't want to kill them. If one tears your arms off or pokes your eyes out you have to say thank you instead of carving her heart out with your teeth," I said. "If a girl hits me, it's fine. She can beat me until I'm bloody and bruised and my bones are all broke. But if I hit her, I get in trouble. They can do whatever they want to us, can't they? Can't they?" I said. "Can't they?"

Mrs. Woodhouse looked somewhere I couldn't see.

"Plus, they're fuckng stupid and they have mustaches," I said.

"Watch your mouth," Mrs. Woodhouse said.

* * *

When I got home after school the place was empty, not even any bikers. The phone was ringing. I picked it up.

"May I please speak with Mrs. Murphy?"

It was Mrs. Woodhouse.

"She's not home."

"And when will she be home, T-Bird?"

"I don't know."

"And your father?"

"He doesn't live with us anymore. He won't be back for a long time."

"If you're lying, I'll make sure you get suspended."

"I'm not a liar," I said. "Try again in a week."

I went outside and into the back yard. The air was cold and the ground was muddy, puddles caked with ice. The dead frosty leaves under my feet cracked. In the middle of the backyard was the tetherball pole Fat Fred had made for me by filling a car tire with concrete and putting the pole in the center of the concrete-filled tire. I lifted the ball and punched it. The ball soared around the pole, and when it got back around to me I punched it again, my forearm meeting the ball on the fly, and the ball went around again, and I punched again and again and the rope shortened and shortened until the ball knotted on the ring at the top of the pole. I jumped and tipped the ball loose and let the ball unwind slow until it was free and then I punched again.

I played tetherball against myself until long after the sun went down, the dark ball against the gray cloudy sky lit by the lights of Oakland, and I didn't quit until my forearm was bleeding.

The next morning, Stephano and Chico, the other members of the Girl Haters Club, were waiting for me in front of the school.

"You told," Stephano said. "You rat-finked, didn't you?"

"I swear," I said. "I didn't say a word."

"You broke Rule Number Five," Stephano said. "You revealed our secret identities."

"This calls for an impeachment," Chico said.

I looked at Chico hard. I wanted to sock him or tie him up to a tombstone. "What's an impeachment?" I said.

Chico smiled and looked smug. "It means, illiterate, that we're going to fire you from office. Or we might have to kill you. Since Stephano's vice president, he'll be the new president, and since I'm vice-vice president, I'll move up to vice president."

"I didn't rat-fink," I said. "But if you impeach me, I *will* tell. I'll tell that you're the other members and that you made the Erector Set bomb. I swear if you impeach me I'll rat-fink."

"You swear on your mother's grave you didn't rat-fink?" Chico said.

"That's no good, swearing on his mother's grave," Stephano said. "His mother is a bitch. Make him swear to God." He pulled his silver cross necklace from under his shirt and shoved it at me.

"That's no good either," Chico said. "He doesn't believe in God. He's a white-boy heathen."

"I swear to you guys," I said. "My best friends in the world."

They talked it over.

"To us?" Stephano said. "You swear?"

"You guys," I said. "What else I got? You're my family."

Every night that week Mrs. Woodhouse called, but my mother still hadn't come home.

Late Saturday afternoon I was smoking Pall Malls I'd swiped from my mother's bedroom and watching *Ultraman* on television. He was fighting a giant dragon that knew judo, and the dragon's tail swung back and forth knocking over the buildings of Tokyo. The red light on Ultraman's chest was blinking, which meant his powers were running down, and soon he'd have to fly back up to the sun to get recharged.

Someone knocked on the door. I put out my cigarette and said, "Who is it?" while I tried to wave away the smoke. No one answered. "Who is it?" I said again, louder. I hid the cigarette pack under the sofa and I got a knife from the kitchen sink and opened the door. It was Mrs. Woodhouse and Mr. Ball, the truant officer. He packed a gun. Mr. Ball took a lot of bull from us kids. We'd ask him how Mrs. Ball was, and how all his little Balls were, and he'd laugh and he'd say, "Hanging in there." For a narc, he was cool. He'd caught some sixth graders in the field smoking pot and not busted them.

"She's not home," I said. "And I haven't been playing hooky, so you can't bust me."

"We're not here to 'bust' you," Mrs. Woodhouse said. "Can we come in?"

"Why?"

"You don't need the knife, T-Bird," Mr. Ball said.

I put the knife back in the sink. I looked around the house. I hadn't cleaned up my stuff since my mother had been gone, and my dirty clothes were all over the place, on the floor, on the sofa, on the kitchen table with my homework. The garbage basket overflowed with empty chili cans and macaroni-and-cheese boxes. I needed to do the dishes.

"How long has your mother been gone?" Mr. Ball said.

"I don't know," I said. "A week."

"She must smoke an awful lot," Mr. Ball said. He looked at me.

I shrugged. "Guess so," I said.

Mrs. Woodhouse opened the refrigerator. She pulled out an old potato, roots growing from it like bony fingers. "What do you eat?" she said.

"Peanut butter. Crackers. Wheaties and Cheerios. There's some cans of raviolis in the cupboard. There's pork and beans. I know how to make grilled-cheese sandwiches."

Mr. Ball took Mrs. Woodhouse outside and they talked, but

I couldn't hear what they said. They came back in, and Mr. Ball had a briefcase with him. He opened it and took out some papers, and he cleared a spot on the kitchen table and began filling out a form.

"Would you like to come to my house for the weekend?" Mrs. Woodhouse said.

"Why?"

"It would be like a vacation," she said. "I can show you the town I live in, Berkeley. And you can meet my children. We're having a barbecue tomorrow."

"I don't like Berkeley," I said. "Hippies, homos, and weirdos." I turned to Mr. Ball. "What are you writing? I didn't do anything wrong."

"A note to your mother, T-Bird," he said. "In case she comes home and wonders where you are."

"Right," I said.

"What happened to your arm?" she asked. She lifted my arm and looked at the scab that ran from my wrist to my elbow.

"Tetherball," I said.

"Get your toothbrush and some clothes," she said.

"What's wrong with my clothes?" I said.

Mrs. Woodhouse drove a car that only had three wheels, two in the front and one in the back and it looked like a futuristic bubble. We got on the freeway and turned off in the Oakland hills and drove through wooded neighborhoods with mowed lawns and paint that looked new.

We drove a while longer through curved streets with only houses, no liquor stores and no Chinese markets and nobody walking on the sidewalks, just house after house after house, not even any factories or warehouses, tree branches hanging over the road like twisted broken power cables.

Her house was the biggest I'd ever been in. Two stories, a bathroom on each floor, kitchen the size of our front room. It seemed like all the walls were lined with books, books everywhere, even in the bathroom, old ones with leather binding and gold lettering on the spines. Her house smelled like a library someone had cooked pot roast in, musty from old paper and sweet from cooked molasses on meat.

It was late, and after she showed me around the house, she showed me the guest bedroom. After I stripped to my skivvies, I started going through the dresser drawers. They were loaded with teenager clothes—a tie-dyed T-shirt, ratty Levi's bell-bottoms, wool Mexican ponchos and a pair of moccasins and flower-shaped brass belt buckles, all the socks matched and carefully folded together.

I turned around and saw Mrs. Woodhouse. She stood in the hall wearing a nightgown. It was creepy seeing her in something other than her teacher dresses. She looked a lot older. She didn't look like Mrs. Woodhouse at all.

"Where's Mr. Woodhouse?"

"Would you like to see a picture of him?" Mrs. Woodhouse asked.

She led me into another bedroom. Between the bookshelves hung old black-and-white pictures in silver frames. She pointed to one of the pictures.

In the picture stood a man in a tuxedo and a young woman in a wedding dress.

"Handsome wasn't he?"

"Is that *you*?" I asked. She nodded. "You were really pretty then," I said.

"He died a long time ago," Mrs. Woodhouse said.

"Where's your son?"

"Canada, I believe."

Sunday morning I woke up to the smell of bacon frying. I put on my clothes and went downstairs, and there was Mrs. Woodhouse, cooking. Eggs, bacon, toast, orange juice. It was like a

Denny's or a Sambo's. I ate so much my stomach hurt.

We got in her three-wheeled car, a Citroen, and drove to the university area. Weirdos walked the streets everywhere I looked, hippies with long hair and people playing banjos and guitars and wooden flutes and blind people with their leaky eyes bulging yellow like pigeon eggs and cripples on crutches and in wheelchairs wearing army clothes. Sometimes there were so many bums and hobos sleeping on the sidewalk we had to step onto the street to get around them. I smelled marijuana and vomit.

We got onto campus and it didn't look any different than the streets—hippies, homos, and bums—people squatted Indian-style in the squares selling silver and turquoise jewelry and buckskin vests and black-light posters of Chinese dragons and skeletons riding Harleys. We walked into a library with marble floors and cigarette smoke floating in the window light.

"Have you ever been in a real library before?"

"No," I said.

"What would you like to know about? Anything you can think of."

"Dynamite," I said.

She cut me a look, then led me to a huge room bigger than the school cafeteria, filled with card catalogs. She pulled out a drawer and took it over to a table and we sat down in big wooden chairs. I flipped through the cards. There were hundreds of books on dynamite.

"Anything you want to know about," she said. "You can learn about it in the library."

She took me to a museum, and in the museum there were suits of armor from the Spanish conquistadores and swords and knives, and there was a skeleton of a dinosaur big as a house. When we left the museum we heard music playing and we sat in the bleachers watching the marching band practice. It was the lamest music I ever heard, and they looked like dorks marching around in their lame uniforms. We went into an auditorium and there were hundreds of tables set up and at each table people played chess.

The Berkeley Mrs. Woodhouse showed me wasn't anything like the Berkeley I'd been to with my mother.

Laureen Miranda got in line at the Girl Haters Club designated "No Girls Allowed" tetherball court the next morning before school.

"You can't play on this court," I said.

"It's a free country," she said.

"No," I said. "It's not," I said. "Murderer."

She shrieked and then she socked me in the mouth. I didn't sock her back, and she socked me again. She kept hitting me, and she was beating me up, and I knew I wasn't supposed to hit girls, but I popped her one anyway. She started crying and she ran to the classroom and rat-finked on me.

Mrs. Woodhouse came out of the room onto the playground and Laureen followed along behind and they walked up to the tetherball court, where I was winning against Stephano.

"T-Bird," she said. "Did you hit Laureen?"

I nodded.

Her face didn't change. She didn't look mad, but she reached out her hand and grabbed the bottom of my ear and pulled me all the way across the playground to the principal's office.

After she left, Mr. Nasimiento looked at me.

"Did you hit Laureen Miranda?"

I nodded.

"Do you know that you're a boy and you're not supposed to hit girls?"

I looked at my shoes. "Yes," I said.

"Then why did you hit her?"

"She's bigger than me," I said. "She hit me first. She was beating me up. She's huge. Have you seen her? She was kicking my ass. It really hurt." I showed him the red marks her fists made on my arm. "Look."

Mr. Nasimiento looked like he was going to laugh at me, and then he straightened out his face and looked serious.

"I'm letting you off with a warning this time," he said. "See that it doesn't happen again."

Stephano and Chico were waiting for me in the hallway.

"Well?" Stephano said.

"No problem," I said.

"Our president!" Chico said.

"Tetherball, anyone?" Stephano said.

We laughed.

We walked down the hallway, and when we stepped outside the doors, there were the girls, all the girls of the fourth grade standing in a line, shoulder to shoulder. They blocked our way. Laureen Miranda stood in the center with her fists clenched.

Mrs. Woodhouse stood across the playground looking at us, and then she turned around and walked into her classroom.

I was going to put on some of Pop's old jazz records after I got home. My mother wouldn't allow me to play them when she was around, but when she'd start her Ford Galaxy in the driveway, I'd play them on the Garrard turntable and picture Pop standing in the front room of the first house I remember living in, surrounded by his tropical-fish tanks, his tarnished silver Conn trumpet to his lips, blowing choruses with the players, his face puffed and red, his eyes closed, scarred and torn fingers tripping over the valves gentle, his entire body filled with love. My mother hated his music as much as she hated him, and one time she came home and heard me listening to *Kind of Blue* and took the record off the turntable and broke it. "Jazz," she said. She broke most of the records, threw them against the walls, ripped the album covers into shreds. The next morning, I found fourteen albums that weren't broken and hid them under my bed.

When I got home, though, someone was playing Creedence Clearwater Revival on the turntable. My mother hadn't come back from wherever she'd gone, but some of her buddies were sitting in the front room drinking beer. They were bitching about women, telling stories about all the times they'd been fucked over by women who wouldn't act like they should act.

"What the hell happened to you?" one of the guys said.

"A fight," I said. "What do you think?"

One of my eyes was swollen shut. I had a bloody nose. I was limping.

"Women?"

"Women," I said.

They let me join in on their conversation.

They gave me a beer.

They didn't want to join the Girl Haters Club, but they told me I was on the right goddamn track if I ever wanted to get anywhere in this world.

CHAPTER THREE

Mama's Boy

I found out the reason my mother hadn't been home for so long was because she'd been in a motorcycle accident. Fat Fred told me that she'd ridden into the mountains on a three-wheeler, and the bike hit a soft shoulder and she got pitched—rammed her head into a barbed-wire-fence post. She'd been in the hospital for nearly a month. He told me it was best if I didn't visit her in the hospital because it was a pretty gruesome sight, her head shaved and stitched together like Frankenstein. I was glad she was gone. I wished she would stay away forever and I could just get on the back of Fat Fred's Harley and ride to the end of the earth, as far away from Oakland as I could get.

In the beginning the guys were always talking about her horrible accident, and I had to pretend like I was sad about it. After a while, though, they hardly mentioned her at all, but with my mother gone, more and more people crashed out in the living room, in my mother's room, wherever there was enough space to stretch out and sleep off a drunk. And they weren't just the Angels. They were hippies, bums, homos—every brand of human shit in Oakland. It was as if Berkeley had invaded our turf.

I didn't mind, though. I almost always got a ride to school, and usually on a Harley. And no one had smacked me around since my mother had left.

* * *

I was lying in bed trying to sleep. It was past midnight, and I had to get up early the next day because I'd been thrown off the school bus. The party in the front room was loud—bottles breaking, men laughing, the stereo booming over and over "Inna-Gadda-Davida." My bedroom door swung open, letting in the stink of beer and men and marijuana.

A dude who'd just come to town stood in the doorway. He was too skinny to be one of the bikers. His pants were too tight, and he wore a tie-dyed hippie T-shirt with the sleeves cut off. His black hair hung halfway down his chest. His face was pimpled up. He looked kind of sad.

He closed the door behind him and he stood there.

"What?" I said. "What?"

But he didn't say anything. He didn't move.

My door opened and the light came on. It was Fat Fred. He looked around the room for an instant, his eyebrows pulled close together. He looked at the guy, then at me, then at the guy again, and then Fat Fred grabbed the skinny guy by the hair and tugged his head back. "What the fuck's going on?" he said.

"Nothing," the guy said.

"He hit me," I said.

"Bullshit," the guy said. "I didn't touch the little fuck. He's a lying little fuck."

"He came in here and he hit me," I said. "He's hippie scum."

Fat Fred grabbed a handful of the guy's hair and twirled it round his fist until it was knotted tight. Then Fat Fred slapped the guy, cracked him upside the head hard, knocked him down. He picked him back up by the ear and dragged him out of the room and threw him to the floor. Everyone in the living room laughed, and some of them slapped the guy around a little just for the hell of it before they kicked his ass right on out of there.

"You set your alarm? That's why I came in here in the first place."

"School sucks," I said.

"Lock your bedroom door from now on," Fat Fred said. "There's all types of freaks around here."

Before he closed my door, he turned and said, "And don't lie to me again."

Earlier that day, Teddy the bus driver had snuck back into the bus when he was supposed to be outside holding up his STOP sign. Stephano was slugging Andrew. Andrew had gotten even more religious than he already was. He had one of those stupid happy-faces God addicts get, one of those faces that says, "I'm a stupid son of a bitch, and I'm glad. Please, please sock me in the face so I can smile at you like an idiot." You'd say something to him, and he'd start rattling off about God and the devil and Mary and Jesus and all the rest of the Bible gang, hillbilly names like Ezekiel, Noah, Jerimiah.

Being happy and stupid didn't stop Andrew from trying to make everyone else unhappy. He must have spent all his time tracking me and Stephano, spying on us, because he started rat-finking on everything we did. He finked to the principal when we blew up a toilet in the bathroom with an M-80. He finked when we broke old Mrs. Woodhouse's car window with my hammer. When Stephano and me crawled underneath the teachers' cars and cut all the wires and cables we could find, Andrew finked. Stephano and I were on probation now, and if we got caught doing anything else, we'd have to go to Oakland Elementary, the reform school that had even more black kids than ours.

"I got you punks this time," Teddy the bus driver said.

He was standing at the other end of the bus. Teddy always needed a shave, but the top of his head was bald and brown, the skin worn and spotted like an old potato.

All the kids on the bus were quiet, some of them watching Teddy, some looking back toward Stephano and me.

"I didn't hit him," I said.

"Andrew?" Teddy said.

"Stephano and T-Bird," Andrew said.

"You know I didn't hit you," I told Andrew. "I didn't hit him," I said.

"Stephano and T-Bird," Andrew said. He gave me a smug look, one of those God loves *me* but not *you* looks.

Stephano started rubbing Andrew's arms, trying to act as if he'd been goofing around, play-boxing or just trying to scare Andrew. But Andrew was sniveling, and tears streaked his cheeks.

Teddy crossed his arms over his chest, forearms bulging. He pointed toward the door of the bus.

I started down the aisle first, and Stephano followed me. Andrew was hamming it up now, squealing like a pig. "Please, Teddy," Andrew screamed. He sobbed and cried and screamed some more. "Please, Teddy, do not punish them. They know not what they do. It is for God to punish the wicked. We must forgive. We must be merciful. We must not judge. Jesus will judge them and God will send them to hell where they will burn forever in rolling pits of flaming sulfur. They will have their reward."

Teddy followed us out of the bus and onto the sidewalk.

"I'm not through with you punks yet," he said.

We stopped and looked at him.

"I don't want to see either of you on my bus again, or I tell Mr. Nasimiento, got it?"

I looked at Teddy's shoes. They were work boots, greasy and old, the leather cracking and the seams coming apart.

Stephano hacked on the sidewalk. "It's a lousy bus anyway," he said.

Stephano and I were better friends before his cousin Kenny came to town. We used to stack up rocks and branches and boards on the railroad tracks and try to derail the trains. Once we got into a Wonder Bread delivery truck and dismantled the entire dashboard, snipping wires and unscrewing the gauges and swiping all the knobs. We'd get chunks of wood rotten and crawling with termites from the dump and we'd slip the wood under people's pier-and-beam houses. We'd mix up batches of sugar water at his house, and we'd pour the sugar water on people's window ledges so the ants would invade. We'd pour bleach on people's flower beds. We took off the lug nuts of some rich dude's Camaro, but we never did find out where he was or how fast he was going when his wheels fell off and he wrecked.

I ate dinner at Stephano's most of the time. Stephano's mother would stand between our chairs, waiting for us to finish so that she could put more food on our plates. She'd feed us until our bellies hurt so bad we didn't even want to go outside.

But now that his cousin Kenny had come, everything had changed. After school, Stephano hurried home instead of playing with me. Stephano and Kenny did almost everything together. They went to Berkeley and hung out with the hippies, or they went to the Haight in San Francisco. Kenny had a great collection of dirty magazines, Stephano told me. Kenny had been to Vietnam. He had a collection of gook noses he'd cut off the faces of the commies he'd killed.

After we got thrown off the bus, I asked Stephano if he wanted to go over to the high school. I held up my hammer and wire cutters.

"I'm not into that kid shit anymore," Stephano said.

I started toward my house. I walked past the row of shotgun shacks built when Kaiser first brought the Negroes to Oakland during World War II to build the ships. When the war ended, Kaiser fired them all and turned Oakland into an instant ghetto, all the Negroes pissed off for good and still. At the intersection were two liquor stores and two bars. Weeds broke through the concrete sidewalk. The branches of the trees were bare and motionless and tangled with the telephone wires that crisscrossed the street. You could hear people screaming at each other, but you couldn't tell which house the screaming was coming from. All the curtains were closed.

It was dark outside when I got up for school. I pulled my pack of Pall Mall's from under my bed. I lit a cigarette and I touched the match to both the candles in my room. I walked to my bedroom window. It was raining. The garage door was open, and many of the motorcycles were parked inside, the chrome forks and spokes and engines sparkling as if lined with strings of tiny lights. A couple men in the front room were talking. Pop had been gone so long I couldn't remember the way his voice sounded. I stood at the window watching the dark rain until the sky started to turn gray.

Before I left the house, the phone rang. Some of the guys who worked were already gone. The rest were sleeping on the couches, in the chairs, some sprawled out on the floor. Fat Fred sat in Pop's La-Z-Boy, his arms at his sides, chin against his chest.

I answered the phone. It was Stephano. He asked me if I wanted a ride to school since it was raining. He was getting a ride from Kenny, and Kenny said I could come too.

A car pulled up in front of the house. It was an old Volkswagen painted up with flowers and peace signs and psychedelic curves and swirls. They sat in the car and waited with the engine running. Black smoke lifted from beneath the car. Heavy clouds of steamy exhaust chugged from the tailpipes.

Stephano got out and let me climb in the back seat.

The car smelled like wet socks and had the Volkswagen odor of scorched oil.

Kenny turned around and looked at me between the black vinyl bucket seats.

His face was gray and gaunt and covered with tiny pits and

grooves. His hair was dark and straight. He had cut himself shaving, and a piece of toilet paper stuck to his chin, a dot of red blood in the middle.

He smiled.

I looked at him. I didn't know what to do. I couldn't get out because I was in the back seat. Kenny was the guy that had been in my room the night before.

"This is my buddy, T-Bird," Stephano said.

"We've met," Kenny said.

The engine was loud. The windshield wipers pumped steadily and a smudge of tar spread across the glass. Kenny's window was cracked opened and nails of rain shot into the car. The right sleeve of my jacket was wet.

"Where we going?" I said.

"Want to cut school today?" Stephano said. "Kenny said he'd write us notes."

"I want to go to school," I said.

"Since when?" Stephano said. "School's for pussies."

It was raining very hard. Leaves and mud and paper and garbage choked the gutters and storm drains. The fog lamps of the avenues faded in and out, now bright, now dull and wavering. The windows of the Volkswagen were steamed bad.

We drove into the Oakland hills, away from the city. I rubbed the window with my hand so I could see outside. The road was winding and lined with pine trees and wet gray bushes. Stephano hummed some crappy Beatles song.

We pulled onto a dirt road. It was slick with layers of muck, and the side windows of the Volkswagen became caked. I stared at my hands. I had never before noticed how pink my skin was.

We stopped in a clearing. A barn was in front of the car. Rain tinked against the roof of the Volkswagen like thousands of tiny ball-bearings. Stephano and Kenny opened their doors.

"Come on, T-Bird," Stephano said.

Kenny walked behind us. Stephano walked to the side of the barn and jimmied aside a piece of plywood. The stink of horseshit hung in the air. My socks were soaked and my feet squeaked inside my sneakers.

Rotting hay matted the floor of the barn. Dark white mushrooms and gray weeds sprouted from the ground. A pool of water was in one corner, and a steady sheet of rainwater cascaded down, sparkling as it caught the light that streamed through the gaps in the walls' wood planks.

They stood close together. Kenny put his hands on Stephano's waist, underneath his T-shirt, and lifted the shirt up over Stephano's head. Then Kenny got on his knees and unbuttoned Stephano's pants and unzipped the zipper.

"It's okay, T-Bird," Stephano said. "Kenny does me all the time."

I started walking backward, back toward the pool of water.

Stephano called my name. Kenny was laughing.

Outside the barn mud and little streams, pebbles washing down the side of the hill, wind blowing, bushes and pine trees bent and sagging as if they were going to be torn out of the ground. It was raining so hard it hurt my face, as if I were being blasted by a giant showerhead. And I ran. I ran as fast as I could, down the side of the hill, on my rear end sliding in the mud, rolling and slipping down the hillside, hanging on to trees and sticks and clumps of weeds, the smell of licorice plants and wet rocks, pine sap sticking to my hands, stickers from the dead berry bushes and the weeds poking through my socks, my pants, the canvas of my tennis shoes.

I came to a path that went across the side of the hill. I could see tennis shoe prints and horse tracks filled with water. The storm was starting to let up, and now it was more misty than rainy. Water dripped off the leaves and pine needles and onto the path. I kneeled down at a pool of water and washed the mud off my face. In the water I found a rock that was shaped like a big arrowhead. Its edges tapered to points, as if someone had sharpened them. I walked along the path, branches of oaks and pines spanning overhead, the path dark and cave-like. A trail of pale brown horse shit steamed in the mud. A dog barked in the distance, loud and vicious like a Doberman or a wolf.

I kept walking, watching the trail, watching the brush, ditching in the bushes every time I heard a rustle of branches or leaves. The mud on my jacket and pants was starting to dry and flake off when I moved my arms and legs. I came to a place where there weren't any trees on the side of the hill. I could see everything, the whole Bay Area fanning out in front of me. It looked like a postcard. It looked a hell of a lot better than it did in real life.

I came to a road and followed it down the hill to a gas station. I called collect and Fat Fred accepted the charges. I told him I was stranded and needed a ride. He was on his way.

I waited on the corner. I could hear the roar of Fat Fred's chopper before I saw it.

"What the hell happened to you? Are you all right?"

"I slipped in the mud," I said.

He didn't say anything.

"What?" I said.

"I told you not to play hooky," he said. "You want to end up like the niggers?"

"Sorry," I said.

"You need a ride to school, you ask me."

"Let's get the hell out of here," I said. "Okay?"

"Don't get any of that mud on my bike."

The sun was out now, and the clouds lifted and scattered in the pale sky.

We didn't go home. We got on the freeway and headed out toward Berkeley.

***

We went to the Berkeley Pier, and when we got there, Fat Fred didn't get off the bike. He sat there, staring out at the dark brown bay, at the waves pushing against the rocks and the wooden pylons on the shore. The pier was so long that I couldn't see the end. I could hear a distant trumpet playing jazz. People were lined along the railing and fishing, bundled up in hats and scarves and thick heavy coats. A man's glasses reflected the sun as he looked out over the water.

Fat Fred gunned the motor a couple of times, and then he drove the motorcycle down the middle of the pier, past the little old black men and their baseball caps and buckets, past the Chinese fisherwomen, past the old black trumpeter who was blowing out over the water and into the distance. When we got to the end of the pier, he stepped off the bike and walked to the end. It was barricaded with wood slats like a cage.

He looked between the wood slats, out at the water, the bay, the distant skyscrapers of San Francisco. Seagulls screamed behind us where a woman was throwing fish guts into the air.

"When I was a kid my old man used to bring me here," Fat Fred said.

The wind was blowing hard, as if another storm was coming, and Fat Fred's hair fluttered behind his round head. The bay churned and frothed. The gulls beat their wings against the wind and hovered.

"My old man never came out this far on the pier," Fat Fred said. "My old man always said there ain't nothing out there. But one time I walked down here and looked through these boards." He put his heavy hand on my shoulder. "You see those," he said.

He pointed.

I looked where he was pointing. The jagged tips of old pylons jutted out of the water.

"The pier used to go out further than it does now," Fat Fred said. "It used to be a lot longer and they blocked it off. Man, it used to go halfway out into the fucking bay."

I tensed up, and Fat Fred took his hand off me. I moved a couple steps away from him. He looked at me.

"What?"

He opened his mouth as if he were going to say something, but he didn't. His eyes were big and copper-colored like new pennies.

He reached into the pockets of his leather coat. "I've only got four, but you can have one," he said, and he pulled out four bottles of Oly. He put a bottle up to his mouth and opened it with his teeth and handed it to me.

"It's not like I can tell you it gets any better," Fat Fred said. "All I can do is help when it's bad."

"Beer helps," I said.

"Sometimes beer helps," he said.

CHAPTER FOUR

My New Father

When my mother finally came home, she started bossing everybody around. She said she was weak from the accident, and she'd tell one of the bikers to mow the lawn, another to go get her groceries, another to pay the phone bill. She'd tell them to clean the toilet, because if she leaned over to scrub the floor, her brains would slip through the cracks between the stitches in her skull. They got fed up with her pretty quick, and they took off. So then she went out and got a new husband.

After school I showed Stephano the Peterbilt oil tanker that was jackknifed on my lawn. Oil and sludge oozed from the rivets. Tar in feathery combs hung from the cables and chains. A pool of oil beneath the tractor shined. Stephano kicked a twisted bumper that was lying in the front yard.

"Scrape the door," he said. "Let's see what it says."

The lettering beneath read *Charlie Gerlach Trucking.*

"Cool," Stephano said.

"I told you."

We went inside. My mother and Charlie were humping on the La-Z-Boy recliner. I led Stephano back outside.

"They're married," I said.

"He's great," Stephano said.

"I've got a new dad."

"So what, I've got a dad."

"He doesn't talk to you."

"Neither does yours."

"Maybe not the old one," I said. "But now I've got a *new* dad."

I met him the night before.

I was listening to *Blue Train* when I heard a truck stop in front of the house. I looked out the window and headlights blinded me. When the lights cut off I saw the truck, the tractor on the front yard and the tanker on the street. My mother got out of the driver's side. Her shirt was unbuttoned and she was drinking wine from a jug. Then a skinny bald guy climbed out. He was holding his crotch. I could smell the dry diesel exhaust through the closed windows.

I took the record off the turntable and ditched it in my room.

A wine bottle broke and then the door opened. The bald guy's head flickered in the light of the television. His scalp was smudged with grease and freckled.

"This is Charlie," my mother said. "He's your new daddy."

Charlie smiled and stuck out his hand.

"Pull my hand," he said.

"What?"

"Pull on this goddamn hand of mine."

His hand was as small as mine, and his knuckles felt like walnut shells. I pulled and Charlie farted.

Charlie laughed. "Never trust a stranger," he said. "Goddamn glad to meet you, boy."

"T-Bird."

"Glad to meet you, boy."

I was leaving for school, and my mother giggled in her bedroom. Charlie started laughing. He laughed, then coughed, then laughed, then coughed some more. The door to my mother's room opened and I smelled cigar smoke. Charlie jumped into the hall. His boxer shorts were at his knees and his T-shirt was tucked into his boxers. His legs looked stumpy like Fred Flintstone's, chopped off at the shins.

"Where's it at?" he said. He grabbed the crotch of his boxers. "Empty here. Where the hell'd it go?" He put his hand into his boxers and poked his finger through the trap, wagging it. "There it is!" he said. He wagged it some more. "There's the little bugger!"

At roll call, when Mrs. Woodhouse called my name, T-Bird Murphy, I didn't answer. She looked right at me. She had become famous because she caught Jose Martinez with a gun and she swung him around in circles by his arm until it broke.

"T-Bird Murphy," she said again.

I looked at her.

"T-Bird Murphy!"

I could tell that everyone was looking at me, but I looked at the blackboard instead of Mrs. Woodhouse, at the white chalk letters drawn in cursive, the history assignment for the day. Twenty-five pages on the Civil War.

"T-Bird," she said. "You will answer when I call your name."

"You didn't call my name."

"I called your name, and you will answer when I do so."

"My name is T-Bird and it isn't Murphy. My last name is Gerlach. My name is T-Bird Gerlach."

Mrs. Woodhouse looked at me. Her eyes were old and sad and tired.

"Mr. Gerlach," she said.

"Here," I said.

While I was supposed to be reading about the Civil War, I practiced writing my new name in cursive. I wasn't good at *G*'s.

I got better by the end of the day. I knew the answers to all the war questions anyway—the Americans always won. All you had to do was remember the names of the presidents and the generals and that the good guys always won, no matter what they did. I didn't see much point in studying history. It was like reading a story and already knowing the ending.

I waited up for Charlie and my mother one night, even though I knew I'd get in trouble for being up so late.

When they got home, before my mother could whack me, I said, "Dad, can you take me for a ride in your truck?"

"Don't call me Dad."

"My mother said you're my new dad."

"My name is Charlie," he said. "You have a dad, but it's not me. No matter who else's around, you've only got one goddamn dad, and that's the man you call Dad."

"What's my last name then? Am I still a Murphy, or am I a Gerlach?"

"Your last name is Gerlach," my mother said. She was looking at Charlie.

"That's it?" Charlie said.

"We're married," my mother said.

Charlie looked at me.

"Gerlach," he said.

One of my back teeth was loose and about to fall out, and I played with it every day with my tongue. It bothered my mother, watching me with my mouth open and my tongue lolling around like a retard. She slapped me whenever she caught me.

She was about to give me a whack one time when Charlie stopped her mid-swing, catching her arm in the air with that little hand of his.

"We'll fix that goddamn tooth," he said.

He got a pair of pliers from his truck.

"This is how *my* dad pulled teeth out," he said.

He stood over me holding the pliers in his hand. I looked at those pliers. They were big as bolt cutters. He could have snipped down a tree with them. He grabbed my jaw with one hand and stuck the pliers in my mouth.

"Hold still," Charlie said. "And don't cry."

He found the tooth and yanked. I didn't scream and I didn't cry.

"Go wash out the blood," Charlie said. "When you're done, come back in here and I'll give you a beer. It'll make it feel just fine."

"He doesn't need a beer," my mother said. "Gargle with salt water."

"But, Mom," I said.

"No."

Charlie wanted to go fishing. He wanted to drive to Folsom Dam outside Sacramento to catch salmon. He wanted to catch salmon because someone had cut the net that funneled the salmon into the hatchery and it didn't take Jesus H. Christ to walk on that water, the fish were so thick in the river.

I'd never been fishing before, except crawdads, which didn't count, because everyone caught crawdads in the ditches, especially right before the checks came in the mail. Nobody had any money until the checks came, but you always knew it the day the mailman brought them. The whole neighborhood went crazy. Dads and boyfriends would fix the broken parts on their cars and they'd get their tanks filled. Moms would buy groceries. You could hear whoops and yells coming from inside all the apartments, and men and women lined up on the sidewalk outside Joe's Liquor store—only three customers could be in the store at a time. The party lasted about three days, the streets thick with broken bottles and paper bags and empty cans and crumpled packs of cigarettes, and then everyone was broke again. Sometimes it was a long time between checks.

We took my mother's Galaxy for the fishing trip. The Galaxy had the coolest exhaust pipe in the neighborhood. Me and Fat Fred made it, sewed old Hunts tomato-sauce cans together with wire. When she started the car, the neighbors shut their windows to keep out the smoke. Charlie put on a country-western eight-track and I knew my mother hated country music but she pretended she liked it and so did I.

I had never been out of Oakland, and I was surprised at what I saw on the way to Sacramento. Past the oil refineries of Vallejo we came down out of the hills and I saw fields without houses or factories. I smelled onions and garlic. I saw a sky that was not brown or gray, streets without potholes. I saw a field of sunflowers, the flowers big as basketballs. A cloud of bees hung low over the field like black smoke.

The grass was so shiny and green it hurt my eyes.

At the tackle shop the man asked Charlie what kind of bait he wanted.

"Three-pronged hooks."

"You need bait," the man said. "If you hook them without bait it's illegal."

"Three-pronged hooks," Charlie said.

I'd never been next to a river before. The creek didn't count, because the creek water didn't move unless it was raining. The Sacramento River was as wide as a freeway and the water was blue with white foamy rollers.

"You see the silver flashes?" Charlie said. "The streaks? They look like strips of chrome."

I nodded.

"Goddamn salmon," Charlie said, and he cast into the river.

We each had jobs. My mother handed Charlie Oly's, Charlie hooked fish, and I killed them.

Charlie reeled them in, and when he got them close to the bank, he yanked hard and swung them over his head and onto the ground in front of me. They were banged up, white foamy bubbles oozing from all over. I stepped on their bellies and ripped the hooks out. He hooked them anywhere—on the belly, in the eye, in the tail, on a fin. Charlie was a great fisherman.

"You got to stomp them," Charlie said. "Because they're spawning, and they're full of sex. You've got to stomp the goddamn sex out of them. Else they don't make good eating."

I liked killing the fish, and I'd stomp the suckers. The girl fish squirted pink streams of eggs in clear jelly. Charlie would put eggs on the hooks before he cast. "Just in case," he'd say. The boy fish squirted mayonnaise.

I stomped the hell out of those goddamn fish.

We caught sixty-two salmon that day. Sixty-two goddamn salmon. I ate salmon every day, both ways my mother knew how to cook it, broiled and baked. Every goddamn day, salmon. My clothes smelled like salmon. The blankets on my bed smelled like salmon. My piss smelled like salmon.

I hate salmon.

One day Charlie told me that I was going to be his work crew, and he was going to be foreman. He gave me a hard hat. The hard hat was plastic with a leather band to fit the size of my head. Grease and tar smeared over the Massey-Ferguson label.

"We're going to turn this goddamn dirt and these goddamn weeds into the best yard in Oakland," Charlie said. "People will want to take pictures of this goddamn yard. Hell, the social worker'll want to give your mom a raise."

"Who?"

We got the rusted push-mower from the carport and oiled it up. Charlie shoved it into the weeds and the blades jammed so bad we had to take the mower apart and put it back together. Charlie looked at the yard.

"I hate mowing goddamn lawns," he said.

He went to the Peterbilt and got a red five-gallon gas can and he doused the knee-high weeds with gasoline. He used his Zippo to set it ablaze.

"It'll burn the house down," I said.

"Nope," Charlie said. "Dirt don't burn."

I watched the fire, first the burst of flame and then the black smoke and the fire washing over the yard red and orange in rapids. I liked the smell of the fire, the gasoline smell, the swirling strands of burned weeds and trash, the way my skin heated up. I wished the fire would keep burning, that it would burn all of Oakland to ashes.

Charlie raked the ashes and planted trees. We tied the trunks, no fatter than my thumbs, to fence pickets we swiped from the abandoned house around the corner.

Mrs. Woodhouse assigned us an art project. We had to make an artwork about another culture. If we were Japanese, we couldn't make Japanese art. If we were Mexicans, no Mexican stuff. If we were Portuguese, no linguisca or homemade wine.

"What's a Greek artwork?" Stephano asked.

Mrs. Woodhouse shook her head and sighed.

I had no idea what to do.

Charlie and me were watching the A's and the White Sox and drinking Oly's and my mother was at the bar working her new job. The A's were winning and in the middle of the game both dugouts emptied when Sal Bando got hit by a pitch and there was a big fight. Two White Sox got sent out on stretchers. It was a great game.

"I need help with a school project," I said.

"After the game," Charlie said.

When the game was over Charlie made biscuits and gravy.

I'd never had biscuits and gravy before, and after two solid months of salmon, it was the best meal I'd ever had. Whenever my mother made gravy, I loaded my mouth and went to the bathroom and spit it into the toilet. My mother caught me one time and punished me by making about ten more gallons of her gravy and making me eat it all before I was allowed to go to bed.

"I have to do an art project," I said. "About another culture."

"Which one?" Charlie said.

"Something other than mine."

"Which one's yours?"

"German, Irish, English, Dutch, Welsh, French, Cherokee, Italian, and Russian."

Charlie laughed.

"Or so I'm told," I said.

We went to work. Charlie hooked up his table saw and his lathe in the carport. My job was to get tree branches and to go to the store for a can of brown shoe polish. Charlie wore goggles and buzzed away at his machines, and I watched and swept shavings and sawdust.

When he was done, we drank Oly's and looked at the final products—a genuine African spear and an African log drum made out of a rotted section of telephone pole. He used an Oly can to make the tip of the spear.

Before school the day my project was due Charlie got up early to help me get ready. My mother was asleep. Charlie tore up my pair of white corduroy cutoffs into shreds and doused them with coffee to make them brown. He greased my hair black and curled it into kinks with tar from a bucket in his Peterbilt. He used the shoe polish he'd sent me to slick my body brown—my forehead, my eyelids, my ears, my face, my chest and belly, my legs and arms, everything. I was brown as a black man. He handed me the log drum and the spear and the coffee-stained shorts.

"Just the shorts," he said.

"I'll get cold," I said.

"It's spring," he said. "It'll warm up."

"They'll laugh at me," I said.

"You're doing different cultures today?" Charlie said.

I nodded.

"Kid," Charlie said, "you'll all be laughing."

I shook my spear and beat my drum and danced like I thought black people danced and the black kids got mad and Mrs. Woodhouse got mad too. She sent me to Mr. Nasimiento, the principal.

"You can't make fun of the Negroes," he said.

"I was doing artwork from their culture."

"You can't go back to class."

"Why not?"

"You can't. I'm sorry, but I'm going to have to suspend you for a week."

"What did I do? I didn't get in a fight. I didn't get caught getting drunk or smoking pot. I didn't do anything wrong."

"Mr. Ball will take you home."

I glanced back at Nasimiento when I was leaving his office. He didn't look mad at me at all.

When we got to my house, Mr. Ball parked in the driveway behind my mother's Galaxy. Charlie's truck wasn't there.

"I'll need to talk to your mother," he said.

I looked at the house, at the broken windows, at the cinder-black yard, the car and Harley parts scattered in the driveway, springs and fenders and twisted forks and a smashed headlight. In the gravel screws and bolts reflected sunlight.

Mr. Ball got out of the car and started walking toward the front door. I ran past him.

"Please," I said. "Please, Mr. Ball."

"I'm sorry," he said. He opened the screen and knocked on

the door. My mother yelled something.

"She's been really sick," I said. "Really sick. The doctors don't want her to get out of bed."

"What exactly is her problem?"

"She's sick," I said. "She's been real sick for a long time. Nobody will tell me what kind of sick. Just sick."

Mr. Ball put his hand on my shoulder and looked at me.

I looked at his shoes. They were old shoes with skinny leather shoelaces. They hadn't been shined in a long time.

"You're on free lunches?"

I nodded.

Mr. Ball dug some change out of his pocket and gave it to me. "Buy some lunch," he said. He drove away.

"Pack up," my mother said. "You're going on a trip."

"Where?"

"You're going on a trip with your new father."

"I like it where I am," I said. "Where?"

"On a trip," my mother said. "I doesn't matter where. You're suspended anyway. You disappoint me. I never got suspended when I went to school."

"You didn't graduate," I said.

She slapped me. I pretended to cry because I'd learned my lesson about crying. If my mother whacked me, I had to cry hard enough to make her think I was about to die, and while I was crying I thought about how some day, when I was a grown-up and bigger than her, I was going to make *her* cry.

My mother was weird about whacking. When she was swinging the spatula or her belt or whatever she was using, she screamed, howled like an air-raid siren. She screamed louder than I cried.

I learned my lesson about crying because of one of my mother's rules. For every piece of dirty laundry not turned right-side-out, I got one whack with the spatula. One time she found twenty-three pieces, counting each sock separately. While she was whacking I cried like she'd cut my legs off. When she got through, she left the room. I stopped crying.

My mother came back in the room.

"What's the matter," she said. "Didn't hurt?"

"It hurt," I said. "It hurt, it really did. It really hurt. It hurt so bad." I started crying again.

She didn't believe me, and the next couple days I couldn't go to school I was bruised up so bad.

So when she slapped me for saying she didn't graduate, I really cried it up good.

I packed a pillowcase with a week's worth of socks and shorts and got in the truck with Charlie. There was only one seat, and I sat on a wooden Campbell's soup crate. The floor of the cab was sheet metal, wires taped down and empty No Doz boxes strewn about with the beer cans.

I looked at the rearview mirror as we drove away. My mother wasn't standing in the charred front yard. She wasn't anywhere.

The neighborhood looked a lot smaller in the mirror.

We were going to Yreka on an oil drop. Before we left town, Charlie stopped at an oil depot in Oakland and filled his tanker. The ground was tarred black and seemed to be held together with screws and springs and nuts and bolts smashed into the oily dirt by the tires of thousands of trucks. The man who took Charlie's money had a peg leg. He took it off for us.

"Whopped me some shitbags with this some-bitch," he said. He swung it like it was a baseball bat. Then he started telling us all about Vietnam.

"Nobody in their right goddamn mind would mess with you," Charlie said.

Charlie bought a pint of Jack Daniel's from him.

"Which way you want to go, kid?" Charlie said. He handed me a map.

"The long way," I said.

We went over the Bay Bridge through San Francisco. The fog made it so you couldn't see the tops of the skyscrapers. The city looked cooped up. San Francisco didn't have a sky, just forty stories. You could yell at people no matter where you were and they could hear you. It looked like no matter what you said in San Francisco, somebody would hear you. They didn't have a choice. The houses and the trees seemed older than I'd remembered. We drove over the Golden Gate Bridge. It wasn't golden at all. It was orange.

We crossed the bridge and Charlie said, "This is Marin County. This is where the goddamn rich motherfuckers live. Unless you're lucky, you'll be working for them some day. Some rich motherfucker'll sit back and tell you what ditch to dig, what burger to fry, what route to pull. I met those fuckers. They don't drink beer. That's right, they don't drink beer. Not because they don't like it, but because if they drank beer they'd be admitting they're like you and me. The fuckers. So at the shindig they drink scotch, which tastes like shit, and no one drinks it unless they're a rich motherfucker, and not because it's good, but because it's what they're supposed to drink. The fuckers."

I nodded.

"You see the houses those fuckers live in?" Charlie pointed through the windshield. "Big motherfucking houses. And you know who bought them? You and me and your mother and even your father. They make money like this—they pay us less than we're worth and keep the change and there's nothing we can do about it. They'll tell you to go to church and believe in God and shit, but God don't help you when you're alive, and the rich fuckers know it. They know the saps will believe it's okay to be poor because they'll go to heaven and so it's good to suffer while they're alive. But God is a millionaire, and he don't give a rat's ass about the poor. He was invented by the poor, but the rich bought the fucker out."

Charlie slapped the steering wheel.

"So take a good look, kid," Charlie said. He pointed at the trees, at the house-dotted hills. "Those fuckers own your ass."

I took a good look. There were too many trees. It didn't look like people could live where there were so many trees.

Charlie was old. His face was wrinkled and his stubble was white. He looked dried up, like an old peeled recap off a semi on the side of the road. His little hands had white hairs springing from the knuckles. He wore glasses while he was driving. His clothes even looked old. He didn't wear bell-bottoms.

A waitress at a truck stop near Geyserville didn't seem to mind. She didn't look any older than my mother, long brown hair that hung over one eye, the other eye with a lot of purple makeup. She was taller than Charlie. Her hands were bigger than his.

She told Charlie her break was coming up.

"That's what I was hoping, honey," Charlie said.

She gave me two more pieces of apple pie, with chocolate ice cream on top. Her nametag read "Martha."

When I finished my pie and ice cream I couldn't find Charlie so I went back out to the Peterbilt. I sat in Charlie's seat instead of on my wooden crate and pretended I was driving, moving the stick shift, clicking the red splitter button up and down, pulling the air-brake knob and listening to the loud long hiss. I tugged the leather strap over my head and blasted the air horn. I blasted it until my ears rang.

The air got colder and the sky bluer than I'd ever seen, blue like the flame of a welding torch, gemlike and hot and reflecting off the asphalt and concrete highways. We wound through grassy hills and when we reached the summit redwood trees rose into the sky to either side of the road so high it got dark, the road in shadow, the sky hot blue above, the air cool and brittle. The trees were as wide as the cab of the truck, and four times as high as telephone poles. Sometimes the highway was so narrow branches slapped against my mirror and came through my window, needles scratching my face. The air smelled like a greenhouse, moist and green and sweet. It smelled so good it smelled fake, like some kind of aerosol bathroom-freshener. It made me sneeze. I got a runny nose.

We passed giant statues of Paul Bunyan and his blue ox. We passed the Enchanted Forest, haunted with Oz-like tree demons, according to the billboards. We passed a place that, if you wanted to pay two dollars, would show you a tree older than Jesus Christ. Charlie asked me if I wanted to see it. I told him I didn't.

We drove. When the sun went down, it just got dark, no sunset, no orange and red sky. The sun clicked off and the sky went black.

The last drop was in a factory compound just south of Yreka, near the Oregon border. Charlie finished pumping the tanker out and started up the tractor.

"Can we go into Oregon?" I said.

"Why?"

"I want to go there."

"It looks the same as here, kid," Charlie said.

"But it isn't here."

Charlie laughed. "Kid," he said. "You've got plenty of time."

And we started back to Oakland. We took I-5 instead of old Highway 101. We stopped once when Charlie needed to pee. It was nighttime. I climbed down out of the tractor. I looked up.

I couldn't believe what I saw. The sky was white with stars, a streak across the middle of the dark like a white rag. Oakland only had about twenty stars, but where we were the sky had millions, stars and stars and stars, as if God didn't like people and only put stars out in the boonies where no one lived.

The sky was dark with rain clouds when we got back to Oakland, but it wasn't raining yet. We had to park a block and a half away from the house when we got home because my mother's Hell's Angel boyfriends were back, and their motorcycles were everywhere, in the driveway, on the lawn, on the porch, in the garage, hundreds of Harleys lining both sides of the street.

"What the hell's going on?" Charlie said.

"Probably nothing," I said. "Let's go somewhere, to the zoo or a park. Let's go to an A's game."

Charlie wasn't listening to me. He walked toward the house. I followed Charlie halfway to the house and stopped. I saw Fat Fred and Domer standing on the porch passing a bottle of booze back and forth and taking shots. I heard my mother's laugh. Charlie walked right past Fat Fred and Domer and into the house. I looked at the trees we'd planted. They didn't look any bigger. Then Charlie came out, my mother following and grabbing at his shirt. I stepped off the sidewalk and stood in a driveway. They walked right past me.

"No," my mother said. "Please."

"I'll get my things tomorrow."

He started up the Peterbilt and put it in gear and when he drove past me, he tossed my bag of clothes out the window. My mother screamed "Please" and "Oh God" and then "Please" and "Oh God" again.

Puffs of black smoke shot out of the exhaust pipes each time he shifted gears.

CHAPTER FIVE

East Bay Grease

My mother decided it was high time to get the hell out of Oakland. Pop was being released from jail, and she didn't want to be around when he came home. She got the Angels to load our things into a pickup truck. Anything she couldn't fit into the pickup, she gave to her friends. The house was empty except for some half-packed boxes of dishes, strewn newspaper, empty cans of Olympia.

When the truck was all loaded up, we had beers in the alley. My mother's friends sat on the seats of their motorcycles, and she stood next to Jimmy Flynn, her newest boyfriend, her arm draped over his shoulders. She was wearing the necklace she'd made from brown and white beads she'd picked off the ground at the Indian burial grounds in Mission San Jose. Whenever it rained, those beads would come up from the graves. Sometimes bones came up too. It was a long necklace, and at the end hung a finger bone and a silver Christian cross with a dead Jesus.

"Fuck this place," she said.

She looked at me.

Jimmy Flynn spun around so that he was facing her and lifted her up into the air. She held on to Jimmy's head. Her beads dangled down his back.

"You guys have been so good to me," she said.

I walked toward the Ford Galaxy with my cardboard box.

She pushed herself away from Jimmy.

"Put your box back on the porch," she said.

"Why?"

"I said put your box back on the porch."

I didn't move.

"Your father will be here at eight," she said.

"Good," I said. She pulled her arm back and slapped me. I looked at her.

"Didn't hit you hard enough?" she said.

She slapped me again, harder.

"Ungrateful little bastard," she said. "He won't even cry."

"Leave the boy alone, Wilma," Jimmy said.

"Keep your ass out of this," my mother said. "He's an ungrateful little bastard."

Fat Fred started up his hogg and gunned the motor a few times.

The sun had set behind the warehouse across the street and a cold bay breeze shot down the asphalt alley.

She got in the Galaxy. She started the motor. A cloud of dust and black smoke rolled from beneath the car. Her friends started their motorcycles and followed her as she backed out of the driveway and started down the street.

I climbed to the flat-topped roof and stood on the scattered gravel and peeling tar paper. The smokestacks of factories on the other side of the freeway rose behind webs of television antennas and telephone wires. Across the bay in the distance the skyscrapers of San Francisco were black against the red and orange sky.

I wondered what it must have been like to have been an Indian sitting on a hillside watching the first Spanish galleon sail through the Golden Gate.

I wondered what it would look like if the earthquake finally hit, if all the buildings shook and crumbled, if the windows shattered and the bridges dipped and sank into the bay, if the freeway cracked and the concrete and the cars slammed to the ground, the city no more than a cloud of dust rising into the air and flames leaping into the sky like the flickering tongues of devils.

Before my grandfather died he told me about what it was like before the bridges, before the war, when you rode a trolley car down the clean new streets of Oakland. People used to paint their houses. They used to mow their lawns. The coloreds didn't carry knives and guns and kill you back then.

I looked out over the bay and tried to imagine ferryboats loaded with Model T's, San Francisco forty stories shorter, the edge of the bay lined with marshlands instead of garbage dumps.

A train was sounding its horn.

An old Ford Fairlane stopped in front of the house. I lay down on the roof and watched Pop walk up the alley toward the porch. He wore new bell-bottom blue jeans held up with a belt embroidered with bright yellow flowers. He was smoking a cigar.

I peeled a piece of tar paper and threw it across the alley.

Pop looked up. "Where's your mother?"

I threw a handful of gravel.

"Where's your mother?"

I shrugged. "She moved."

He looked at me, then at the house, then at his car. He looked at me again.

When he went inside, he slammed the screen door open so hard it slapped against the house.

"Bitch," he said.

He stomped around, opening and closing doors and cupboards, saying bitch, bitch, goddamn bitch. I climbed down off the roof and stood in the alley next to my cardboard box. Pop came back outside.

"Bitch," he said.

He walked past me and down the alley. His bell bottoms

flapped against his legs.

I followed him to the carport. He walked back and forth across the oily concrete, kicking empty boxes and Olympia cans.

He bent over in the corner and picked through some old newspapers. From underneath them he pulled out a black-handled hunting knife. He held it up to his eyes.

It looked like a sword.

"The bitch didn't say where she was going?" he said.

"No," I said.

He waved the knife in front of his face and laughed.

"You sure?" he said.

"Yes."

"Goddamn bitch," he said.

He tossed the knife back and forth, from one hand to the other.

He smiled.

Now that Pop was out of jail, his old boss gave him his job back at the Mohawk gas station, and he let him live next to the station in a trailer next to the rest rooms. The trailer looked like a fat aluminum torpedo with plastic windows. A high wall of stacked truck tires surrounded the trailer.

He made me sleep on the floor.

"If the bitch doesn't call tomorrow, I'll tear down the kitchen table," he said.

He stabbed out his cigar in a Styrofoam coffee cup.

"It turns into a bed," he said.

Pop woke me at six in the morning. He turned on the radio to the news station and walked from one end of the trailer to the other in his underwear, getting ready for work. His body looked like it was made up of two different people. He had a tiny rear end and skinny white legs, but his upper body was huge and tanned. Thick black hair covered his chest like steel wool.

His Jockey shorts were old and gray and spotted with battery-acid holes. The elastic around his legs was stretched and the shorts bagged down beneath him. I'd seen plenty of naked men before, seen them four or five at a time on top of my mother, but I'd never seen Pop naked.

I'd never before thought of Pop as having balls.

His balls frightened and repulsed me and I couldn't stop looking at them, the way they bagged and drooped, how hairy they were, how dirty and huge and magical and evil they seemed.

He scratched his nuts and I turned my face into my pillow.

"I'm going to work now, kid," he said. "You do whatever you want. I've got a TV and a radio. The catering truck brings breakfast at seven and I'll get you a doughnut."

He took his keys from the counter.

"We'll do just fine, kid," he said. "Don't walk around by yourself, though. There's niggers everywhere."

That summer, I didn't leave the lot of the Mohawk station.

Pop taught me how to pump gas. He taught me how to patch inner tubes using the grinder-chuck. He taught me how to change oil and how to look up the oil filters in the Mohawk auto-parts manual.

He showed me how to unlock the gas pumps and set out the oil racks and towel dispensers in the morning, how to turn on the air compressor that ran the air hoses and the car lifts. By the end of the summer, he'd let me open up the station while he slept in.

While he'd close the shop at night, I'd light the barbecue pit and cook his steak and my hamburgers.

Pop made an outdoor table from some old car tires and a rusted sheet of tin. We ate dinner outside next to the trailer after work, and when we finished dinner, we'd walk down to Loard's Ice Creamery and eat ice-cream sundaes. At night we'd sit outside, surrounded by the wall of truck tires, Pop smoking a cigar, and on a transistor radio we listened to Monty Moore announce the Oakland A's play by play.

Fall came, and my mother still hadn't called.

Lunchtime the first day at my new school, Hoover Elementary, I sat down at a table by myself. Almost all the other kids were blacks and Mexicans. I tried not to look at anyone. I stared at my spaghetti and played with my paper milk-straw.

Someone stopped and stood behind me.

"That's my seat."

I turned around. It was a big Mexican kid with a black mustache and a stringy little goatee. He wore a heavy black coat even though the weather was hot.

I lifted my tray and stood. He bumped me as I walked away. I sat down at the next empty table.

"That's my seat too," he said. "This side of the cafeteria is my seat. The other side's for pussies, right, Hiro?"

Hiro was a short Japanese kid. He sat on the other side of the cafeteria, in the farthest corner, by himself. He looked at the big Mexican, his eyes wide.

"Right, Hiro?" the big Mexican yelled.

"Right, Alfonso," Hiro said.

"Right what?" Alfonso yelled.

"Right this side is for pussies," Hiro said.

I needed a baseball mitt for PE, so Pop bought me one at K Mart. It was my first mitt, a Sal Bando autograph model. The leather smelled so good that I kept burying my face in it and sniffing it all the way back to the trailer. Pop bought himself a mitt too, and a baseball.

We went behind the gas station to play catch.

"Keep your eye on the ball," he said. "Here it comes."

I heard it hiss. I had never before heard a ball going so fast that it hissed.

I let it hiss past me.

It hit a car parked overnight for repairs.

"What's the matter? Didn't the bitch's boyfriends ever teach you how to play baseball?"

I shrugged.

"Don't just stand there," he said. "Get the ball."

I got the ball and wound up to throw it at him.

I wanted to knock his head off.

The ball sailed over his head and hit the side of the station.

Pop walked to the ball and picked it up.

"What in the hell do you think you're doing?" he said. "Now this time when I throw it stand there like a man and catch it."

He threw the baseball. It hissed like a broken air hose. It looked huge and seemed to move in slow motion. The red stitches rolled toward me, over and over. My arms hung at my sides.

The ball hit me in the mouth.

I had a split lip, so we called off practice.

"You didn't even try to catch it," Pop said.

Being the new kid at school sucked. The second day of school Alfonso and the four Jarimallo brothers and Raymond Alvarez waited outside Miss Patusco's class for Hiro and me. Mrs. Patusco wasn't tough like Mrs. Woodhouse. Mrs. Patusco didn't look like she could break a kid's arm if she tried. She looked like she belonged on the other side of town, where the kids wore new sneakers and got haircuts at fancy barbers at the mall.

We watched them through the classroom windows. Hiro had told me about them during lunchtime, which we spent in the classroom with Mrs. Patusco. He said they'd been beating him up every day after school for about two years now. He said that unless I thought I could take them—and not just one of them but all of them at once—that we should become friends and help each other. As the new kid at school, getting a new friend the second day of school sounded like a good idea to me.

Outside, the Mexican kids swung chocko sticks and slapped miniature baseball bats against their palms.

"Come out and play with us," Alfonso said.

Miss Patusco finished gathering her papers together.

"I'm sorry boys," she said. "You have to leave now."

We walked alongside her to her car.

Alfonso and the Jarimallos and Raymond Alvarez followed behind at a distance.

Miss Patusco wouldn't look at Hiro and me. She got into her Volkswagen, and she drove away.

We ran.

I climbed over a fence into someone's yard and landed in a flower bed. The flowers smelled good.

They caught Hiro on the other side of the fence.

They swore at him both in English and in Spanish.

Their chocko sticks and baseball bats cracked against his bones.

The thin redwood boards of the fence slapped each time they kicked Hiro against it.

I crouched in the flower bed and I cried.

Hiro and I mapped escape routes on graph paper. The escape routes were of varying complexity to keep the Mexicans off guard. We numbered the routes so that we could call "audibles" in the event our opposition's defense seemed impenetrable. We stockpiled 33 plans and studied them until we had them memorized.

The plans did not always work.

I came home to the Mohawk station later than usual one day.

"What's your problem," Pop said.

"Nothing."

"If you come home crying one more time, *I'll* give you something to cry about."

A car drove up to a gas pump.

"Wait here," Pop said. "Don't you fucking move."

I sat in the office and watched Pop wash the rear windshield, check under the hood and put air in the tires.

I hoped that the car's gas tank would never get full.

When the car left, Pop came into the office and put the charge receipt in the till. He sat down on a tire display and lit a cigar.

"So," he said. "The bitch's boyfriends didn't teach you how to fight either."

He drew a long drag off his cigar, closed his eyes and exhaled thick blue clouds of smoke. He looked at me. "After work, you and me are going for a walk."

I went into the trailer and waited. I didn't turn on the radio or the portable TV.

I'd never noticed before how noisy it was at the station.

Cars and trucks ran over the black cords and made the station's bells ring. Out on the street horns honked and brakes grated and squeaked. People hollered at each other from inside their cars.

I heard a hissing noise not too far from the trailer, then smelled the hot dry odor of overheated antifreeze.

The wind gusted. The plastic windows of the trailer slapped closed, and the trailer creaked, rocking slowly on its tires and the jack.

I heard the glass doors of the station's garage slide down along the metal rollers.

I had to jog to keep up with him.

He hadn't changed out of his grease-soaked Mohawk coveralls. The pant legs were too baggy and the upper part strained against his back and shoulders.

"Which way do you walk to school from here?" he said.

"It depends," I said.

"It doesn't matter," he said. "Come on."

We walked past rusted sheet-metal warehouses with broken windows, past the railroad switching yards where trains pulled forward and backward, coupling and uncoupling. Their spinning headlights cut through the now dusky air. The cars clunked against each other so hard the ground shook.

Between the Del Monte canning plant and a factory where they made tanks and armored cars was a residential neighborhood. The paint of the old wood-frame houses was a uniform dull gray. The trim peeled like sunburned skin. Broken-down cars cluttered the driveways and weed-strewn yards like dead iron buffalo. Oil slicked the sidewalks and gutters. My sneakers smacked each time I lifted a foot.

Pop stopped in front of a sagging picket fence. He looked up and down the street.

"You see this?" he said. He pointed at the fence.

"What?" I said.

"This," he said. He kicked one of the pickets. It snapped in two. He reached down and clutched the top half of the picket in his hand and ripped it from the fence.

He held the picket in front of his face. The nails were bent and rusted.

"This," he said. "This. You know what this is for?" he said. "Do you know what this is for?"

He clutched the picket tighter. His hands shook.

I stepped back.

"This is for niggers," he said. "You understand? Do you? Niggers. This is for niggers."

"But it's the Mexicans," I said.

"It's niggers," he said.

He wheeled around and threw the broken picket down the middle of the street. It sailed like a javelin.

He grabbed my forearm and pulled me along. We stopped in front of a burned-out house. The charred black beams smoldered. Spindly burned bushes rose from the puddles in the yard, and the sourness of wet furniture hung in the air.

Pop splashed through the yard and kicked at the porch steps. He knocked loose a brick and leaned down and picked it up.

Transformer towers disappeared into the fog in the distant horizon, looming above the brick and steel warehouses and the concrete silos of the Kaiser Permanente Company's batch plant and faded billboards. The burned-out house crackled and a beam broke and fell into the coals and ashes. And in front of the burned-out house stood Pop holding that brick in front of his face.

"This is for niggers," he said. He turned around and threw the brick into the smoldering heap of house. Sparks dusted the air. "Over there," he said. He pointed. "There, over there. You see that? Do you see that?"

He charged through the flooded yard, water splashing up into his face. He ran across the street. I followed behind. He stopped, his chest heaving. He pointed.

"You see that? Do you see that?"

He was pointing at an overflowing Dumpster.

"What you see?" he said. "What do you see?"

"Garbage?" I said.

He dropped his arm and ran to the Dumpster and tore through it, throwing paper and cereal boxes and beer cans and bottles into the air. He picked out a metal coffee-can lid.

"Come here," he said.

I backed up.

"Get your ass over here," he said. "Now."

I walked toward him. He grabbed my arm and twisted it behind me.

He put the coffee-can lid to my neck.

"You know what this is for? Do you? Do you?"

"Niggers," I said. "Niggers."

"Right," he said. "Don't forget it."

He let me go and tossed the lid back into the Dumpster. He stood and his breathing slowed. He wiped his forehead with his sleeve.

He pulled a cigar from his chest pocket and peeled off the cellophane wrapper. He ran the cigar along his tongue wetting the tobacco leaf. He lit the cigar with his Zippo and inhaled deeply. He exhaled.

"There's no such thing as a fair fight," he said. Smoke wisped from his mouth and nostrils as he talked. "Someone always wins, and someone always loses. It's stupid to be the loser."

Pop unlocked the station's office door and told me to follow him. The station smelled of solvent and musty rubber. It was dark. Everything looked gray and black, the Goodyear promotional banners, the Mohawk oil and transmission-fluid cans, the red-and-white checkerboard floor tiles. Pop didn't turn on the lights.

He reached behind the counter and lifted out a cardboard box.

"It's from your mother," he said.

The box was opened.

Inside was a new pair of Hush Puppies, a white dress shirt, bubble-bath soap, a chessboard with wood pieces, dried fruit, and a wallet. I opened the wallet. There was a fifty-dollar bill and a note.

> *My dearest darling little boy,*
>
> *Hope you like these little things—I picked them out myself! I've missed you so much. But I've been ever so busy! Run run run, you know! See you soon!*
>
> *Love you!*
> *Mommy!*

Pop had watched me unpack the box. He sat on a black plastic chair leaned back against the gray metal wall. He twisted a cigar and stared at the checkerboard floor.

"She'll be here tomorrow," he said. "Tomorrow night."

He tore the cellophane from his cigar and smoked. His glasses reflected the inside of the shop window.

"You don't have to go with her if you don't want to," he said.

Hiro and I used Escape Plan #14 after school the next day.

Escape Plan #14 went like this: Hiro would make a dash for Hung Lee's Market. At Hung Lee's, Hiro would try to outwait them, or, if they didn't go away, he would make a break for Sosa's Liquor Store, which stayed open later. Meanwhile, I would run down the railroad tracks and try to make it to the shipyards, which stayed open all night long.

The Jarimallo brothers went after Hiro, and Alfonso went after me.

But I was ready for Alfonso, that Mexican piece of shit nigger. I was going to give him some nigger back. I was going to show him some nigger shit he never saw. Some real Oakland nigger.

After I opened the station that morning, I went back into the trailer. I dug through Pop's toolbox and took his hunting knife, the one he found in the carport of my mother's house.

I wrapped the knife with greasy gas-station rags and put it under my shirt, holding it in my armpit. I carried it that way all day long at school.

Near the shipyards a boarded-up concrete pedestrian tunnel cut beneath the railroad tracks.

Alfonso lagged about a block behind me, but I made sure he saw me climbing through the boards and into the tunnel.

I hid deep in the tunnel's dark and pulled the knife from under my shirt.

The floor of the tunnel was slick with muddy silt, runoff

from rains. Ropes of light filtered through the boards at the tunnel's entrance. Water seeped from the cracks in the walls, and the dripping sounds echoed as if tiny tongues clicked against the walls of a great whale's empty stomach.

I gripped the black handle with both hands. The weight of the knife felt good.

I saw Alfonso crouch down and squint into the dark of the tunnel. He stayed there a long time.

He walked away, kicking the rocks that lay around the railroad ties.

I didn't move. Come on you Mexican nigger.

I heard his sneakers grind into rocks as he ran back toward the tunnel.

"Pussy," he said. "If you don't come out of there, I'm gonna kill you. Gringo ass pussy son of a white whore bitch."

He threw rocks through the opening, one at a time at first, then fistful after fistful. I flattened myself against the cool damp concrete wall and listened as the rocks flew through the darkness and slipped into the slimy mud floor.

A rock hit my leg but I didn't yell. I looked at the knife. In the dark I could barely see its shine.

"Pussy," Alfonso yelled. "Fuck you."

His feet crunched in the gravel as he walked away.

"Fuck you," he yelled. "Gringo." His voice was distant. He yelled something in Spanish.

I walked up the stairs toward the entrance.

At the top of the stairs I stopped. I looked through the boards. Alfonso was far down the tracks. He looked very small.

I sat on the mud-slicked stairs and looked into the dark. I held the knife in front of my face and looked at my distorted reflection.

I threw the knife as far as I could.

Wind shot through the cracks in the weathered wood and made low moaning noises like faraway whistles of ancient trains.

* * *

My mother leaned against a new Oldsmobile. She wore a red suede miniskirt and a lacy white blouse. She had a new hairdo.

An older man with a blue suit and silvery gray hair stood beside her. His face was pink like a white rat's nose. His arm was wrapped around my mother's waist.

They watched Pop carry the towel dispensers into the shop. They watched him lug in the oil racks. They watched him empty the oil-barrel trash cans into the station's Dumpster. They watched him sweep the lot. He lit a cigar and smoked it. He unzipped his coveralls and put his hand in his Jockey shorts and scratched.

"You see that, honey," my mother said. "He's a pig. That's right, a pig. No class."

"That's life in the big shitty," Pop said.

"Pig," my mother said.

Pop continued scratching with one hand, smoking his cigar with the other.

I was ducked down behind a parked car at the edge of the lot.

"Where'd you put him?" my mother said. "Where are you hiding my darling boy?"

"I hid him in a stack of tires."

"Honey," my mother said, "search the tires."

The pink-faced old man searched the tires that surrounded the trailer. He shrugged and then stood brushing tire soot from his suit.

"Actually," Pop said, "I sold him to the circus. He shovels monkey shit."

"You see what I've been telling you, honey," my mother said. "I don't know how I ever married a pig like that."

"*I* do," Dad said. He clutched his crotch.

She slapped Pop.

Pop smiled. He blew her a kiss.

"Your juvenile conspiracy is not going to work," she said.

"We'll be back, won't we, honey?"

"You leaving so soon?" Pop said. "I was almost beginning to remember how nice it was having you around, honey."

My mother and the man walked toward their Oldsmobile.

"Pig," she said.

"Oink," Pop said.

She slammed her car door. The man started the motor and they drove away.

Pop sat on the metal step of the trailer. He stared at the wall of tires. He smoked a cigar.

"What's for dinner?" I said. "Did Mom come? Sure hope I didn't miss her."

I smiled.

Pop looked at me over the top of his glasses.

"She came. Where were you?"

"You want me to put on the food?" I said.

"Start the fire up," Pop said. He tossed me his Zippo.

I emptied a sack of new charcoal briquettes into the barbecue pit and doused them with lighter fluid. I touched the lighter to the briquettes and watched the fire spread slowly across the pit, growing bigger and bigger, until the flames were as high as my face.

Pop came out with steaks for each of us and stood on the other side of the fire.

The fire lit up the side of the trailer, making it shimmer in oranges and yellows.

Pop's silhouette stretched high across the rounded top and disappeared into the shadows of the station walls.

CHAPTER SIX

Kuyashii

By the next year, Hiro and I were tight. We were a team.

We were the smartest kids in the sixth grade. Hiro was a lot better friend than the ones I had at my old school. Hiro wasn't a fag like Stephano, and he didn't waste his time on Jesus like Andrew. I never even called Stephano and Andrew on the phone. I had better things to do.

Lots of kids at Hoover Elementary were famous for being good thieves. Armondo Costello was the most famous. He'd been to juvy twice already for stealing. But even though other kids were famous, Hiro and I were the best thieves. We were the best because no one *knew* we were thieves.

No one ever would have suspected us, and that made copping off with whatever we wanted easy.

When Hiro and I became stealing partners, he told me about his parents. I had asked about the dull brown scars around his father's wrists.

"My parents lived in the Mojave Desert when they were kids," he said.

"What's that have to do with the scars?"

"When Japan bombed Pearl Harbor my parents had to go to

relocation camps."

I'd read about relocation camps in History. We helped out the Japanese who lived in America. We gave them safe homes away from people who might accuse them of being spies and beat them up or kill them.

Hiro looked at his feet, then looked back at me.

"My grandparents died there," he said. "I don't have any grandparents."

"Is that why your father never talks?"

"He talks," Hiro said. "When he has something to say."

"I've never heard him say anything."

"He never has anything to say that *you* need to hear," Hiro said.

We found out we were smart when Dr. Danielson, the principal himself, called us into his office. Dr. Danielson wasn't like the principal of my old school, Mr. Nasimiento. Nasimiento wore tennis shoes and hardly ever shaved. Nasimiento cussed and smoked cigarettes on the playground while we were at recess. Dr. Danielson, he was a different type. He wore a suit and tie. He wore shiny black shoes. His face was always so clean-shaven it looked like he'd never had a whisker. Hiro and I were scared when we got called to Dr. Danielson's office because we thought we might have been snagged stealing the wooden chessboard and metal chess pieces from the library. We'd gone into Royal Music, the music store on 14th Street in downtown Oakland, and we'd swiped polish rags, one for my trumpet and another for Hiro's sax. We went downstairs and watched the trumpet master making his trumpets, and when he wasn't looking, we stole a mouthpiece. Also, we'd been selling firecrackers for Pop—he let us keep a dime for every pack we sold.

Dr. Danielson looked at us, his face pointy and his eyes beady and black like greasy ball bearings socked into white dough.

"You two boys are very talented," Dr. Danielson said.

I thought about all our heists, the time we stole the PE stuff—baseballs and footballs and the school's only soccer ball. I thought about how we swiped Mrs. Weismann's grade book from her desk right under her nose. I thought about that chess set. I thought about all those packs of firecrackers.

"Hiro," Dr. Danielson said, "T-Bird. How would you two boys like to take classes at the university?"

"I'm going to go to MIT when I grow up," Hiro said. "I'm going to be a nuclear physicist."

Dr. Danielson smiled.

"I'm going to be a cop," I said. "Nobody's going to get away with anything when I'm a cop. I'm going to kill anyone who breaks the law."

"I'm sure you will," Dr. Danielson said. "However, why I've called you two boys into my office is that we have a new program which enables us to send our brightest students to the university to study with the college students. You will find it a challenge and a valuable educational experience."

We told him we'd do it, because he told us that we'd get to leave school twice a week to go to Berkeley.

After school, Hiro and I broke into Dr. Danielson's office. Breaking in was easy because Hiro set us up. When he was leaning against Dr. Danielson's wall, Hiro slid his hand along the window pane and unlocked the window. That night, after Cederick the janitor finished up, we pushed the window open and climbed in. We searched the file cabinet and found folders with our names on them. We discovered that we'd had IQ tests.

We found the tests and the answers we'd given and our scores. We remembered taking those tests. The tests were stupid. They gave us both the same questions. One of the questions was, "If you lost a quarter in a field of tall grass, how would you go about finding it?"

My answer was, "I wouldn't look for it. I'd take out someone's garbage or mow a lawn or something and get another quarter."

The lady who tested me told me that I had to tell her how I'd look for the quarter—I couldn't just earn another one. Right then I knew she was stupid, because it would take more time to find a quarter in a field of grass than it would to earn another one.

I told her, "I'd pay someone a nickel to find it and keep the change."

She didn't like that answer either.

Hiro's answers were different. He told her that he'd get a metal detector. She told him that he had to *look* for the quarter. He said, "I'd wait until nighttime and sweep a flashlight over the field. The quarter would shine."

The lady told him it was a dirty quarter and he couldn't find it that way.

I had to get Pop to sign a permission slip so I could leave school twice a week to go to Berkeley.

He was underneath the hood of a Ford Futura when I got home to the Mohawk station. His knuckles bled from where he'd slipped the wrench and shredded the skin.

"What?" he said.

"I said I need your signature so I can take classes at the university."

The wrench slipped again. Pop hit the air cleaner with the wrench and made a dent in the metal. "What's it look like I'm doing?"

"Working," I said.

"That's right," he said. "Working. More than I can say for some people around here."

He turned his head sideways and looked at me. "Now, if I'm at work, do you think I care about signing permission slips?"

"No."

"Damn right no," he said. "When I was your age, I could take an engine apart and put it back together again. You might get straight A's in school, but you flunk out in real life."

* * *

Hiro and I did the college classes for a while, and it was great. A professor taught a bunch of kids from all over the East Bay who were just as smart, and lots of them smarter, than Hiro and me.

We learned a lot of things. An economics professor taught us about capital and resources and labor and the stock market and how to make money without working. Hiro and I already knew how to do that—you just swiped it or returned deposit-bottles—but the professor taught us how grown-ups did it on a big scale, how they bought and sold foreign money for favorable exchange rates, how they bought stock low and sold it high, how rich people never had to work at all because people paid them interest to use their capital reserves.

We learned about Adam Smith. He lived on an island with two guys named Caliban and Friday, and they divided up labor according to whoever did the job best, and then they traded with each other. Caliban and Friday did all the lousy jobs, and Adam Smith wrote equations and drew blueprints and figured out what plants were good for medicine and which ones were good to eat. Adam Smith had the easy job because he was smart and Caliban and Friday were stupid.

We went to the cyclotron at Lawrence Lab Berkeley and learned how new elements were made. We learned to cut up frogs and cats. We went to Lawrence Lab Livermore and saw where they made nuclear triggers for the bombs.

During the year Hiro had been my best friend, I always had breakfast at his house. He lived across the street from Hoover Elementary. Every morning we played chess on our stolen board and pieces. We told Hiro's parents the board and pieces were mine so they wouldn't wonder where he got the set.

His mother was shorter than me. She made us rice with sugary syrup, and Hiro's father read the newspaper. He was taller than anyone I'd ever met. He ducked through the doorway when he walked out to his car in the morning. He looked at Hiro's mother and she bowed down low, her hands pressed together as if she was praying, and then he left. Pop always made fun of the Japanese because they were so short, but he never met Mr. Kawaguchi, because if he had, he would have changed his song. I saw Mr. Kawaguchi every morning, but I never heard him speak even a word.

Mr. Kawaguchi had given Hiro a collection of old baseball cards, and they were worth a lot of money. Hiro had a cedar chest filled with them, old yellowed cards with the edges worn and some of them creased and all of the cards sorted by year, position, and team. He had a card of Willie Mays when he was with the New York Giants. The players wore baggy clothes back then and they shaved their beards.

Hiro showed me a book that had card prices, and I couldn't believe my eyes. The Willie Mays card was worth three dollars! He told me there were baseball card conventions all the time, and all the collectors set up tables and sold and traded cards. His father took him to every convention.

"Hiro," I said. "I've got an idea."

The next convention was in a month. I borrowed Hiro's baseball card price books and spent those weeks building up a collection. I stole money from Pop's change stash—a giant plastic beer bottle he emptied his pockets into after work. Every night at the gas station I asked the regular customers if they had any old baseball cards they'd give me. Joe Clausi, the boss of Clausi Carpets, gave me three shoeboxes of old cards, Topps and Bowman and Goudey bubble-gum cards and Zee-Nut and Pee-Chee Nut cards and caramel cards and cards that came with packages of cigarettes. By the end of two weeks, I had capital to work with.

Then I found out who the other kids were who collected cards. I found out that Tim Courageous' dad had a great collection, and I knew Tim liked to set things on fire so I traded him ten packs of firecrackers to steal all the cards from his father. Joe McGhee had the best collection, four thousand cards. He was the best fighter in the school, and he had two big brothers who were even better fighters.

"I want to trade," I said.

"I don't trade," he said. "I flip."

"Flip?"

"Flip," Joe said. He smiled. "Come to my house after school tomorrow, and bring a stack of cards."

Joe's parents' house smelled like wet dogs and the sweat of old people. Joe's room was the garage. He had his own bench press and free weights and a punching bag mounted to the rafters. He punched the bag for me. He could hit the bag with his fists and then his elbows and even with his head. He was good at punching the bag.

"Here's how it works," Joe said. "I look through your stack and pick three cards, then you look through my stack and pick three. We lean them against the wall and try to knock down the cards with the cards from our stack. We take turns. Whoever knocks the last card down wins all the cards we've flipped."

I'd brought over all my best cards, the ones Joe Clausi had given me. Joe's stack was nothing but junk, new cards of players nobody cared about.

Joe lined up all of my best cards against the wall, my 1911 Tris Speaker and a Pee-Chee Nut Mickey Cochrane and my 1933 Goudey Babe Ruth.

We stood behind a strip of masking tape he'd stuck to the concrete floor and we flipped cards. Joe let me flip first. I spun my card at the cards lined against the wall and the card I flipped was off by about six feet.

He waited until almost all my cards were on the floor, and then he flipped a card that hit the wall like a plate. It knocked down two of the six cards.

"What kind of card was that?"

Joe shrugged. "Someone dipped it in hot wax," Joe said. "To protect the card from getting old."

"How many more do you have?"

"A few," Joe said.

I lost all my best cards to Joe McGhee and his waxed flying saucers. I didn't accuse him of cheating because I thought about that punching bag and those weights of his.

But I still had my plan. The convention came and Mr. Kawaguchi had a carload of us kids. You see, I'd recruited Tony Romero, Roger Chavez, and Armondo Costello to come along and help. I promised them each a pack of firecrackers for every shoebox they filled with baseball cards. Hiro had money he'd saved from his allowance, and he promised a dollar for each boxload. We all wore our stealing jackets, baseball jackets with elastic waistbands so cards wouldn't fall out when we loaded up.

The convention was held in the gymnasium of Corpus Christi High School in Alamo, a rich suburb on the other side of the Oakland hills. The sky was bluer on the Alamo side, and they had trees and cars I'd never seen before, new cars with weird shapes, and instead of names like Falcon or Galaxy or Impala the cars just had numbers or letters—240Z, 600D, XKE.

Inside, hundreds of old men sat at tables loaded with cards. The old men looked dumb as grandparents, and ripe for being stupid enough to trust my band of thieves.

The acquisitions program went according to plan, with one exception. I had already stolen a stack of cards from an old black guy and I was eyeballing his display of Topps Fold-Ups from the fifties when he looked at me and smiled.

"You know who these players were?" he said.

His face was wrinkled and shriveled. He reached for a card with his hand, and his fingers were so knotty that he couldn't pick up the card, so he pointed. He didn't have regular fingernails—they were like yellow pieces of cracking pipe glued to his brown shiny skin.

"That's me," he said.

I looked at the card. It was a Roy Campanella. I looked back at the old man.

"I was younger then," he said.

"Campanella's crippled," I said. "He got in a car wreck."

The old man pointed at the wall. A wheelchair leaned, folded up, against a stack of boxes.

He smiled.

I waited until he wasn't looking, and I put back the cards I'd swiped from him. I felt like a rat. I went to another table.

Hiro and I divvied up the goods when we got home. Mr. Kawaguchi came into the room and looked at us, the eight shoeboxes full of cards. He stared at Hiro, then at me, for a long time. Then he left the room.

"Dad knows," Hiro whispered.

"How do you know?"

"Because he didn't say anything."

"But he never says anything."

"It was the *way* he didn't say anything," Hiro said.

"Big deal," I said. "You're not in trouble."

"I'm not in trouble," Hiro said.

He closed his eyes and tears squeezed out from beneath the lids.

"I'm not in trouble," Hiro said. "I am kuyashii."

I shrugged and started sorting through the cards again.

Hiro's lower lip trembled.

"What?"

"I am shamed," Hiro said. "You can't understand. It's the worst thing in the world."

"There are worse things," I said. "You could have gotten a whipping."

"That would have been better," Hiro said.

* * *

Hiro didn't realize it, but the biggest score of the convention was a set of 1933 Goudey reprints, and that's how I ended up with the whole set. I convinced Hiro they were worthless and let him take a 1957 Hank Aaron, his favorite player, in exchange for the whole set of reprints. The original 1933 cards were worth plenty, so whoever made the reprint set printed the cards on thinner paper so that collectors would know the difference.

It only took me a week to make those reprints look even older and more genuine than originals. I soaked the cards in a bucket to get the paper to separate, making the cards thicker. While the cards were still wet, I rounded the edges with my fingernails. I set the cards to dry in the sun every morning before I went to school, and they turned yellow. The cards would have fooled anyone.

At Joe's house I handed him the stack of cards.

"Are these worth anything?" I said.

"No," he said. "They're old. Old cards are like the old bubble gum that comes with them. Worthless."

"No way," I said. "I read Hiro's card book. I know what these are worth."

"Want to flip?"

"I want to trade," I said.

"I'll have to ask my dad," Joe said.

Mr. McGhee was the fattest man I'd ever seen. Even his fingertips were fat. He used a cane to get up out of his chair, and he wheezed every three or four words. His eyes were solid blue, no whites, no pupils, just blue like clear marbles. Joe showed him the cards. Mr. McGhee looked at them, over and over, flipping through the stack. He told us stories about when he was a kid and he used to buy Goudey bubble-gum cards in Brooklyn and his eyes got watery. He told us ballplayers were gentlemen back then.

"Give him," Mr. McGhee said, "whatever," he wheezed, "he wants."

"But, Dad," Joe said.

"You heard me," Mr. McGhee said.

I took home three thousand cards.

Pop was smoking a cigar and sitting on a car tire when I got home to the gas station. Pigeons lined the tin canopy above the pumps and cars honked their horns on the freeway. Traffic was jammed at the stoplight, and you could hear people's radios and sometimes people yelling at each other when the light turned green.

I showed him my box of baseball cards.

"How'd you get them?"

I told him the story of how Hiro and I stole them.

He nodded. "Good job," he said.

We sat on tires together.

Pop smoked his cigar.

Every morning Hiro beat me at chess. No matter what I did, what books I read, what famous openings I memorized, he always beat me. One time he beat me without moving anything but his pawns.

Before school one morning I took my trumpet from its case and hid the horn in my clothes cupboard in the trailer. The trumpet was a loaner from school, and I was getting pretty good at playing it, already lead trumpet in the band at school.

I went to Hiro's with the empty trumpet case. Mr. Kawaguchi opened the door and let me in and I ate breakfast with the family, Hiro and his sisters and his mom and Mr. Kawaguchi. Hiro and I went to his room to resume the game we'd been playing the morning before. He was beating me again, and he'd set it up so that my queen and my king's rook were forked, and no matter what, he'd get one of the two pieces. Hiro's mother told him to brush his teeth.

When he went to the bathroom, I opened the empty trumpet case and started loading it up with Hiro's baseball card collection, taking half of each of his twenty-four team stacks. I heard the water running in the bathroom, and I knew Hiro was still in the bathroom, but I looked over my shoulder anyway toward the doorway.

Mr. Kawaguchi was standing there, looking at me. He closed his eyes and lowered his head, then slowly raised his head back up and then he took a deep breath and then let the air out slowly. He opened his eyes again. I had Hiro's stack of Cleveland Indians in my hand. Mr. Kawaguchi looked at me. The water in the bathroom stopped running. He turned around and walked down the hallway. His shiny black shoes made a sound so quiet it hurt my ears.

I didn't have time to unload all the cards from the trumpet case and back into Hiro's cedar chest, so I put the stack of Cleveland Indians into the case and locked the snaps.

Hiro and I went stealing at Hung Lee's Market before school, and I swiped a whole box of baseball cards and gave them to Hiro. He wanted to divide them up, but I wouldn't let him.

"You keep them all," I said.

Hiro shrugged. "You take all the candy, then," Hiro said. "But you're not dealing with supply and demand very well."

"I know."

The next morning I took the trumpet case to Hiro's again. I knocked on the door and Mr. Kawaguchi answered. He let me in just the same as any other day.

"Where's Hiro?"

Mr. Kawaguchi didn't say anything. He sat down on the couch with his morning paper on his lap. The sweet smell of syrupy rice made my stomach growl.

After breakfast Hiro got up first. He came back from his room holding the chessboard. He set the board on the coffee table in front of the couch and sat down next to his father. Mr. Kawaguchi lowered his paper.

"We're playing chess in the front room from now on," Hiro said. "We won't be playing in my room again."

The trumpet case was still filled with Hiro's cards. I was going to put them back into the cedar chest when Hiro brushed his teeth after breakfast during our morning chess match.

Hiro took my rook, the one he forked with his knight the morning before. He looked at me. Mr. Kawaguchi looked at me too.

"Your move," Hiro said.

I couldn't think of what to do. They both sat there staring at me.

"Your move," Hiro said.

CHAPTER SEVEN

Malaga

For an entire year I tried to sneak Hiro's baseball cards back into his room, but he always made sure there was no way for me to do it. We stayed friends, since we really didn't have much choice—neither of us had any other friends. But even though we were still friends, we kept our guard up against each other. And he wouldn't let me make things better by giving back his cards. So I sold them.

I sold the cards I'd gypped out of Joe McGhee too. I liquidated my entire inventory, went to a convention and sold my collection, some of the cards to the same old dudes I'd stolen them from, and I used the cash—a thousand bucks—to buy myself a new trumpet.

The school loaner at Jack London Junior High School was junk, and Pop wouldn't let me touch the family trumpet. The loaner was a dented-up Bundy held together with rubber bands and peeling solder. Air hissed from the rotted cork of the spit valves. The bell buzzed from a bad solder joint. When I'd drop it on the floor or ding it on the music stand, I wouldn't even cringe.

My new trumpet was a hell of a lot better than Pop's old hand-me-down. I had it custom built by the trumpet master at Royal Music on 14th Street in downtown Oakland. His trumpet factory was in the basement beneath the music store. You could smell the bubbling flux from the solder, the heated brass and silver, the chemicals from the tempering vats.

"I want you to build me a trumpet," I said. "I have a thousand bucks."

He looked at me over his safety glasses. He wore a leather apron that went down past his knees and was blackened with tarnish and chemicals and burns. Stiff jets of hissing flame roasted the air at the workbenches. The smell of ozone heavy in the air, the sulfur odor of silver polish nasty and rotten, the walls blackened and blistered and sweating, brass and silver and copper tubing hanging in racks along the walls, lathes spinning and grinding mouthpieces, the shavings spitting into a fifty-five-gallon oil-drum, trumpets were in every stage of craft. They hung by leather strips from the ceiling—valves, bells, slides, bodies. In the center of the basement room was a furnace smoking with heat, and next to the furnace was a metal rack with dozens of hammers and punches and files. Against the wall in one of the corners was a neatly made bed, and next to it a dresser. Work clothes and black dress coats and slacks hung from a dowel that was attached to the ceiling with leather straps.

"And you are?" he said as he took a pad of paper from one of the pockets of his apron. His face was darkened with soot.

"T-Bird Murphy."

"Murphy?" he said. "By any chance son of Bud Murphy and grandson of old man Murphy?"

"That's me."

"They were fine trumpeters," he said. "Whatever happened to your father? He's still around, I take it."

"He married my mother," I said. "They had me."

"I'm sorry," he said. He wrote my name on his pad. "I mean I'm sorry your father quit playing."

"Everybody is."

"Silver, brass, copper, or nickel?" he said.

"Silver."

"Standard bell, or oversized?"

"Oversized."

He wrote on his pad. He opened a drawer in the workbench and pulled out a bag of balloons. He handed me a green one. "Take a deep breath and then blow up the balloon until you run out of air."

"Why?"

"Checking lung capacity."

I blew up the balloon and tied a knot and gave it to him. He held it in his hands, then touched it to a hissing flame and popped it. "You need a .468 bore already, young son of Murphy. If you grow any more, you'll need a .472. Think you'll grow?"

"I'll grow."

He wrote on his pad. "It'll be hard to play at first—it'll seem like you're blowing into a tuba. You'll reach for a note and you won't be able to grab it. But you only buy one trumpet like this in your life, and it's better that you grow into it than out of it." He reached into another drawer and pulled out a ball of clay, then took the clay over to the sink and got it wet. He handed me the muddy ball. "Hold it like you'd hold your trumpet."

I sank my fingers into the clay, molded it to my hand.

"Now hand it to me, and be careful not to move your fingers," he said. I reached my hands out and he took the ball. He set it on a counter. There were five other balls of clay there with handprints.

"Bell tuning or standard slide tuning?"

"What's the difference?"

"A bell tuner gives you the chance to switch bells if you ever decide you want a gold one or a different size."

"Bell tuner."

"That's what I'd do," he said. He wrote it down. "You a high-register player like your father and grandfather?"

"Lead trumpet in the Jack London Stage Band," I said.

"What mouthpiece you on?"

"7C."

"You need to get off the school-issue mouthpieces. If you're not lying about being a high-register player," he said, and he looked at me over his glasses again to check if I had the face of a liar, "then I can grind you *my* version of the Shilke 6A4A. I've made a modification that brings the player's range up another third of an octave." He smiled. "I carve out a shallow double-cup."

"Do it."

"A thousand dollars?" he said.

"That's what I've got."

"You going to quit like your father?"

"I'll never quit," I said.

"If you quit, you'll have to live with knowing that you stole from me," he said. "You see those?" he said, and he pointed to the wall behind me. Tacked to it were newspaper clippings and concert flyers and pictures of old black dudes in tuxedos. "Those men played horns I built. You'll notice your father isn't on that wall."

"I'll be on that wall."

"Then we'll grind that mouthpiece of yours right now," he said. "And I'll give it to you free of charge, on this condition: if you ever quit playing your trumpet, you have to walk back down here and hand it to me personally and tell me that you quit. You have to tell me to my face that you don't want to play the trumpet I made for you."

When my new trumpet was finished, I took it to school. The trumpet master gave me an old beat-up case, and so when I made a big deal about turning in my loaner because I had a new trumpet, the other kids snickered. They weren't snickering when I opened that case, though. They gathered around and I told them about the trumpet master, how he made the trumpet specifically for my hands and lungs, how there wasn't another trumpet like it on the planet and how it didn't even have a brand name, just a date stamped to the middle valve. I was the only kid in the band with a silver horn.

Hiro played alto sax in the band, and though we were still friends, things were different since I'd ripped off his baseball card collection. He wouldn't let me in his house anymore, and at school he wouldn't let me copy his math homework if I hadn't done mine. If I asked him to borrow a quarter to buy myself a pizza square, he told me his capital reserves had been plundered, and that he didn't have money working for him anymore.

Since Hiro was being a dork, I got a new friend, Rich Gonzalez. Rich played second trumpet in stage band. His mother bought him a new brass King trumpet, and he shined it every day before practice with a T-shirt he'd cut specially for the shape of his horn. He was as smart as Hiro and me, and he was just as good a thief. He'd come to school every day with a half-pint of booze he'd stolen from the supermarket, and Hiro, Rich, and I would drink it down at lunchtime while the tough kids wandered the neighborhood smoking their cigarettes and pot. Rich shared everything he had, and he had a lot—and whatever he didn't have, he'd swipe. He could walk into a store and come out with five big bags of potato chips stuffed into his jacket. He could steal a pair of Converse All Stars without Hiro and me even noticing. One time he swiped a teacher's purse right off her desk, and we divvied up all her cash. Rich lived in a three-bedroom house his mother bought. He had a green Pea-Picker Schwynn five-speed with a sissy-bar and shock absorbers and a front drum brake. He had his own bedroom. His mother worked as a photographer for a big company in San Francisco. She had a degree from Oakland Community College. Rich and me wanted to fix his mother and my father up so we could be brothers.

Mrs. Gonzalez hated my father, though. The first time she came into the Mohawk station, Pop said, "That's one terrific set of major league yabos."

"I beg your pardon?" Mrs. Gonzalez said.

Pop wiped his hand across his forehead and left a smear of axle grease over his eyebrows.

"You got your face greasy," Mrs. Gonzalez said, offering Pop a white Kleenex.

Pop smiled and took the Kleenex and wiped his hands with it. "I bet you like my greasy face," Pop said. "I bet you'd really like my greasy hands, wouldn't you?"

The first day back to school after spring vacation, Dr. Scheidemann, the music teacher, walked into class wearing a tuxedo and smoking a cigar. Dr. Scheidemann was a huge, dark-skinned man who spoke Spanish. He was from Cuba, and he played all the instruments, the drums, the piano, the saxes, the bones, trumpet, string bass. He had thousands of records lined up on shelves in the practice rooms, and every day when we came to practice a different record was playing, and Dr. Scheidemann was playing along with the record with whatever instrument he felt like playing that day. Before we played any music, he told us about the record, told us about the men and women who were making the music, told us the stories of their lives, of the additions they'd made to the history of the art.

His black hair was slicked back, and he had a brandy snifter in his hand. He stood there and looked at us for a while, and then he reached into his briefcase and pulled out a folder. He held it up as if he were flashing a wad of hundred-dollar bills.

"For Reno," he said, "Malaga."

Our stage band at Jack London Junior High was legendary.

The school had won the Reno International Jazz Festival seven years running and had been to the Monterey Jazz Festival four of those years. With guys like Don Dolly, Skip Freitas, Walt Jardine, Hiro Kawaguchi, Henry Pratt, Rich Gonzalez, Adam Alvarez, Art Azurdia, Phil Koski, Kevin Hamilton, Daryl Sale,

Loretta Branco, Keith Weiskampf, Oh-Bee Gim, my brothers—Kent and Clyde, who Pop had sprung from their foster homes—and me, how could we not be great? Most of us gigged around town in bands, and we got paid. We were pros. A few guys played in Night Life, a disco band named after an Oakland low-rider club. Some of the guys had a band called Souled Out, and they sounded as good as the Isley Brothers. I played with a band called Ticket, and most of our songs sounded like Chase or Malo or Blood, Sweat and Tears or Chicago because we had a full horn section and we horn players wrote the songs. We wailed on Tower of Power tunes, like an Oakland band should. Most of us could play more than one instrument, and sometimes, just for the hell of it, at competitions we'd switch instruments—Walt Jardine would play drums instead of trumpet, Dave Borges would play guitar instead of lead trombone, I'd play bass instead of lead trumpet—and we'd win anyway.

When we all had our parts to "Malaga," Dr. Scheidemann told us to close our eyes.

"I want you all to imagine that you're out of high school, you're wealthy beyond anything you can imagine. You have more money than the rich people in the hills. You drive a Cadillac and when you go out to dinner you don't look at the prices on the menu. Your girlfriend is beautiful and owns houses on the French Riviera, and Loretta, your boyfriend is a Spanish prince. You're on the coast of Spain, and everyone around you is as rich as you are. The weather is hot, and the palm trees glitter as if they're laced with diamonds. You're at a casino, and you're playing roulette or craps or cards, and you've just lost twenty thousand dollars on a single bet, but you don't care, because you have millions of dollars. Spending twenty grand is like dropping a nickel on the street. Sometimes you don't even bother to pick it up."

And we listened to Dr. *Scheidemann*, listened to him as he described the scene, money everywhere and booze flowing and everyone smoking cigars like the one he was smoking, everyone wearing tuxes, the women beautiful and all shades of skin, the men perfect and none of them fat and all of them tall, dozens of languages being spoken and everyone understanding all of them.

"And you feel tough," Dr. Scheidemann said. "You feel reckless and tough and invincible and drunk and *free,* free like you've never felt before, free to do anything and be anything you want to do or be. And what you want to do is *something you shouldn't be doing.* You want to keep on drinking until sunrise, or you want to steal someone else's wife or girlfriend, or you want to race your Cadillac, a Cadillac *convertible,* along the beach at a hundred miles an hour. You drive like a madman even though you might lose control, even though you might die."

The next sound was the crackle of a needle on a record, and then blazing trumpets, trumpets screaming sixteenth notes up in the stratosphere, and beneath the trumpets the saxes and the bones hammering out counterpoint sixteenth-note punches, a wild fugue of fury and fire. It sounded like there were a thousand trumpets and saxes and trombones blasting out the head, and at the same time you could hear a melody coming through in a 3/4 time signature, a crisp and neat tune snapping through the measures.

Then the pace slowed, the tempo calming and easing to a full stop, out of which, almost imperceptibly at first, you could hear the drum set playing a Latino beat in 4/4 time and then the trumpets, quiet at first, sneaking in and the pitch rising, getting louder and higher, the drummer louder too, and then the saxes and the bones on the same melody and the entire band playing at fortissimo, brasses near exploding, drums steady and insistent, cymbals shimmering.

The band cut and a trumpeter screamed solo, his notes piercing and high like Maynard Ferguson or Cat Stevens, high and loud and clean, screams not of terror but of passion and need, of triumph, of sheer and utter joy. I'd never heard anything like it on Pop's old jazz albums. On Pop's albums, the trumpeters were easy and cool, their whole point in playing to express a strut and a meal and a lover and a humid stormy evening with music. But this music, this "Malaga," this was anything but cool. This scorched. This trumpeter sounded like he was blowing flames out of his bell, like his keys were too hot to touch and his fingers had to dance over the melting metal.

Then the tempo switched again, and it went swing, straight time, a key change, echoing the themes of all that had gone before but riffing variations on those themes, going raunchy, the bass walking through the changes in jazz, the horns going chaotic and wild above, the drummer syncopating in ways that seemed not to make sense but which always found the downbeat. And I imagined the town of Malaga, saw myself sitting at the bar and watching the gamblers, saw myself dressed well and older. I saw myself—calm.

"When you go home tonight," Dr. Scheidemann said, "I want you all to change your radios from KJAZ to 88.7, KLTN, the Spanish-language radio station. You are to listen to nothing but KLTN until after Reno. You're to live and breathe Spanish music."

"But I can't even understand Spanish," Rich said. "My mom and dad speak Spanish, but I don't."

"You don't need to know what the words of a language mean to understand the music the language makes," Dr. Scheidemann said. "You listen to the music with your balls," he said. "Even you, Loretta."

There was no way Rich and I were ever going to get to be brothers. One day, when Mrs. Gonzalez was giving us a ride to school, she said, "I'm sorry to have to say this."

She turned down the radio.

"It is no reflection on you, T-Bird, but your father is the filthiest lowlife I've ever met. I'm not accustomed to being around such people. I'm sorry you have to have him as a father, because you're such a well-behaved young man. I can't believe that beast is really your father. You don't look at all like him, you know. You must take after your mother's side of the family."

"He's told me that before," I said.

Mrs. Gonzalez shook her head.

"Where's *your* dad?" I asked Rich.

"A drunk," Mrs. Gonzalez said. "He lives in a trailer park and drinks tequila and cans vegetables for a living. That's no life for a man."

Before school each day I told Mrs. Gonzalez stories about my family and she would make me sack lunches to take to school. Whenever I went over to Rich's house on the weekends his mother offered me something good to eat: pot roast that had been simmering in its thick molasses all day, mashed potatoes that didn't come from a box, squash from her garden. I'd tell her about the Angels, how they ate up all the food and left nothing for my brothers and me, how they shot up and smoked pot and drank beer and whiskey until they were all passed out on the living room floor or in my mother's bed.

"Little boys aren't supposed to know of such things," Mrs. Gonzalez would say. And later she'd say, "Tell me more."

When I'd finish, she'd look at Rich and nod smugly, as if to let him know how good he had it.

I was lead trumpet, and the solos usually went to second chair, but Rich couldn't cut the solo in "Malaga." The high notes the trumpet needed to solo properly were beyond Rich's range, and my range had gone up, just like the trumpet master said it would. So Dr. Scheidemann told me I'd be playing the solo in Reno.

I was practicing my solo in the trailer after school. Outside, the gas station bells rang like crazy as if someone were dancing on the rubber bell-cord. A diesel was laying into his air horn.

Someone was lowering a car in the lube bay, and the air hissed as the rack came down. The trailer door opened, and Pop stood outside looking at me. Garbage swirled over the asphalt lot behind him. His face was smeared with black grease, his beard matted and his glasses smudged.

"Put a sock in it," he said.

"But I need to practice," I said.

"I didn't say don't practice," he said. "I said put a sock in it. You're bothering the customers. A sock, like goes on your foot. In the trumpet. In the bell."

"What I need is a mute," I said. "A Harmon mute or a straight mute."

"You got all that money," Pop said. "Buy your own goddamn mute."

"I don't even like using a mute."

"Then use a fucking sock."

Pop had spent the summer before I started junior high trying to get my brothers, Kent and Clyde, away from the foster homes they'd been put in after Pop got thrown in jail. He had to pay lawyers, he had to take time off work for all the hearings and court dates, he had to buy a tie and fancy black shoes. He had to write an essay about why my brothers would be better off with us in the trailer than with the foster parents. I helped him write it. We told the Children's Protective Services board that my brothers needed to live with their real father, not some person who wasn't even related to them. We told the Board that Pop had conquered his temper, that he didn't hit people anymore, especially women—he was divorced now, and he would never have to hit my mother again. We told them he had a steady job and that Kent and Clyde would benefit from the quality of the school district, which had the best junior high school band in California and had been producing great musicians for fifty years. We told them that my brothers would ben-

efit from the cultural opportunities of East Bay, from the community feeling of our working-class neighborhood and how it instilled proper moral values and attitudes toward work and responsibility and family.

The board approved Pop's petitions finally, and the four of us packed into the trailer, Pop on the foldout bed, and two of us kids sleeping on the floor each night, one on the other bed.

They'd been living in swanky towns like Anaheim and Reno with families that owned houses and had new cars and bought them things like new baseball mitts and different kinds of shoes for every kind of sport. Hell, they had shoes for basketball and tennis both. They had cleats for football *and* baseball, as if there's a difference.

Clyde, the youngest, played trombone, and he'd been living in Anaheim and wanted to be a movie star when he grew up. He was only a sixth grader, but he was so good on the trombone that he played for the Jack London Junior High Stage Band. Clyde was Pop's favorite. Clyde worked on cars. When Clyde moved in, he took over my spot as Pop's helper at the Mohawk station. One day I came home late from school, and when I opened the trailer door Pop was under the covers with a fat woman. She pulled the sheet over her floppy titties. The sink was filled with empty jugs of Spanada wine. Pop was smoking a cigar.

"Don't you ever knock before you barge in?" Pop said. "Don't you have any fucking manners?"

"Sorry."

I went to the back of the trailer. Clyde was necking with a Japanese girl. He had her shirt off. Her bra was black.

"Get out of here," Clyde said.

"Sorry."

The trailer rocked. I heard Pop get out of bed. I turned around. Pop was naked and still smoking his cigar.

"What's the matter with you?" Pop said. "I've got a girl, Clyde has a girl. I've never seen you with a girl. What are you, anyway? Some kind of faggot?"

I didn't say anything.

Clyde and the Japanese girl laughed.

"Well?" Pop said.

My older brother, Kent, didn't spend his time being popular. He was an eighth grader and a cello player. In stage band he played upright bass. The family he'd been living with in Reno bought him the cello, and when he strung his cello, the sound was full of pain and joy and compassion and rage. When he played that cello, it was as if some god had dropped into his soul and sang for him, as if Kent heard that song and he could spread it through his body and then out of his body and into the cello and into the world.

The week before Reno, Dr. Scheidemann made us play a lunchtime concert for the rest of the kids at Jack London Junior High. We set up in the cafeteria, and Dr. Scheidemann snapped his fingers and counted us off, and we nailed the opening to "Malaga," played it perfectly and with the precision of a band of seasoned old cigarette-smoking pros.

The kids in the cafeteria were not impressed. They thought we sucked. They threw their food at us.

Clyde and Kent, my brothers, were surprised when the food started flying. They'd never before had people throw food at them when they were playing. I wasn't surprised, though. I knew that when we played for those goons we'd be laughed out of the cafeteria, called pussies, heckled, and reconfirmed as faggots all.

Roger Alvarez threw a book at me, and he hit my trumpet and it fell to the floor. The bell was crushed, wrinkled up like tinfoil.

The black kids didn't throw anything at us, at first. They looked down at their lunches while the Mexicans and the white kids hurled their chow our way. Then Dawsey Jefferson stood up and yelled, "Let's *pay* these boys," and he reached into his pocket and pulled out his change and threw it at us. Then the rest of the black kids stood up, and they started throwing their pennies and nickels and dimes at us. The coins pinged against our horns, and Loretta got plunked in the eye with a quarter.

When Kent's cello got hit by a flying lunch tray and cracked, Kent packed it into the case and started toward the crowd of black and Mexican hyenas in the cafeteria.

I tackled him.

"Get off me," he said.

"They'll kill you," I said.

"They cracked my cello."

"And they wrecked my new trumpet," I said. "You don't understand," I said, and I looked at him hard. "They *will* kill you."

I took my trumpet to the trumpet master. He felt the bell with his fingers, and then he smiled.

"The animals ruined my trumpet," I said. "The fuckers. Can you fix it?"

He smiled. "Sure, I can fix it. No problem. Happens all the time."

He walked to a bench and he went to work on my horn. He used the forge and the anvil, he used a torch. He beat on the bell with a mallet. When he was done, he polished it up on a buffer and handed it to me.

"Real trumpeters play rough crowds," he said. "The trumpet was invented to play rough places. Battlefields and bars."

Pop and Mr. Gonzalez, Rich's father, agreed to chaperon the Reno trip for the jazz festival.

The day before we left for Reno, Rich took me to his father's trailer park. It was on the edge of the dumps. Seagulls screamed, and the trailers were all big nice ones. They had sewer hookups. They had television antennas. They had windows that slid open instead of cranked. Each trailer had a mailbox of its own planted in a little patch of lawn. We knocked on the door of Rich's father's trailer, and his father answered in a T-shirt and boxers. He had tattoos, but they were so old and faded you couldn't make out what they were.

He stood in the doorway holding on to the jamb with one hand, a bottle of tequila in the other.

"Come in, my little mariachis," he said. "Come in, come in."

The inside of the trailer smelled of food, of sweat, of tequila and beer. The garbage cans were overflowing with beer cans of many brands. Old black-and-white pictures of men in bolo ties and women in frilly dresses lined the counters and the window ledges. There must have been fifty pictures of Rich too, pictures of Rich as a baby, Rich wobbling around in a diaper, Rich's school pictures, Rich sitting in a chair with his trumpet across his lap.

"You are lucky that I was home," Mr. Gonzalez said. "I should be at work, but today I called in sick. I am preparing for the trip to Reno."

He took a swig of tequila and then cracked a beer, a Hamm's, and sipped the foam from the top of the can. Then he handed Rich an Oly and me a white can that said BEER in big black letters.

"I am very much looking forward to this Reno trip," Mr. Gonzalez said. "I haven't been to Reno since I married your mother."

A helicopter hovered above. Its blades chopped so loud the windows buzzed.

"You married Mom in Reno?" Rich said.

"At a drive-through chapel I married your mother." Mr. Gonzalez had to talk loud over the sound of the copter. "She was pretty hot for me, young man. She really liked me, then. We got drunk together for a week solid, drinking and having fun and gambling away all our money, and we'd only known each other for a week and we got married, right there at the drive-through."

The helicopter dove away, and shouts came faint from the distance.

Mr. Gonzalez smiled and knocked back his beer and cracked another. "You, my son, were born nine months after I met your mother."

"Quick work, Dad."

"Then your mother wanted me to stop drinking, which didn't make any sense to me. If she liked me as a drinking man, liked me enough to marry me after only knowing me for a week, why would she want to see me sober?"

"Variety?" I said.

"I was not asking a question," Mr. Gonzalez said.

The next day, Pop rolled the truck tires off the back of one of the Joe's Tire Service trucks, a flatbed with wood-slat guardrails.

"All aboard!" Pop said, and we climbed up onto the back of the truck. When we were all on, Pop slipped the rear guardrail into place. Clyde rode in Pop's passenger seat, and Rich rode with his father. Dr. Scheidemann took the instruments in his black Chevy van so they wouldn't get rained or snowed on, and Loretta sat in his passenger seat. Kent and I sat next to each other, and we shared one of the tarps Pop had thrown on the back of the truck to keep us warm during the trip. Pop looked at us through the wood slats.

"All my boys playing together at the Reno International Jazz Festival," Pop said. "That doesn't happen every day."

"And we're going to win," I said.

"I expect nothing less," Pop said.

* * *

By the time we got to Reno we were frozen solid. It rained on us when we drove through Auburn and the foothills, and once we hit the Sierras it started snowing. When we got to Donner Pass, the snow was so deep you could only see the tops of the trees. The road was a tunnel cut by snowplows. But when we saw Reno, we forgot about being cold. Kent had a look of relief on his face when he saw the lights in the distance, since he'd spent half his life there with his foster parents, and, though he'd never said anything, I'm sure he'd have rather been living in Reno than in Oakland. Almost anywhere on the planet is better than Oakland. We saw the city lights from twenty miles away, the casinos rising neon into the desert night. We drove under a sign that said, "Reno, The Biggest Little City in the world!" and it did seem huge, high-rise flashing buildings, limousines and Cadillacs with the racks of Texas longhorns on the hoods, pawnshops with guitars and drum sets and saxophones in the windows, hookers standing around on the street corners and walking up to cars stopped at streetlights, liquor stores, wedding chapels, gigantic hotels, doormen. It was like Dr. Scheidemann's Malaga, classy and rich and decadent.

The next day, we played "Malaga" at the preliminary competition at a high school near downtown. Mr. Gonzalez and Pop were so sure we'd make the finals that they went off gambling together. And we did make the finals. When we played the opening measures of "Malaga" the audience gasped and the judges stared at us as if they couldn't believe what they were hearing. We could have just walked off the stage without even finishing the song and we would have made the finals. We got 97s and 98s on a 100 scale from each of the five judges.

I was rooming with Rich and Hiro, and when Mr. Gonzalez got back from gambling, he came to see us.

"We made the finals!" Rich said. "We're in the night show at the concert hall downtown."

"Then there is a reason to celebrate," Mr. Gonzalez said, and he pulled a bottle of tequila from the pocket of his coat.

It was Mexican tequila, the label written in Spanish, and Mr. Gonzalez held the bottle up to the light to show us the worm. He took a swig, and he passed the bottle to Rich. Rich took a pop and passed the bottle to Hiro, and then I had my turn, and we passed the bottle around again. We'd damned near finished the bottle, and we were drunk, giggling and wobbling around. Hiro jumped up and down on the bed, and Rich opened up the twelfth-floor window and he pissed away. We laughed it up good about that one. Rich laughed so hard that he almost missed the window. And even if he had, we wouldn't have cared.

Mr. Gonzalez tipped the bottle and finished it off, worm and all. He went for more booze, and Hiro and Rich took turns barfing in the bathroom, hurling their guts out into the toilet, into the sink, the bathtub. There was puke everywhere, and it smelled flammable and nasty.

"Wimps," I said, and I headed on out of there.

When I hit the street, the cold air woke me up. The sun was setting behind the Sierras, and the sky shimmered with spooky yellow light, the mountains to the west snow covered and purpled with sunset. Everyone on the streets was as drunk as me, and people were crashing into each other, stumbling, barfing in alleys, smashing bottles against the walls of buildings. Prostitutes cooed at me when I walked past them. Hot air blasted onto the sidewalks from the open doors of the casinos, and the hot air when it hit the cold turned to steam, billowing clouds smoking into the sunset night.

I stood on the Virginia Street overpass that spans the Truckee River, and I looked down at the clean clear water bubbling through the snow-covered boulders and rocks, and I felt the wind at my back, and when I looked up at the mountains I couldn't see them anymore. They were black as the night that had fallen.

I went back to the hotel, and inside the room Rich and Hiro were crashed out on the beds, asleep and stinking. Mr. Gonzalez was snoozing in the chair, a half-empty bottle of tequila nestled against his chest.

Mr. Gonzalez made us take showers before we went to the concert. He gave us breath mints, and he made us slap Old Spice aftershave on our faces and necks. He made us eat toothpaste. We smelled pretty damn good by the time we headed out.

The concert hall was a golden dome a couple blocks from the Truckee, downtown, and to get in you went down elevators. It held five thousand people, and the place was packed. We stood around backstage while our competition, a band from Switzerland, played the Maynard Ferguson version of "MacArthur Park." Their lead trumpet player was a girl. None of us had ever seen a girl trumpeter before, and certainly not one that had balls like her. She nailed each note, and the crowd cheered like crazy. That girl trumpeter was some kind of mutant to be able to play like that.

"You guys doing all right?" I said.

"My head hurts like a motherfucker," Rich said.

Hiro nodded.

"I'm feeling pretty damn good," I said. "Must be that drunken Irish blood in me."

We took the stage. The lights were hot and pointed in our eyes from above. The seats rose in tiers into the vaulting dome. You could barely make out the people in the audience, but I spotted Pop. He was standing in the back on the ground level, leaning against the wall, and he was wearing a trench coat and a fedora. When we finished getting into place, and Phil Koski finished getting his Rogers drum set arranged, and we all had "Malaga" open on our music stands, Dr. Scheidemann walked onto the stage, and the way he walked, the cool glide of his feet across the hardwood floor, let the audience know that they were in for something good.

He leaned into a solo mike and said, "Malaga," and the

word boomed through the hall.

He turned to us and said, in a whisper and with a sly smile, "Horns up, gentleman—let's give these folks a ride."

We had our horns to our lips, Koski had his sticks in the air, Kent hovered over his bass, and we waited while Dr. Scheidemann swayed back and forth tapping his shoe, getting the beat, giving us the rhythm before he counted us off. He started swirling his hand in circles, snapping his fingers on "one" and whispering the count of the beat, one-two-three, one-two-three, one-two-three, one-two-three, looking us all over, looking at our eyes, making sure we had the beat in our blood, in our souls, making sure we had the beat in our bones. Then he began the countdown, four-two-three, three-two-three, two-two-three, one-two-three, and when he said "one-two-three," instead of waiting for the next round of beats to begin the song, I played the opening sixteenth-note B's and C's and I played them high and sharp.

But I'd come in at the wrong time, I'd started the song a measure early and since I was first trumpet, since I was the leader of the band, half the band followed me. And the half that didn't, the half that was watching Dr. Scheidemann, they didn't play when I started the head, they waited for their cue, and when Dr. Scheidemann landed on the cue, they began.

And there we were, rattling away at our parts, all of us in different places in the song, all of us knowing we'd screwed up, all of us wondering what the hell we were going to do about it, how we'd ever get back in sync, how we'd straighten out this mess of noise that was supposed to be Stan Kenton's "Malaga."

The look on Dr. Scheidemann's face was disgust.

He dropped his hands to his sides and stood there looking at us while we played our scrambled parts, none of us stopping, all of us playing straight ahead and hoping the other guys in the band would somehow align their parts to ours.

"Stop!" Dr. Scheidemann yelled. He swept his arms across each other like a football referee signaling an incomplete pass.

"Stop!"

And some of the guys stopped, and then more stopped, and finally we were all silent. The concert hall was frozen quiet.

Dr. Scheidemann clenched his teeth together and he growled. He growled loud enough for all of us to hear, loud enough for the sax mikes in the front of the band to pick it up, and it roared low through the concert hall.

I looked to the back of the hall, and I saw Pop. He was walking toward the exit. He opened the door and the light from the lobby swept into the darkness, and Pop walked through the doorway and was gone. The door shut.

Dr. Scheidemann looked at me.

He looked at me and he saw my drunken eyes. He looked at me and then he looked down at the stage and then he looked back up again, not at me but at no one in particular, and then, slower than normal, he raised his hands with the horns-up signal, and he hunched toward us, and "Now," he yelled, and we ripped to attention like a military band, like we were the band playing for a Mexican execution squad.

"One," he said, "one," he said, rolling his hand, and said, "one, one, one-two-three-one."

We hit the opening of the song square and tight, our horns singing. Man, we nailed that fucker. And when I played my solo, I played it well. I played it as if it mattered. I played it as if Pop hadn't walked out and were still there, as if after the show Pop were going to take me to a bar, and tell me he was proud, and buy me a drink.

CHAPTER EIGHT

Some Get-Back

I came home one day and found Clyde trying to play my trumpet and I decked him. He finked to Pop, and Pop restricted me to the trailer for the rest of the summer. There was no escape, because Pop was sure to catch me if I tried to leave. No privileges: I could only go outside once a week to empty the toilet's holding tank into the gas station toilet.

I discovered a lot that summer.

I discovered pot, thanks to Hiro, who'd given up being good in school and become a minor drug lord, dealing pot and purple microdot. He didn't care about his baseball cards anymore, loaded like he was from the new business, and he'd sneak me joints and acid through the plastic porthole near the rear of the trailer. I'd pay him with change I swiped from Pop's big plastic Heineken bottle. Hiro was pretty sharp about his drug dealing—he never sold to anyone at our school. He only sold to people from the rich side of town, where the prices were better and he was less likely to get caught.

I discovered, in Pop's decanters, scotch. I discovered mushrooms. I discovered, while reading the letter my mother sent me, that she had been saved by Jesus. I discovered, in the same letter, that my mother had played second clarinet in elementary school, and that's why I was a good trumpet player. I discovered, from that letter, that everything I'd ever done good in my life was because of her, and everything I'd done lame was the fault of Pop.

From the Funk & Wagnall's encyclopedia set I kept stashed in the drawers beneath and above my bed I learned that every scientific theory except the ones we believe in now has been proven false. I learned that if you divide a second in half, and then in half again, and again and again, you can divide it forever, and therefore there's an infinity between every tick on a watch. I learned that you can know where you are, or how fast you are going, but not both. I learned that you can't predict the path of a quark, and therefore everything in the cosmos is shit.

I decided I was going to live in the woods in Oregon when I left Oakland and shoot animals and build a log cabin and kill anyone who came near me. I decided my mother must have mated with an intelligent milkman when Pop was at work and produced the zygote that became me, because there was not a chance in hell I was born of the ape who was allegedly my progenitor. I decided, after reading about Marx, that I was a communist.

I grew six inches and twenty pounds and went from being fat-boy to being a monster. Every day of the summer I did push-ups for an hour in the morning and an hour at night. I did hundreds of sit-ups each day before noon. I put my hands on the counters and did dips as if the counters were parallel bars. Veins popped out of my arms and neck. I clipped my hippie hair off with a pair of tin snips. I did a bad job on purpose. I could throw truck tires around like they were Styrofoam life preservers. I could swing the sledge against split rims like John Henry. I had to start shaving. When I'd cut myself I'd let the blood run down my neck.

I could hardly wait for school to start.

There were some people I wanted to talk to.

* * *

It was the end of summer, it was hot, and the shit stank fierce. I was emptying the holding tank one bucket of chemical-green shit at a time, I was carrying the buckets around the back of the Mohawk station and dumping them in the ladies' room toilet, I was paying my friend Hiro half of my allowance to help, when the idea came to me.

Even though I was a fat-boy, I was one of the best athletes at Jack London Junior High, because every day for many years I'd been running home from school being chased by herds of cawing Mexicans and blacks. I was no sprinter, fat-boy me, but I could run my fastest without ever slowing down. I could run for hours at full-tilt. If I got a couple minutes' head start, I could get home to the Mohawk station without being touched. When they caught me, though, they beat me bloody. All of my fingers have been broken from being stomped on. I have an ugly nose. One kid sliced me up so bad I got thirty-one stitches. I limped for six months when I was in sixth grade. My head's been knocked so many times, I wouldn't be surprised if I was permanently stupid.

And if I showed up at the Mohawk with tears in my eyes or limping, Pop would smack me around too for being a coward. Unless I could prove I'd taken one out. Proof: my own bloody knuckles.

Being a whitey isn't as easy as it seems.

When I got home, I worked out. I slung truck tires at the Mohawk station, stacked them and restacked them. Instead of using the air gun on the lug nuts of the trucks I used a T-bar. I could lay beneath a car and hold up the tranny while someone bolted it on. I could climb the tire racks without using my feet.

But I wanted to make sure not to get the shit kicked out of me by Pop for being a coward. So sometimes—hell, lots of times—I ripped up my knuckles on the sidewalk, scraped my knuckles raw to bone so Pop would think I kicked some ass. I'd have dangling chunks of skin I could flap back over the meat. I'd grind them up good.

I was too chicken to ever hit the Mexicans and the blacks back. I was too chicken because every time I'd hit one of my own brothers, Pop had beat the shit out of me. "You're bigger than they are," he said. And then he popped me. "That's what it feels like when someone bigger hits you." The thought of hitting someone had always terrified me. My brothers, Clyde and Kent, could cry at will. They could be standing there pumping gas or scooping dogshit with the shovel and if they felt like it they could break out in sobs and tears. "T-Bird hit me," they'd say. I'd deny the charge, and get popped double for lying as well as for beating up my brothers.

Pop had two rules.

1: Take one out with you.

2: Remember.

"Never, never forget," he said. "You keep a list. Your 'get-back' list."

He reached behind the marble-topped counter in the shop and pulled out an old pad of paper. He showed it to me. The words were written in pencil, faded and smeared and smudged with grease and oil, and on the pad was a list of names, with columns, and the columns were "Date" and "Offense."

"A list," he said.

I noticed my mother's name was on the list. In capital letters. Big.

His father's name was on the list.

His boss's name.

Nixon and Agnew.

The offenses were vague: Shame. Too many. The Night. Cops. A woman's name.

The dates went back to before I was born.

"Never, *never* forget. Never. You keep a list, so you can be sure. And before you get even, you wait until *they* have forgotten what they did to *you*. Then there's two ways to proceed," he said. "One: remind them of what they did to you when you're nailing them."

And then Pop looked up from beneath the hood of the car he'd been working on, and he smiled big and his eyes shimmered with joy. "And two: make them *think* you're doing them a favor while you're destroying them. Some day, when they're groveling, when they're drooling on themselves and vomiting in the gutter, when they have the gun to their head and they're ready to check out, they'll look back and know it was *you* who orchestrated everything, you who were the puppeteer, you who were pulling their strings. And when they pull the trigger anyway, and they know it was you that brought them to this, then, *then* you have proper get-back. It might take you ten, maybe twenty years to get the right and perfect chance to shell out some get-back. But remember, get-back isn't worth the while unless it's forever, unless it's the *final payment.*"

Pop put his list back under the counter, and he stood there for a second with a blank face, stood there as if time had stopped and he were somewhere else, as if he had vanished. And then his lips began slowly to curl and twist, to slide upward on his face and into a smile and he said, slowly and with a voice that sounded like the first time he'd used his true voice instead of making sounds he'd thought he wanted people to hear. "Payment," he said. "*Payment in full.*"

I kept a list. It was a long list. It could take me the rest of my life if I waited for the right moments. I would never be bored.

Pop was on my list.

Hiro was a Japanese shrimp, I was a fat-boy whitey, we both wore black-rimmed glasses, and there was no way either of us was ever going to get any nookie, ever. Nookie was almost something mythological. The school's fat-boy four-eyed punching bag is not the likeliest candidate for nabbing a girlfriend. I asked six different girls, four Marias and two Lucys, to the seventh-grade dance. Five of them said no, and Maria Amaral thought it was so hilarious and ridiculous that *I'd* asked *her*, that she went into the cafeteria ahead of me and told everyone. When I walked through the doors, everyone was laughing. I mean they were really laughing. They were choking on their food laughing. They were having a good old time.

Maria Amaral went on my list.

Kids coming home from school had seen me going in and out of the trailer next to the Mohawk station. They were on welfare, but at least they lived in apartments. I was trailer trash that didn't even live in a trailer park. And they'd seen me emptying the buckets of slimy green, chemically treated turds. Someone would spot me, and then they'd round up all the kids they knew, and soon I'd have an audience, all of them laughing and holding their noses and squatting along the sidewalk as if they were dropping shitloads for me to haul away to the ladies' room toilet.

The ass-kickings were the worst when report cards came out. At Jack London Junior High, if you got caught with As on your report card, the beating was especially bad, and then the ridicule that followed was even worse. The girls? They didn't want nerds: they wanted real men, men who could protect them at the Laundromat when they were washing the family clothes, men who were already sixteen and had Camaros and Firebirds and Monte Carlos. And we had plenty of sixteen year olds in the eighth grade, kids who couldn't speak much English, kids who'd flunked plenty of grades. Our basketball team was ten kids, six-foot mutants—virtual retards—with driver's licenses and stringy goatees. Our team would scare the shit out of the other teams, showing up for games in their Bondo-mobiles, all of them drunk, making sure that at least five of them fouled out each game, and fouled out in style. They used to send the opposing teams home bloody. One of the local schools—from the fancy side of town—wouldn't even come to play our team. They'd forfeit every time we came up on the schedule. The more our school's goons flunked out, the better they were in sports, since each year they stayed behind, they got another year older than the other kids. Hiro and me got younger every year, and the odds of us getting any nookie when everyone else was six feet tall and drove cars and smoked pot and snorted coke and had good part-time jobs at the canneries and UPS and the loading docks surrounding the rim of the bay—the odds of getting laid if you were a little whitey fat-boy who got As in school were nil. Zip. How can you compete with those kinds of guys? At my school, flunking was the epitome of cool. So when report cards came out, Hiro and I would be absent.

I'd grown, though. I had grown, and I had a list.

Emptying those buckets of shit, the kids from my class watching as the green slop lapped onto my blue jeans, the sky Oakland gray and the breeze curling and twisting and eddying around the courtyard of the Mohawk station's brick-surrounded lot—cigarette wrappers swirling and me and Hiro dodging dog turds as we walked through the alley behind the station with the plastic buckets so heavy our shoulders drooped—emptying those buckets and watching the faces of the kids, the girls, two of whom I'd asked to the seventh grade dance and who'd rejected me, I decided what must be done, and to whom, and just how—and how splendidly—it would be done.

I was a kid with a plan.

I was glad when school started. The only kids who recognized me were the ones who came every Saturday to the shop to watch me empty the buckets of turds. I had cuts on my face and my hair was so short I didn't need to comb it and I was bigger than everyone by twenty or thirty pounds. Some of the flunkees were taller than me—Joe Gonzalez, Joe Borges, Joseph Alvarez—but they were skinny dudes with sunken chests and pointy heads. I could take them out in a flat second.

And they knew it. When I walked down the hall, my hair

shorn ragged like Cro-Magnon man, and my arms pumped up like ham hocks, people kept out of my way. And I liked it that way, and I encouraged it—I made my eyes look crazy. My eyes are gray like old plaster. I made them look creepier, though. I kept my eyes wide open and bulging like I was insane, like I'd never before blinked them and never would again. I had dry eyes that looked like they saw something beyond the world out there, something that would spook normal people but that I was in cahoots with.

Number one on my list was Alfonso. Alfonso Joseph San Miguel.

So I made it my personal mission to make friends with him.

I'd read a book by a Chinese writer named Sun-Tzu. Hiro had loaned it to me. It was his father's book. There wasn't a person on the planet who could look at Hiro's father without knowing that if they crossed him they'd pay *the final payment.* Even his name, Shig, sounded like an ancient Japanese weapon, like a sickle or a sacred spear used to ram enemies. You could tell that he'd dice you up clean and nifty, and he wouldn't do a victory dance afterward, no—he'd stand up straight and he'd pull out a handkerchief and he'd wipe the blade clean and walk slowly away, as if he'd found a good parking place downtown and paralleled without nudging a bumper.

When Hiro handed me Sun-Tzu, he said, "Read this."

"Books are for queers," I said.

"Not this one," Hiro said. "Look," and he turned to a dog-eared page.

Make the enemy's road long and torturous, the underlined paragraph read. *Lure him along it by baiting him with easy gains.*

"And this," Hiro said, and he showed me another passage.

Know the other, know yourself, and the victory will not be at risk. Know the ground, know the natural conditions, and the victory will be utter.

I nodded. "Sounds good to me."

"It's my father's favorite book," Hiro said. "He keeps it on the nightstand in his bedroom. He gave me a copy after the Chavez brothers pounded us last year. He gave me a copy of the book and a new chess set."

So I swiped a copy of my own from the Oakland Public Library downtown, and during my summer on restriction, when I wasn't working out, I read the book over and over. *The Art of War. The Art of War. The Art of War. The Art of War.* I nearly memorized the sucker.

The first item of business when school started was to lull my enemies, to infiltrate their camp, to make them believe I was *one of them.*

I set out to make friends with Alfonso.

Lunchtime the first day of school, I walked up to his table in the cafeteria and sat down.

"This table isn't for faggot culeros," he said. "Puta madre mojon gringo maricon."

He looked at me. The other Mexicans looked down at their sloppy joes and coleslaw.

"Maybe *you*," I said, "should leave. You know, I saw your mother on San Pablo Boulevard," I said, "with the other whores," and before I knew it he was across the table with his hands around my neck.

But I was ready for him. I'd rolled pennies from Pop's change bucket and my fists banging on his head were like hammers. It only took two punches to knock him dizzy and sprawling across the slop on the table. He looked up at me, and his eyes were twitching. He was breathing funny.

I took the rolls of pennies from my fists and peeled the paper and sprinkled the pennies over his face.

The cafeteria was silent.

I leaned close to his ear.

"Together," I said, "we can kick some holy ass."

***

After school, when I was walking through the parking lot toward home, I saw Alfonso. He was standing next to his '68 GTO. He was only in seventh grade, and I was in eighth, but he was three years older, and he had his driver's license.

"T-Bird," he said. "Come over here. I'm needing to talk some words with you."

I walked over to his GTO. It was Bondo-gray and had a set of Krager mags and 50-series monster BFGoodrich tires on the back, 60s in the front, raised whites.

He opened the passenger door. I got in.

"I could cut you up like a pig," he said. "Like a gringo pig."

We drove.

"My little goat the cabron has a four-barrel Holley double-pumper, traction bars, and glass-packs," he said. "I got the upholstery done in TJ."

The diamond-tuck job was crushed red velvet. *Everything* was diamond-tucked. The door panels, the glove compartment, the dashboard, even the floorboards. The inside of the trunk was diamond-tucked. It was a serious car.

"I builded the fucker my own self, the fucker," Alfonso said. "My little Goat, my cabron."

"It's boss," I said. I pulled a joint from my wallet. "Thai stick," I said.

"Panama Red," he said, and he took a joint from his shirt pocket and he lit it and smoked, then passed the joint to me. He smiled, and smoke leaked out from where one of his teeth was missing.

"How do you know so much about cars?" I said. "My pop works in a gas station and I live next door to it, and I don't know half as much as you."

I passed the joint back. I was getting stoned, and I felt good. I almost forgot I was sitting in a car with Alfonso Joseph San Miguel.

Rumor had it he'd killed someone.

He leaned his head back and exhaled. We smoked with the

windows rolled up so we could inhale the clouds over and over. The windows were crusted yellow with pot tar. I scraped my fingernail against the windshield and rolled a brown ball of resin between my fingers.

"I work at Santos Rentals," Alfonso said. "Seven dollars an hour. I can fix anything made of metal."

And that's the way it went for a month. Every day after school we'd smoke a joint in Alfonso's Goat, and we'd tell stories about our families. I told Alfonso how my mother used to ride with the Angels, and *he* thought that was *really* cool. I told him how my father used to play trumpet in the Oakland symphony, and he told me how his grandfather used to play violin in a mariachi band in Mexico. He told me how his father was illegal, and how his father and his uncle shared a green card between them, how sometimes he'd have to stay at his uncle's apartment for a month at a time when the federales were getting feisty, and he'd have to pretend that his uncle was his father and his aunt was his mother. He told me how someday he wanted to build dragsters himself, how he wanted to make the world's lightest rail so the horsepower/weight ratio alone would compensate for any problems he might encounter with aerodynamics.

One weekend, when he didn't have to go to work, we drove out to Berkeley and walked out to the end of the Berkeley Pier to smoke a joint. We stayed there until sunset, the bay shimmering orange and purple, the fog in the distance matted atop the Golden Gate and San Francisco. You could hear the seagulls crying happy over the garbage dumps, and you could hear the tugboats hooting their foghorns. A pelican dove into the water and came up with a fish and slowly lifted itself into the air, flapping hard and heavy. A yacht slipped past, and the people on it were having a party, dancing on the deck and throwing their empty champagne glasses into the water. They looked really happy.

"My papa's a wetback," he said. "In Mexico, he was an engineer. He went to the college in Mexico City and he designed bridges gringo tanks rolls across when the Mexicans buy them and bring them home. But when he gets to America and tries to become the engineer, they make him go to junior college to get the American credentials, the gringo papers. He failed that fucking freshman English every time he taked it, every motherfucking time, every semester for ten years, twenty times he took freshman fucking English, twenty times he fucking flunked. His *English* not good enough to build *bridges?* His *English* not good enough to draw *blueprints?* His fucking ingles? Fuck college. Fuck the fucking college and the fucking school. So he's just a wetback. But I'm not. I'm not a wetback because my papa worked hard all his life to hide from the federales. In Mexico he was a government inspector, he was a boss, he told people what was right and what was wrong. Here, in the fucking America, he's a garbage fucking man."

Alfonso looked out at the yacht and shook his head.

"When you throw something away, my father is the pinche mierda that picks it fucking up," he said.

"I'm sorry," I said.

"Don't be sorry for me. I'm no fucking wetback, and I can fix anything made of metal. And I'm going to make the fastest dragster ever *did* the quarter mile. My childrens will be motherfucking proud of their papa reata."

The fog was sweeping toward us. The sun behind had set. The bay clicked from orange and purple and red to battleship gray. We stood silent a long time.

"You know," he said. "Even though you a fucking gringo and you get As and shit in school, you okay, man. In my book, you okay."

I shouldn't have felt flattered, but I did.

I still had plans. In PE the first fall sport was wrestling. Wrestling was especially suited to my needs.

For wrestling, Coach Butler made us weigh in on the scales while he noted down the numbers on a pad. Only three guys were heavier than me, all of them fat-boys, geeky nerd friends of mine—Nelson Van Sickle, my science partner, Chaim Goldstein, the school whiz at anything that had to do with math, and Load Hansen, who played tuba in band. All two-hundred pounders. Coach Butler grouped the four of us together, and we were #1 Mat. As your weight got lighter, you moved down mats, all the way down to #15 Mat. The goal was to move up mats by beating the people at your starting mat. If you were a loser, you moved down mats and wrestled lighter and lighter kids, until you got to #15, where the runts were, Tito Campos, Joe Garcia, Joseph Guiterrez, and my friend Hiro. Since I was on #1 Mat, my job was to fend off challengers.

That's not what I had in mind, though.

Master Sun said, *Better to seem to lose the battle and actually win, than to seem to win the battle and actually lose. Sometimes the seeming loser is in truth the victor. One must know the definition of victory before one engages the enemy.*

I won by losing.

Everyone on my list was on a mat beneath mine, and so, to get to them, I had to lose.

During wrestling month, I'd pretend to wrestle, then let myself get pinned, and down a mat I'd go. Until I met with someone on my list, someone who'd pummeled me years before, sometimes someone who'd knifed me or stuck my head in a toilet four or five years before, and when I got to him on the mat, I'd crush him. I'd smash his face into the mat with my forearm against the back of his neck, I'd twist his arms behind his back until he screamed so loud everyone else stopped wrestling and Coach Butler had to pull me off.

I got sent to Mr. Hanover, the vice principal, who told me that I was a rough ball of clay, and it was education's job to shave off the rough edges.

When I got all the way down to #12 Mat, I met up with

Francisco Alvarez, who only weighed ninety pounds. We were in "referee position," Francisco on his knees and me behind him, and I whispered into his ear, "You remember in fourth grade when you punched me in the mouth in basketball practice?"

"No," he said.

"You chipped one of my front teeth," I said. "You don't remember? I had to go to the doctor?"

"I don't remember," he said.

"I do."

When Coach Butler blew the start whistle, I picked Francisco up into the air over my head and slammed him down so hard I knocked him unconscious. Coach Butler had to slap him around to get him to come to.

And when he came to, I was standing over him, smiling.

I started a trend. Everyone started losing. No one cared about winning anymore. All the fat-boys, all the big nerds and geeks, started losing and moving down the mats to the lower mats and pounding the runts when they got there, following their enemies from mat to mat by losing and winning as necessary. It got so bad, with no one really caring about winning or losing, that Coach Butler had to cancel wrestling and move us to weight lifting, where we wouldn't have to touch each other.

We didn't get to play football that season.

But I got to cross six names off my list.

Alfonso helped out a lot too. It was like having my own private hit man.

"Anyone fucking with T-Bird Murphy," he said, "fucking with Alfonso. I don't care how old we are, and where we living, if the motherfucker fucks with you, he fucks with Alfonso. And if you don't tell me, you, too, fucking with Alfonso."

All I had to do was say that someone had looked at me cross-eyed, and it didn't matter if it was one of his other friends or not, he'd shred him. I was helping Alfonso with his homework, and he was teaching me about cars and engines and electrical systems and fuel combustion, and if anyone fucked with either of us, he was meat. So I'd put the finger on a kid who'd thrown a football at the back of my head in sixth grade, and Alfonso would break his finger or slap him rummy in front of his friends. I could have asked Alfonso to assassinate someone and he would have done it for me, his amigo gringo.

On my way to school one morning, as I was walking through the shop to put back the dogshit shovel, Pop pulled me aside. He was working under the hood of an old Chrysler Newport.

"The toilet in the trailer stinks like shit," Pop said.

"Sorry," I said. "I forgot the chemicals this week."

"Sorry," Pop said. "Empty the fucker."

"After school," I said.

"Notice you have a new friend," Pop said. He slipped the wrench and banged his knuckles against the manifold. "Son of a bitch," he said. Blood seeped through the grease on Pop's knuckles. "Son of a bitch."

"He's not really a friend," I said. I rolled up my sleeve and showed Pop my scar. "You remember when I got this?"

"Thirty-one stitches," Pop said.

"Alfonso," I said. "My new friend."

Pop smirked. He smirked and looked at me over his glasses and he just stared at me, smirking. And then his smirk widened into a grin, a full smile, both rows of teeth showing. "Get out of here," he said, and I looked back before I turned the corner and saw Pop, and he was standing in the middle of the lube bay, wiping down his hands with a red rag, and he was watching me, and he was still smiling.

Things around Jack London Junior High had changed for me lately. I still had my geeky friends, and we still did all the geek things together—chess club, band, California Junior Scholarship Federation meetings, study group at lunchtime, drama club. But now no one else would talk to me. They wouldn't even *look* at me. When they'd see me coming down the hall, they'd look down at the floor and they'd back off, scattering. The school seemed much more spacious.

In PE, I could do just about anything I wanted. During basketball, I didn't mind fouling out, and so when I had the ball, I'd run over anyone in my way and do a layup. Rebounding, I'd swing my arms and elbows, and one time I smacked a Jarimallo so hard in the mouth he bit the inside of his own cheek off. There was blood everywhere, and I got sent to the vice principal's office again.

"You're a straight-A student," he said. "Why are you doing this?"

"Doing what?"

"Fighting all the time, doing what," he said.

"They're the thugs," I said. "They've been beating the hell out of all of us for years now. You know that."

Mr. Hanover shook his head.

"You can't run around taking justice into your own hands."

"Where's the justice supposed to come from, then?"

"Justice?" he said. "*Justice?* How long have you lived in this country, justice."

He stood up. He walked over to my chair and put his hand on my shoulder. He lowered his voice. "Look," he said. "I don't give a damn what you do to the little shits."

I looked up at him.

"Just don't do it on school property."

He sent me home for the day. When I walked past the idiot math class I peeked in and caught Alfonso's eye. He asked for a hall pass and came out to meet me.

"Suspended," I said.

"No big," he said. "Why?"

"Nailed a Jarimallo."

Alfonso nodded in approval. "Fucking bueno."

"I have to do some work on the trailer," I said. "Pop wants me to fix the shower pump, and I don't know what the hell to do."

"Let's go," Alfonso said. "I will help you."

Alfonso parked his Goat next to the trailer.

"You *live* here?"

"And my father and my two brothers."

"Fuck," Alfonso said. "I didn't know."

"Didn't know what?"

"Let's fix that pump," Alfonso said.

"I'll go get the toolbox."

Pop stopped me. "What are you doing home from school?"

"Alfonso's going to help me empty the holding tank, and in return I told him he could use your tools to work on his car for a while. Please?"

"If I need them, that's the end of playtime with the tools."

I wheeled Pop's huge red Snap-On toolboxes through the lube bay and around the side of the station to the trailer. Alfonso was smoking a cigarette.

"You know," Alfonso said, "I gave you your first real battle wound, didn't I?"

I rolled up my sleeve and showed him my scar.

"That's a good scar," he said. He nodded proudly. "A good fucker, that scar. I'll show you *my* first cabroncito."

He lifted his T-shirt and showed me his chest. It was mapped with scars, red ones, white ones, black ones. It looked like he'd been whipped too, white and hardened streaks of scar across the breadth of his back.

"You see this one?" he said. He drew his finger along a small white scar the length of a tire valve. "This little fucker was my first one, and just look at the fuck. It's nothing. If I show people this scar, they think nothing. It's a pussy scar, and I got it making play-fight with my brother. No nothing in this scar. But yours," he said, and he walked over to me and lifted my shirt-sleeve and ran his finger along mine, and the way he did it, the way he touched my scar, was as if he *loved* that scar, as if the scar were not a part of me but a creature living on its own in the world, a splendid and beautiful creature that Alfonso was petting, that Alfonso was in awe of, "—yours is a *scar,* a scar earned in battle. Some day you will tell your childrens and your grandchildrens that you were scarred by Alfonso."

"Let's get to that pump," I said.

I showed Alfonso the part of the trailer where the problem was, underneath, and he lay on his back on the asphalt and shimmied himself between the truck tires I'd arranged that morning.

"Tight fucking fit under here," he said.

"Get your head all the way up against the tire," I said.

"Got it," he said. "It's dark, though. I can't see a fucking thing."

"I'll get you a flashlight," I said.

I wheeled the toolboxes over his legs, and I put a flashlight in his hand.

"See anything?" I said.

"It doesn't look like there's anything under here that has to do with a pump," he said.

"There's not," I said.

"What?"

"There's not," I said. "I just wanted you under the trailer, pinned."

"I don't understand."

"Do you understand what the word shit means?"

"What the fuck you talking about?"

"When you knife little fat-boys, they don't forget," I said. "They feel like shit. They feel like this," I said, and I reached under the trailer and I pulled the handle and the shit flowed. Every shit I'd taken that week, every shit of my brothers and

Pop, every turd of their girlfriends and even the turds of some of the preferred customers—slipping and sliding onto Alfonso's face.

I stood back and listened to Alfonso curse, and man did he curse. He cursed my father, my mother, my cousins, my aunts and uncles. He cursed every member of a hundred generations of Murphys. He cursed us back to Adam and his whore wife Eve.

The shit and piss and puke and spit spread out on the asphalt beneath the trailer like gurgling tar, and Alfonso kicked his legs and punched at the undercarriage of the trailer but he couldn't get loose.

Then, suddenly, his noise stopped. His legs went limp and I couldn't hear anything.

"Alfonso?" I said. "Alfonso? *Alfonso?*" But no response. "Alfonso!"

I ran to the lube bays. Pop was there, and Joe Clausi, the owner of Clausi Carpets, was pumping his own gas on the island. "There's been an accident," I said.

"What," Pop said.

"Alfonso's choking."

Pop looked at me. He winked. "Got him good?"

"Pop," I said, "he might be dead."

"Son of a bitch," Pop said. "*Son* of a *bitch*." And he called Joe Clausi and he went to the trailer and Joe Clausi and me followed. Pop pulled the toolboxes away, and he grabbed Alfonso's ankles and he pulled. Alfonso was limp.

"It was an accident," Pop rehearsed. "You were emptying the tank and he got caught and he drowned. By the time you figured out what was happening, he was gone. You didn't know. It was an accident."

"It wasn't an accident," I said. "It wasn't an accident," and I slammed Alfonso's chest with my fists knotted together. He lay there corpsed. I slammed him again, and I slammed him a third time, and he coughed, and runny browned shit bubbled from his mouth and trickled down his cheeks. I sat him up and slapped his back, again, again, again, and I slapped his back again. His eyes, when they opened, couldn't see a thing.

"Alfonso," I said.

His head hung like a drunk's.

"Alfonso," I said. I slapped him. "Alfonso!"

The station bells rang.

"I'll give you a hand with the customer," Joe Clausi said, and went to the islands. When he came back, he had a ten-pound sledge hoisted over his shoulder. We stood around Alfonso, Pop, Joe Clausi, and me, and Alfonso stood slowly up, and he began taking off his clothes, his shirt, shoes and socks, his pants, his shorts. He stood there naked, dripping. You could see the scars on his chest through the slime. It looked like they were bubbling, like they were heated up and boiling through the shit and piss and vomit.

He walked toward us and we moved away and let him through, and he walked through the alley behind the station and cut right. A few minutes later he was back, and he'd wrapped himself in the rolling towel from the rest room. He looked like an Incan warrior, his hair wet and slick and black, his brown skin glistening with water.

"You don't know a fucking thing about fighting, little gringo," he said. He looked each of us in the eye. Then he stared at me. "You might be big, but you will always be a little gringo."

Joe Clausi switched his sledgehammer from one shoulder to the other.

"Tomorrow," Alfonso said, "tomorrow, my gringo fucking amigo, *I* will be clean."

And he walked off, left his Goat there next to the trailer and walked off, buck naked under the washroom towel, walked down the street and into Oakland.

In the middle of the night I heard Alfonso's car start and drive off.

I didn't tell Hiro about what I'd done. I didn't tell anyone. Pop, though, would tell everyone who came into the station. He kept changing the story around to make it funnier—and he left out the part about nearly killing Alfonso. Once he got the story fixed up, he thought the Alfonso event was just about the funniest damn thing that ever happened.

For the customers, he'd put on a Mexican accent and he'd tell the whole story, and when he got to the end, he'd say, "Tomorrow, my gringo fucking amigo, I will be clean," over and over again, and everyone would laugh so hard his stomach hurt. "Tomorrow, my gringo fucking amigo, I will be clean," Pop said, and an old dude laughed so hard his choppers shot right out of his mouth and onto the ground. "Tomorrow, my gringo fucking amigo, my *teeth* will be clean," Pop said, and everyone laughed some more.

Alfonso never did come back to school. During Christmas break, I went by Santos Rentals, and they told me he'd quit. I didn't know where he lived, or where his uncle lived.

Eventually I started telling my own version of the Alfonso story.

In my version, I made Alfonso beg like a coward.

In my version, I left out the part where we'd become friends.

CHAPTER NINE

Los Asesinos

When I started at Oakland High, I answered an ad in the newspaper for a trumpet player. A Mexican answered the phone and told me the auditions for the band were being held in Hayward, about twenty miles out of Oakland.

Instead of the music hall I expected, I stopped my ten-speed at a house. Mexican ladies in halter tops and cutoffs sat on the lighted porch beneath clouds of mosquitoes and moths. They drank beer and smoked cigarettes as I unstrapped my trumpet case from my bike rack. A gold tooth blinked yellow in time with the streetlight behind me at the intersection.

A girl my age stood up when I got to the porch. She had long black hair and wore an almost see-through white bikini top and very tight cutoffs. I tried not to stare at her breasts and lowered my eyes to her belly, and then I tried not to stare at her belly, and then I just closed my eyes.

"They're in the garage," the girl said.

The other ladies looked at me, and I could tell that when I walked away they would laugh.

"Follow me," the girl said.

I followed her into the house, which smelled like broiled beef and fried flour and cumin and cilantro and jalapeno and red wine, and like grandparents and babies and fathers home from work. I heard men laughing and then the sound of a Hammond electric organ, the thump of a bass drum, the tones of trumpet players warming up. I watched the girl's cutoffs switch back and forth, watched her legs and her bare feet.

She led me into the backyard, stopped, then pointed to the garage, a weatherworn gray wooden shack. She turned and smiled, tilting her head to the side. Her black hair covered one eye, and the other sparkled like black glass. I stood there, staring at her face, her bikini top, and the night shadows outlining her figure. She walked past me and tossed her hair to the side, and it brushed my arm.

I opened the side door of the garage, and inside were men and equipment and six Mexican trumpet players. The walls were lined with cardboard egg cartons, mattresses, and blankets, and I felt very white and more blond than usual. They looked at me. The man at the Hammond organ smiled. He was skinny, with black sideburns and a black mustache, and he wore a tank top with a picture of Shakespeare silk-screened across the chest. He laughed.

"Hey, boy," he said. "Muchacho gringo, you needing something?"

"Audition," I said. I held up my trumpet case. "T-Bird Murphy. I play trumpet. Trompeta?"

The men looked at each other, smiling.

Amid the electric riffs of the organ player and the tuning of the electric bass, the guitarist playing his own versions of Santana solos and the drummer hammering his Rogers set like some rockster, I listened to the other horn players warm up by playing the highest notes they could, their faces contorted and red and purple like puffed bruises, nostrils flared and eyes bulging as if about to pop like swollen cysts—except for one old player, a short, fat man in a jogging suit. Clean shaven, he rifled through scales, major and minor and then harmonic minor and pentatonics, and then thirds in all the scales, and then fourths and fifths, and then octave leaps with delicate fingers—all with a blazing clean tone that reminded me of Lee Morgan at his best. Never a sign of effort except the sweat that beaded above his thin Spaniard eyebrows. The other players—warm-up artists, blowing their chops out even before the audition began—ripped their lips ragged with failed attempts at triple C's.

I watched the old man, lifted my horn and played my own warm-up tones, long notes, full, whole, calm. The warm-up artists screamed a mess of noise that didn't sound anything like music. Me and the old man played scales.

I hadn't warmed up by playing scales in a long time.

The Hammond organ player laid one arm across the keys and turned up his volume, then raised his other arm into the air, fisted. We all went silent. He looked at us, looked at our eyes, each player in turn.

"I am Claudio," he said. "This is my band, Los Asesinos. I need two trumpet players. Five of you I do not need." He smiled. "Tonight we will find out *which* five I do not need."

Claudio played a death march on his organ and laughed, and then he reached into a trunk and pulled out a folder of sheet music and put it on a music stand in front of the old trumpet player.

The old trumpet player stepped aside, yielding the stand with a gracious sweep of his arm, trumpet in hand, to the player next to him.

"I don't need music," he said.

"No?" Claudio said. "Thinking you're pretty good, don't you?"

"I am Ricardo Ramirez," the old trumpeter said.

"Senor," Claudio said. He nodded his head and bowed slightly. "Gracias."

I looked at Senor Ramirez. Senor Ramirez looked at me. The expression on his face did not change.

The trumpeters lined up and Claudio called the name of a tune, but I didn't understand what he said because the title of the song was Spanish.

"What?" I said to Senor Ramirez.

"Los Asesinos," Ramirez said. "The Assassins."

When it was my turn to audition I played the head as written, but when my solo came, I didn't quite know what to do. The others played something I'd never heard before: repetitious staccato riffs with the organ hitting the chords on two and four—not in a jazzy way, not relaxed or vicious, but with all the notes inside the key and no altered chords, a strange foreign polka set to Mexican oompah chords. And then there was me, who'd been listening to nothing but black jazz and Pop's classical music since I could hear. I blurted out a Clifford Brown-Miles Davis type of solo over the chords of "Los Asesinos," breaking every rule there was—playing dissonant chords over the bass, leaving open space like Miles, dragging the notes like Freddie Hubbard.

When all of the trumpeters had played Claudio looked at Senor Ramirez.

"Who would you like to be your assistant?" Claudio said.

"El gringo poquito."

They argued about something in Spanish that I couldn't understand. The other trumpet players yelled at Claudio. Everyone kept looking at me, and the word gringo seemed to come up a lot, and that was one Mexican word I knew.

I got the job.

After practice I walked with Senor Ramirez to his car, carrying his five trumpet cases. He wheezed with every step. He was very old.

"I have a sick heart," he said. He pressed his palm flat against his chest. "The doctors say I should not play the trumpet, or I will die. But if I don't play I die too. I will die playing the trumpet. Better to die playing."

When my older brother Kent and I had been ready to leave for school the morning before the audition, Pop hadn't opened up the Mohawk station yet. The doors to the lube bays were closed, the office was locked, and Pop hadn't brought out the oil rack or the tire display or the paper-towel dispensers. Next to the rest rooms, Kent and I found Pop and Clyde. Clyde sat on a pile of tires with his face in his hands, Pop standing over him in his green Mohawk coveralls, yelling.

"A name," Pop yelled. "Give me a fucking name."

"It was my fault," Clyde said.

Clyde looked up. His face was caked with dried blood, smeared and streaked now from fresh tears. One of his eyes was swollen shut, purple and red, oozing. His right ear looked like a flattened and rotten tomato. It wasn't even an ear, just a bloody hole.

"It was my fault," Clyde said.

"Whose sister?"

Clyde looked at Pop's feet and started crying, choking like he was going to stop breathing.

Pop grabbed Clyde's shoulders and shook. "Whose? Whose? Whose?"

"Jarimallo," Clyde said.

We took Clyde to the hospital then. The doctor said that after the place healed where his ear had been, someone would be able to make him a fake ear that would look good as new, but until then he'd have to wear a patch. His eye they'd have to wait and see about, because until the swelling went down, nobody would be able to tell.

On the way to the hospital, Clyde told us his story. He had been caught screwing Toby's sister, Maria, in the backyard. Toby pulled a gun on Clyde and made Maria tie him up with fishing line. Then Toby called the Alvarezes and the Jarimallo brothers and Papa Jarimallo, all of whom were partying at the Alvarez house. Soon the backyard was filled with Jarimallos and Alvarezes, all yelling and screaming in Spanish, while Clyde lay buck naked and hog-tied. Maria had gone inside. Clyde said he could hear her crying.

Then they kicked and hit Clyde, first taking turns, and then all at once, and it hurt so bad after a while that Clyde couldn't feel it. It was as if his body had gone to sleep and he could just see and hear them. And then someone cut off his ear and threw it into the neighbor's yard, and he heard the neighbor's dogs fighting over it, yelping and growling.

Then Clyde came to, he had his clothes on again and he was on the BART train beneath the bay, in the tube, on the way to San Francisco. Someone had duct-taped a washcloth to his head where his ear should have been. People were not looking at him.

He got off at the Powell Street station and started walking. He walked a long time, and the only other people on the streets were bums and street sweepers, and sometimes he heard sirens. He ended up on the Golden Gate Bridge, standing against the cold iron railing. The fog started to come in and swept over his back from the ocean behind, and Clyde looked across the bay and tried to see our part of Oakland before it got swallowed in the rushing mist. He saw the lights of tugboats and barges and the sparkling of the Oakland skyline, the Tribune tower lit up green and red, the Mormon temple's fairy-castle golden spires. He watched Oakland disappear. He stayed there until the sun came up over the hills, and then he walked into town and scored some coke and smeared it on his swollen-shut eye, and then where his ear should have been, and then in his mouth.

Standing next to Senor Ramirez after he told me about his heart, about how he wanted to die, I said, "Senor Ramirez," and he said, "Ricardo," and I said, "I would like to ask you for advice." He said, "You may ask me for advice," and I told him the story of Clyde getting his ear cut off.

"What was the family name of the people who hurt your brother, who your brother hurt?" he asked.

I told him. He closed his eyes and crossed himself. "I know these peoples," he said. "We share the blood. The blood is thin, but the blood is shared."

He looked at me. "I can give you no advice in these things."

"Why not?"

"It is not the proper thing for me to speak," he said. "Trust your heart, and the hearts of your brothers and the heart of your father. The hearts of men of flesh and bone know these things."

After the audition, when I got home to our trailer next to the Mohawk station, Pop was there. Clyde was still at the hospital, and our older brother, Kent, wasn't home either, was probably still practicing his cello or studying at the library.

Pop sat in the dark on the metal step of the trailer smoking a cigar. The red tip lit up his glasses, and I could see him looking out at the stacks of tires and rubber tube-flaps and heaps of old batteries and worn-out brake shoes.

He looked at me. "It's time for you to learn how to drive."

"I don't have a license," I said. "I'm not sixteen."

"It's time for you to learn how to drive."

Before we left, Pop filled two red five-gallon cans with gas—ethyl, 94 octane—and then he bundled all the rope he could find in the station: rope from the tire racks, from the rolling glass doors in front of the lifts, from the side panels of the tow trucks.

Pop had a '56 Ford Fairlane, brown with white trim, and bashed up on the passenger side, the doors held closed with greased rope.

"Drive," Pop said.

He'd never been so patient with me before. I killed the engine four straight times, and he didn't even say anything. And soon I was driving. Man, I was driving all over town, driving the streets I knew on foot and on bicycle, driving over bumps that had busted my ass when I was on a bike. Then Pop started giving me directions, and soon we were going through a neighborhood near the Mohawk. He stopped me in front of the Jarimallo house. “Keep the engine running,” he said.

He climbed out the window on his side and reached back in for the gas cans and the rope, which he hooked over his shoulder like a fireman from a movie. The Jarimallos’ house was lit up with black lights, purple and blue, and strobes flicked and popped white daggers of light. The silhouettes of people danced behind thin white window shades to disco—some bass-pounding music with trumpets and a synthesizer. Pop roped the front door to the burglar bars on the porch window, and then he went around back with the rest of the rope and the gas. A dog started barking. Then the dog stopped barking. As Pop came back around the front, he was emptying the gas cans, splashing gasoline on the windowsills, on the porch, on the bushes. He climbed into the car and lit a cigar with his Zippo. “Drive,” he said, and he tossed the Zippo.

In the rearview mirror I saw the flames.

We stopped at a 7-Eleven and Pop bought us a six-pack of Olympia. When we got on the freeway, we could see the flames from the double-decker over Cypress Street. We drank beer together, and Pop gave me one of his Roi-Tans and we smoked.

I felt like a son.

Oakland High held memorial services for the dead Jarimallos and the dead Alvarezes and some of the other kids and their parents who’d been burnt up. Right before lunch we went to an assembly in the gym, which smelled like basketball games, and we sat quietly for forty-five minutes while the vice principal, Mr. Hanover, told us about how really rotten revenge was and how God and his badass armies of avenging angels were the only true judges of the souls of man.

We heard that the surviving Jarimallos and Alvarezes now lived in the Alvarez house. We heard that only grandparents and women were left in the families.

I sat next to my brothers at the assembly, and what Clyde

couldn't hear, I whispered to him in the undamaged ear. Everybody was looking at us, and they didn't seem to be mad at all.

Pop got called into the police station that day while we were at school. All told, there were six dead Mexicans—two Jarimallos and four Alvarezes. It didn't even make the news. We never figured out who finked, but it didn't matter, because the investigating officer was Eddie Martinot. Eddie had graduated from Oakland High, ten years before, and when Eddie was at Oakland High, he had worked part-time at the Mohawk with Pop. Eddie asked Pop where he was the night before, Pop told him that he was at home with his children, Eddie gave Pop the charred Zippo, and that was the end of the matter.

Months had passed since the Jarimallo house had burned down, and we figured things were square between the families.

Right before Easter, the night of the Oakland High spring concert, Pop had spent his entire day busting truck tires, 10.00 X-20s—the ones that go on the big rigs, with split rims that might chop your head off at any moment while you're airing them up. He swung his sledgehammer to break them down, took them apart, then put them back together again and aired them up. And even though he'd spent the day doing the worst work in the world, he walked into the trailer after work, and while Kent was tuning his cello strings and polishing the wood of his cello, Pop shaved.

Kent was being featured as a soloist at the concert, playing a song he wrote himself. I didn't play in the symphony—I hated classical music. I only played in the jazz band, and whenever I got the chance, I slipped away to Archibald's Playhouse, a jazz club where the old black dudes hung out. I'd hang around with an old black dude named Mr. Beasley and drink gin with him and listen to the old jazzmen play.

Pop lathered up his neck and the space between his cheeks and his eyes, and he shaved. I'd never seen him that way, his face clean and white, the skin beneath his glasses showing. When he put on a jacket and tie and his fedora he looked like someone from Berkeley or San Francisco, or like a character from a movie about New York, where they dress like that all the time.

"I could play 'Carnival of Venice,' you know," Pop said. "When I was at Oakland High. Trumpet."

Kent looked at him. "That's a difficult piece," he said.

Pop smiled, and then he looked sad. "I was very good then."

"You're still good," Kent said. "When you play."

"I was *really* good then," Pop said. He stared at Kent. "I bust tires so you can play cello. This concert better be good."

"It'll be good, Pop," Kent said.

The concert was held in the gym, and Pop led us to seats in the front row. The program was a folded ditto, purple and smeared, and it announced that the symphony orchestra would be playing three pieces: Prokofiev's *Piano Concerto No. 1,* Stravinsky's *Rite of Spring,* and Murphy's *Symphonic Concerto for Cello.*

The Prokofiev wasn't that good, the piano player flubbing it during some of the arpeggios and overdramatizing the parts that should have been playful, making the concerto sound like the soundtrack to a melodrama. And during the Stravinsky, the director, Dr. Boyd, a bald-headed elf, thought he was God or Zeus or something and had the whole audience laughing, he was so corny, sweeping his arms and squatting and spinning circles and snapping his elbows like he was throwing thunderbolts.

When the Stravinsky was finished, Dr. Boyd gave Kent a good five minutes of hype, telling the audience about his awards, who he studied with, what symphonies he'd soloed for, how he had won a national high school award for the piece we were about to hear.

Kent walked out in front of the orchestra and took the mike. "This piece I wrote for my father," Kent said, and he bent over the cello and strung a long, low note, a groan like a foghorn sounding far across the San Francisco Bay.

Dr. Boyd walked off the stage and Kent conducted the orchestra himself, swinging his body toward the sections of the orchestra he wanted to pipe up or tone down, pacing the tempo with the stroke of his bow, directing the nuances with a sudden arch of his back or a sweep of his upper body across the band.

And Kent played. He played and worked that instrument and Pop and Clyde and me sat there and didn't say a word to each other, and I felt ashamed of myself for how I didn't practice, and I knew by the looks on their faces that Clyde and Pop felt ashamed of themselves, too—Clyde for being deformed now that his ear was cut off and his face was messed up, and Pop for not ever becoming the trumpeter he could have become, should have become.

While Kent was playing, the Alvarez and Jarimallo girls entered the gym through all four entrances, one or two at each door. Everyone turned and looked at them. They wore black Derby jackets and red bandannas tied across their foreheads, clothes like their brothers had worn. Maria Jarimallo had tattooed tears down her cheek.

"Pop," I said. "At the doors. Jarimallos and Alvarezes."

Pop looked at them but he didn't say anything.

The third movement began, and Kent set down his bow and started plucking. First he did a jazz walk, slow and sleazy and dark like the lights and mirrors of nightclubs, and then he cut into double time, triple-fingering the strings and hitting chords on that huge fat-stringed cello which was now a string bass. Someone backstage lowered the lights and spotted Kent in blue, and the audience cheered and Kent was off somewhere in the bowels of Oakland, off into the nightlife, hammering that cello like it was a truck tire, slapping the strings and hunched over it almost kissing the wood, his ear against the cavity, listening to the echo of bass, his whole body concentrated into the light, the sound, the strings, the void.

Then he stopped, picked up his bow, and turned back to the orchestra. He began stomping his foot like he was going to kick off a jazz tune, one-two-three-four, but when he hit the next downbeat a dark hot wash of sound rolled over us like a huge wave, like a roll of molten iron, iron that would become the girders and beams and cables and hammerheads and bolts that held Oakland together. And there we were, hundreds of us, cooking in the heat of that molten note, that eruption from the cauldron heart of the earth. The note seemed to last forever.

When the music kicked in again, Pop leaned over to me. "That Kent," he said.

Murphy's *Symphonic Concerto for Cello* ended, and the crowd applauded as they had at the end of the other pieces. When Dr. Boyd came out and bowed, and then made Kent bow, the crowd stood up to clap.

Standing outside the gym after the concert Pop bristled with pride. He never really smiled, but his face was stretched so far with not-smile it looked like his cheeks hurt. People came up to him, people we didn't even know, and they shook his hand. Pop stood there, all clean shaven and dressed in his tie and his fedora, looking like a gangster and smoking a Roi-Tan.

When Kent and the rest of the orchestra finally came out, everybody cheered again.

Standing back from the crowd, in the shadows, were the Alvarez and Jarimallo girls, huddled, staring at us from the dark.

Los Asesinos had gigs every weekend, sometimes two in a day. The money was good—about $40 a night and all the drinks I could slam. We played cumbias, rancheras, and salsa—sometimes a Santana tune so the guitar player, Julio, could stretch his fingers. Sometimes we did concerts in the civic centers of San Jose, Hayward, Milpitas, Sunol. But mostly we did lousy gigs, quinceaneras, weddings, dance jobs at Mexican bars and nightclubs where everyone wore silk shirts unbuttoned to their navels and drank fruity drinks and cheap beers. I wasn't kidding myself—I wasn't big-time. I was a cheap trumpet player still in high school playing with a band of broken-down old Mexican dudes who wanted to get away from their wives long enough to get laid once in a while.

Except Senor Ramirez. He was famous, and he didn't have a wife to fool around on. As far as I knew, he didn't have any family at all, and for some reason, he couldn't go back to Mexico. Everywhere we went, the crowd cheered when he walked into the bar, people crowding around him for autographs, women kissing his round brown cheeks. Senor Ramirez was a star, and we all knew that the only reason we were going on tour was because he was in the band. With Senor Ramirez on the stage, we could pack a house anywhere there were Mexicans within driving distance. And in California, that meant everywhere south of San Francisco. But we had to play a lot of gigs as fast as we could, because Senor Ramirez had a bad heart, and there was no telling when he would drop dead on us and kill Los Asesinos.

When Senor Ramirez dropped me off at the Mohawk after the gigs, I'd sit outside on a tire for a long time. I'd listen to the cars on the Nimitz Freeway cut the night air and whisk through the fog, and I could hear owls sometimes, owls perched with their claws grabbing on to iron rails in the broken-glass window frames of abandoned warehouses or flapping through alleys and hooting it up before a graceful deadly swoop. Those nights were the best times of my life.

Senor Ramirez picked me up for a gig on the Saturday of Easter weekend. He didn't say anything to me when I got in his car, and when I tried to make conversation, he didn't talk. He lit a cigarette.

"You're not supposed to smoke," I said.

"Smoking is something I am not supposed to do." He kept smoking.

"What?" I said. "What's the deal?"

"If you do not wish to play today, I will share my pay with you."

"I always play," I said. "What are you talking about?"

"Today is the quinceanera of Maria Jarimallo."

We didn't speak the rest of the way to the gig, but we opened with "Los Asesinos," and I didn't take a solo when my turn came. Senor Ramirez nodded toward me when he ripped up to a high F at the end of his solo, but I looked at the base of the mike stand and pretended I had missed my cue. The guitar player picked up the slack, and I watched the dancers—the tuxedoed men, the women in long and elegant frilled taffeta dresses, and the little girls and the boys and the old people. Dancing in the middle of the floor, dressed in bridal white lace and veiled and wearing a withered red-rose corsage on her wrist, was Maria. She was with a grandfather, white-haired and somber and his face streaked with pain and dignity, dancing with him and yet alone. In the embrace of the older man, her sway seemed to choreograph a history, her body and face and eyes the markers of ancient blood. And she grew older. She became a woman. She was beautiful.

The next song was "La Playa Blanca." This time I soloed, and when Maria stared at me I played for her, looked straight into her eyes and played like I never had before. My head stopped thinking about what I was playing and what came out was not what I wanted but something different, something that boiled and rumbled up from inside, something that burst from my lungs, forced its way through my throat and whipped through the silver tubing of my trumpet. What came out was *song*—not notes, but a song I didn't know I had, a song that charted through time and mapped the souls of my own family: vague flashes of long-dead farmers, tradesmen, and beer-soaked Irish tribes staggering and jigging to long-forgotten melodies.

At the end of my solo, the other guys in the band held the triple G I'd landed on, I was screaming out, and they kept holding the note with the organs and the guitars, and the drummer rolled and the bassist triple-strummed the lower neck of his ax, and then I felt my head go numb and things started to wobble, and my eyes ceased to see and the room went red and then purple and then everything went black.

When I came to, Maria was kneeling over me. She held my face in her hands and I looked at her eyes, at the tattooed tears dripping down her cheek. She lifted my face and it was as if I floated to my feet, and when I stood the crowd cheered and the band kicked off the next tune, "La Mugura." Maria led me out to the dance floor.

When Senor Ramirez began his solo, Maria pulled me close and pressed her cheek to mine, and it felt as if the tattooed tears burned right through my flesh and into my blood.

It was past midnight when Senor Ramirez dropped me off at the Mohawk. The sliding glass door of the bay was rolled up, and Kent was backing a tow truck off the alignment rack and onto the asphalt yard.

"Got a call?"

"What's it look like?" Pop said. He dragged on his cigar and he inhaled the smoke, holding it in his lungs a long time.

"Los Asesinos is going on tour," I said. "They want me to go. The valley. Los Banos, Fresno, Modesto, Bakersfield."

"Are you asking me a question?" Pop said.

"We leave in two weeks."

Pop looked at the tow truck. Kent sat with his foot on the accelerator to keep the engine from dying. White tubes of smoke chugged from the rattling exhaust pipes.

"*He*'s not afraid to get his hands dirty," Pop said. He walked inside the bay and yanked the chain to bring the door down. The chain whirred and clacked and the door slammed shut. As I walked toward the trailer, I heard him snap the padlock and come out through the office door. He got into the tow truck with Kent.

***

Inside the trailer Clyde was asleep, and I sat on my bunk looking at him. He twitched and shuddered as if he were cold, as if some night wind were snaking through the aluminum shell of the Airstream, a night wind that etched his bones with scrimshaw needles of ice.

I stuffed a tube sock into the bell of Pop's trumpet and began slowly playing the first movement of "Carnival of Venice." Pop's trumpet had been his father's before him. It was an 1886 Conn silver concert model. Grandfather Murphy used to tell us he had played it in Bayreuth, played *The Ring* when Wagner was there—Wagner in his gray-gloried rage, pagan, barbarian, terrible and filled with the lust of ancient song. At rehearsal one time Wagner had accused Granddad Murphy of missing a note, had stopped the entire orchestra and made him play his passage solo. Granddad Murphy played it perfectly, and then he told Wagner that his music was hay for plow horses, pennies for peasants, and that if Granddad Murphy was going to play his trumpet for him, there'd have to be some volume other than fortissimo.

Wagner threw his baton at Granddad Murphy.

When Granddad Murphy was still alive, he told the story of the baton every Christmas. He told it as if he were killing Wagner each year. He told it as if he had stolen Wagner's soul and was passing it along to us to do with as we would.

Years later, when I was graduating from high school and after Granddad Murphy had died, I discovered that Wagner had died in 1883—before the trumpet was made.

By three in the morning my lip tingled and bled from playing so much—practicing in the morning, playing the quinceanera in the evening, trying to master the trumpet concerto after hours—and finally when I blew nothing came from the horn but a strained hiss of sputtering, bubbling air.

I hadn't been worried yet, since sometimes calls could take a long time, but by four o'clock in the morning I knew something must have gone wrong. I opened up the shop with Pop's spare set of keys and looked at the chalkboard.

The address of the call was in a neighborhood I knew.

I drove alongside the alongside the Nimitz, down Cypress Street, the double-decker freeway quiet above. The Oakland Tribune tower rose neon-lit and obscene in the distance like the immense finger and painted fingernail of a whore.

Everywhere I drove the lights were green. So I drove faster and faster, rolling along the street as if I were coasting downhill, the weight of the car dragging me down toward a black distant point.

The neighborhood got darker. There were fewer streetlights and fewer houses lit by porch bulbs. Trees arched over the street and weeds grew from the gutters, and the road grew narrower. I turned down 14th Street. Sagging rain-soaked gray houses with red doors—row after row—were lined up like dominoes. Only the arrangements of the birdbaths and plaster angels and Chevy Impalas and Bel-Airs and palm-up Jesuses made the homes distinguishable from each other.

Pop's tow truck was parked at the intersection of Peralta and 14th Street, the emergency lights spiraling atop the cab.

Yellow paddles of light swept the pale concrete walls of the projects.

I pulled the Fairlane up to the curb across the street from the truck and shut off the engine. I heard a foghorn sounding deep in the wash of the San Francisco Bay. Somewhere a dog barked. A bulb hung from a wire like a pin-dot star behind the paper shade of someone's apartment window. The spinning emergency lights of Pop's tow truck made an electric noise that whirred like a dynamo.

I got out of the car and stood looking over the hood at Pop. He sat on the cast-iron front bumper of the truck. He held a tire iron in one of his hands, and he pinched a cigar between the fingers of the other. The cigar wasn't lit.

Kent lay on the ground in front of Pop, gutted.

Pop looked at me, and then he looked down at Kent. He looked at me again.

"They didn't have a flat," Pop said.

We stared at each other.

"There wasn't anything wrong with their tires," Pop said. The lights of the tow truck coptered yellow across closed windows.

"Nothing wrong," Pop said. "Nothing at all."

CHAPTER TEN

El Musiquero

When our school stage band played a concert for the fancy high school across town, I got myself a girlfriend. She liked the way I played. She was the first real girlfriend I'd ever had, the first one I'd held hands with and kissed in public, and she was a doozie. She was kind of short, but her figure was good anyway. Her father owned a bank. She had blonde hair. She went to church with her parents. She wanted to go to Mills College and study liberal arts. She wasn't going to have sex until she got married. She was perfect.

When I told her I was going on tour with Los Asesinos, she started yelling at me. "You're not going on a band tour without *me*," she said.

"They'll hate you," I said. "They'll treat you like shit. You'll be the only white girl in every club Los Asesinos plays."

"I know how you like those Mexican girls," she said. "All dark and sweaty and steamy."

"The only reason I'm welcome is because I'm in the band," I said.

"Either I'm coming," she said, "or you're not going."

Pop was fixing a flat at the Mohawk station, buzzing down the inside of the tire with a grinder.

"I need to take some time off from school," I said.

Pop didn't say anything. Someone had taken down all the girlie calendars and posters, and someone had cleaned everything—everything—scrubbed the floors, the lifts in the lube bays, the toolboxes, the tire racks. Even the sink everyone pissed in had been scoured.

He'd changed, Pop, since he killed the Jarimallos and Alvarezes, and since they killed Kent. He was quieter now. He looked older. He cut his hair neat and short. After work each day, he scrubbed his face clean before he ate, not after.

When Pop finished buzzing down the tire, he popped off the chuck and snapped on the air attachment and then blew out the dust. Then he painted Camel cement on the raw rubber and he replaced the brush and, without looking at me, walked into the office. He took a pen and a pad of Joe's Tire Service stationery and wrote his name at the bottom of the sheet of paper. Then he flipped the paper back and wrote his name at the bottom of the next. And the next and the next until he'd signed his name to all the sheets.

"Do whatever you want," he said.

I walked around the side of the shop and into the trailer, and I stuffed my clothes into a pillowcase.

When I was walking toward my navy-surplus station wagon, Pop called me to the lube bay. "How's your oil?" he said.

"I don't know," I said.

"Pull it onto the rack," he said. "We'd better change it, just in case."

The first gig of our California tour was in Modesto, a dusty shithole in California's Central Valley. It's the kind of town where tractors drive the main drag, and Mexicans work for shit wages picking heads of lettuce in 110-degree heat. The men drink Budweiser, and the women are fat with destitution and boredom. Everyone has three or four cars, but only one of them runs, and the children run naked through yards burred with foxtails and sticker-weed.

Before the gig, Senor Ramirez pulled me aside. The air was iced with frozen fog and dew dripped from the lamps that lit the parking lot of the neon strip-mall nightclub. Low-riders—dropped Impalas and Monte Carlos with their springs heated into mush, and even a pathetic low-rider VW—glittered metal-flaked and custom-detailed under the darkest sheet of sky you can imagine. The stars were ringed with light as if each were a moon, nimbi circling each star like the chrome split-rings of 10.00 X-20 18-wheeler truck tires.

"I am sorry," Senor Ramirez said, "for you," he said, "that your brother was killed by the women of the Jarimallo and Alvarez families." He opened the trunk of his car and, one at a time, lifted his trumpet cases and set them on the asphalt lot. "But everyone knows that your father killed their brothers and their fathers."

"It was never proved," I said.

"Nor did anyone prove who killed your brother," Senor Ramirez said. "But everyone knows."

"Yes," I said.

"The matter is settled," Senor Ramirez said. "I have been told to tell you this, although this you probably know."

"Yes," I said.

"You are no longer held to accounts."

"Yes," I said.

"You are settled?"

"I'm playing with a Mexican band," I said. "What do you think?"

Senor Ramirez smiled but showed no teeth. It was kind of a not-smile smile, pained and forced. "Will you help me with my trumpets?" he said, looking down at the cases. "They have become too heavy for me to carry."

"What do you think?"

"I think tonight you will play well."

"Don't I always?"

Senor Ramirez smiled. "Help me with my trumpets," he said.

Claudio, the leader of the band, had come in early to the club and set up the equipment, and so all I had to do was play when I got there. But I got there early with my girlfriend and Senor Ramirez, and so I sat down at the bar.

The barkeep said something in Spanish to Senor Ramirez, and Senor Ramirez nodded, and then the barkeep pulled a Polaroid from beneath the bar. He handed it to me and ducked beneath the bar and stood next to Senor Ramirez, putting his arm around his shoulders, nodding at me to take the picture. I snapped the shot, and the bartender took the camera and waited for the exposure. When the photo came, he wagged it in the air to help it dry. He asked Senor Ramirez to sign it. The barkeep took a hammer and a nail from behind the bar and nailed the photo to the wall.

Senor Ramirez began setting up his horns—he had five of them, a coronet, a flugelhorn, a C-trumpet, a pocket trumpet, and his Benge Claude Gordon model with three interchangeable bells, brass, silver, and copper. My girlfriend sat down next to me in her frilly white dress. She sat the appropriate middle-class distance from me, as she'd been taught by her fancy mom. The Mexican men and their daughters all assumed that I was at the bar alone and only happened to be sitting next to the only Caucasian at the bar because she'd claimed me like a dog protects its favorite hydrant.

"Why don't you pay any attention to me?" she said.

"I'm paying attention to you," I said.

"No," she said, "you're not."

"I told you not to come," I said. "I'm at work. I act different when I'm at work."

"This isn't work," she said. "This is play. You *play* the trumpet, you don't work it. People don't drink when they're at work."

I couldn't help it—I laughed.

I suppose I loved my girlfriend, but I didn't like to be seen with her at my gigs. For some reason, I was ashamed. It wasn't right bringing someone to a Mexican bar who didn't understand anything about the music, the language, or the people. Not that I was much better, but at least I knew the music, and I learned more every time I played alongside Senor Ramirez.

My girlfriend always accused me of liking Mexican girls, and truth be told, I did like them. I'd never been bitched out by a Mexican gal—instead of thinking I was a Neanderthal, they liked that I was strong, that I wasn't a wimpy gringo who tried to negotiate his way out of every conflict, that I wanted to make money instead of wasting time in college, that I wanted to have a big family instead of a vasectomy.

My girlfriend wanted me to go to college instead of being a trumpeter. I listed off all the great jazzers, none of whom had gone to college.

"But they're all *black*," she said. "Aren't they?"

"What's that got to do with it?"

"They can play around doing things they think are fun," she said. "They can take chances because they have nothing to lose."

"What do I have to lose?" I said. "I don't have a damn thing to lose. I live in a trailer next to a gas station. My mother's a psychopath who marries a new guy every year. My brother's dead. My father smokes cigars and watches television. What the hell do I have to lose?"

"Me," she said.

I didn't want to lose her, but even if I did, it wouldn't kill me. No white woman had ever cooked a considerate meal for me, including my mother, who I hadn't seen since I was a kid. But one time, when I was dating a Mexican gal and ate a whole chicken at dinner at her parents' house, her mother went to the kitchen and got another chicken, put the whole bird on my plate, and let me tear it apart myself. The father too was proud that I'd eaten those chickens, and he didn't give me the suspicious eye most fathers give teenage men—he looked at me like I was a possible son-in-law.

A Mexican gal in a red silk dress sat down on the other side of me, and when I looked at her she smiled. She put her hand on my knee. I didn't want my girlfriend to see, so I sat there with her hand on my knee, acting like I didn't even notice. When my girlfriend went to the bathroom, I smiled at the girl, and I bought her a drink.

Senor Ramirez called me to the bandstand after he finished setting his horns on their stands.

"We need to practice the duets," he said.

"What's wrong?"

"Just because we played them correctly last time," he said, "does not mean we will play them correctly this time."

"Where are the rest of the guys?"

"They are out back."

"I'll go get them," I said.

"No," Senor Ramirez said, and the way he said no was strange. It was an instant no, not a no he had to think about.

"I'll go get them," I said. "We could all use the practice."

"We will practice our duets together without the band."

Playing alongside Senor Ramirez was both an honor and torture. He was so much better than me I felt ashamed standing alongside him on the stage. Every note on the register was his and his purely, as if no one had ever played the note before. Very few trumpeters can be identified by sound only—Miles Davis, Clifford Brown, Chet Baker, Freddie Hubbard, Louis Armstrong, Maynard Ferguson, maybe Dizzy, and Senor Ramirez. The thousands of other trumpeters are imitators, or simply part of the great mass of music makers who will never truly be trumpeters who can call themselves artists. Senor Ramirez was an artist, and I was not, and anyone who ever heard us play together knew it.

But at the same time he taught me things about music and

the craft of the horn every time we played, and he, at least, thought there was hope for me. One time he told me to lie on my back and play. When I lay down, he put his foot on my stomach.

"Play," he said.

So I played, and as I played, he put more and more weight on my stomach—he's a 350-pounder, Senor Ramirez—until I couldn't play anymore.

"Now you stand on me while I play," he said, and he lay on his back and struck a note so high I didn't even know what it was.

I put my foot on his stomach then increased the pressure. Still he played the screaming high note, and so I put more pressure and then more until finally I was standing, I was balancing on his belly. Still his note sang true and clear. He must have held that note for more than a minute.

"How'd you do that?" I said.

"A trumpet player does not play with his belly and his lungs," he said. "He plays with the muscles behind his belly. I am fat, and I am old and weak. But these muscles," he said, and he turned around and put my hand to his lower back, "these muscles are the strength of the note."

Usually I did whatever he said, but for some reason, his "no" made me want to find out what was going on out back, so I went through the rear exit. The air outside was cold, frozen as if it were going to bust pipes and kill park-bench hobos. At first I couldn't see anything at all, the sky black and no lights anywhere on the horizon, no stars above and not even a distant highway. But I could hear, and what I heard was all of the guys in the band laughing and hooting and whooping, and I heard the giggle of a girl, all the men chattering away in Spanish I couldn't understand, and then I heard them calling my name, "T-Bird, T-Bird, T-Bird!"

I started backing up toward the door, and they kept calling my name, and when my eyes came into focus I saw them standing around a woman. She was lying on her back in the dirt, and her dress was hiked above her waist. Carlos, the drummer, had her panties around his neck and Miguel swung her bra around in the air like a bola. Claudio, the leader of the band and keyboard player, was snorting coke bare-nosed off a broken piece of glass, and Domingo was pulling his pants up. Clouds of air froze as they pumped from their mouths and nostrils. They looked like cartoon bulls snorting at some matador.

"T-Bird," the woman said. "Come here, my little T-Bird. I have a present for you."

I retched. There she lay, naked and asking me to come to her, and I knew I should have done the right thing and dropped my pants and gone to it, but instead I was terrified and I retched again and backed up against the door, reaching for the handle. I swear I saw steam rising from between her legs. Pop would have been disgusted with me.

The guys in the band laughed and laughed, some of them doubled over in laughter, and even the woman laughed, and I stood there stiff and feeling like I was a wimpy faggot.

Claudio walked toward me, and I looked to my sides for a way to escape. Then he put his arm around me. "You have never before been with a woman?" he said.

I shook my head.

"This is not the right woman for you," he said.

I pulled the door open and went back into the bar.

Senor Ramirez was sitting on the barstool next to my girlfriend.

The Mexican girl whose beer I'd bought gave me a sexy stare, and I looked away.

"Are you ready now to practice duets?" Senor Ramirez said.

I unpacked my horn.

There's not a lot of money playing for bar bands, even if you are on tour. You play because you love to play, and because you get free drinks. By the end of the second set, most of the guys are well on their way to being hammered. That's when the bands start stretching out the songs, playing longer solos, and either letting the rhythm of the slow songs ooze along, or, if the song is upbeat, soloing away aimlessly. You start getting lazy and saying that someone has requested a song you've already played. Hell, the last set is usually a bunch of songs you've played twice already, but everyone is so drunk they don't even notice. By the end of the night, everyone in the band is smashed, but so is everyone in the bar, and even though what you're playing is sloppy and out of tune and out of rhythm, because you're drunk you think you're some kind of goddamn music giant. You think you're Coltrane or Carlos Santana or Tito Puente or Oscar Peterson. And the people in the bar, the drunks dropping off their barstools and the horny couples doing the hip-grind on the dance floor, they think you're the best damned band they've ever heard. You could fart into the mike, and if they even bothered to notice, they'd cheer. Once you start getting drunk at the gig, you start looking forward to the breaks between sets more than the sets themselves—at least I do. But if I had it to do over again, I wouldn't have taken a break that night. I would have stood on the stage and played a solo to the sounds of ice cubes clinking in glasses. I would have done anything to stay up there on that stage.

During the break before our next-to-last set, I zagged toward the bar to get a scotch on the rocks. Scotch became my drink of preference in high school, because it was the only booze I could bring to parties that no one mooched. While I was waiting on the barkeep, my girlfriend came up behind me and put her arms around my waist and said, "Let's dance, baby."

"What?"

"Ooo," she said. "Let's dance."

"The band's not playing," I said. "There's no one on the dance floor."

I turned around and looked at her. I'd never seen her drunk

before—she always said that she was morally against it—but there she was, all frothy and foamy and liquored up, and smiling big like I'd never seen her smile before. She was rippling and rolling around like a sexpot. If her father had seen her like that, he would have locked her away in the vault at his rotten little Oakland bank.

She grabbed my crotch. "Let's dance, sweetie-pie," she said.

She dragged me onto the dance floor, and everyone was looking. The music was jukebox-low, and clinking ice and Spanish conversation was louder than the speakers, but my girlfriend's body was somehow tapped into the idea of music, and her body involuntarily rhythmed around, not to the beat of the song on the jukebox, but to some cadence only she could hear.

Me? I knew the Mexican dances. During breaks I'd learned how to dance cumbias, rancheras, how to dance salsa. With a couple scotches in me, I could mambo like nobody's goddamn business. During breaks, and even during songs that didn't need trumpets, I'd dance with the Mexican girls, and that was always part of what I considered gig pay. The Mexicans do something that gringos don't do when they dance: they touch each other. Hell, I'd have *paid* to go to a bar where the girls touched me. Playing in Mexican bands was the best job in the world.

But my girlfriend—she'd never even heard a Mexican song before, unless it was a blast from a passing low-rider with a power-booster. Her idea of dancing was disco-slinking around, an erotic solo performed in front of an anonymous manikin worshiper who stood there like a totem pole with a weather-worn woodie. So when I tried to take her hands and lead her through the dance—a ranchera—she turned away and wagged her fanny at me. She wagged that fanny in a way, I guess, that was supposed to make me lusty. But that's not what happened.

Everyone in the bar laughed, that's what happened. And while they laughed, she kept wagging her fanny at me, and the laugh grew louder and more loud as she wagged that fanny more and more, not facing me, but staring at the bandstand and wagging away. Hell, her dress had white lace around the collar. The laugh turned into a roar, and the guys did the Mexican whoop, and the women were hysterical and red-faced. I stopped dancing and stood there, a fire hydrant plugged into the floor, but my girlfriend kept on grinding away at the air behind her fanny, wiggling and wagging and never turning around even once to look at her dance partner, me.

I looked around the bar, and all I could see was mouths, open mouths laughing, white teeth bucked out like a hundred laughing mules, until I spotted the girl I'd bought a drink for. She was looking at me, and she was smiling. Her smile was sad and sympathetic and sexier than anything that wagging fanny could ever have conjured. When the song finally ended, everyone in the bar applauded and whistled and catcalled and whooped like someone had just cut the ear off the bull and thrown it to the queen of Spain. My girlfriend? She finally turned around, and she wrapped her arms around me and opened her mouth and stuck her tongue down my throat like a plunger. Everyone started cheering again, and I tried to push her away but she wouldn't let me go.

Oh boy, did they cheer whenever I played a solo during the next set. I was a goddamn star. I'd start playing, and they'd scream and whistle and hoot and whoop so loud that I couldn't even hear myself on the monitors. Senor Ramirez would play, and everyone would fall silent until he was done, just waiting for the chance to cheer at me.

Fifty-thousand scotches were lined up on the bandstand at my feet. And I made use of as many of them as I could. Soon I was pretty damned hammered, playing like an idiot, missing cues, blurting the head of the tunes over other players' solos, cracking notes like nobody's business. Basically, I sucked.

But I didn't much care, because my girlfriend was out on the dance floor dry-humping some Mexican dude whose hands were burrowed into her buns, and she didn't mind at all. She was kissing away at him and grinding his groin like a titty-bar lap-dancer. Her eyes were fuzzed over like a bitch cat in heat. I knew I should have been mad at her, but I wasn't. I watched her kissing on the dude and rubbing on his hard-on, and I didn't even know what song we were playing.

Senor Ramirez nudged me.

"Que paso?"

"Nada," I said.

"She is drunk," he said. "It is no worry."

"I never worry," I said.

And then his cue came and it was his time to solo, and he lifted his horn, and the band cut, and all was silent. But instead of wailing a screamer or rattling off an arpeggio or a blistering scale, Senor Ramirez pushed the mike aside and stepped to the fore of the bandstand and played a quiet tone, an almost imperceptible whisper of a note. And the band, instead of kicking in when it was supposed to, the band held still, the drummer holding his sticks aloft, Claudio standing with his hands poised over the Hammond keyboard, everyone in the band frozen, the dancers on the floor slack and yet alert, not dancing but standing, not thinking of each other but instead focused, listening. Even my girlfriend and her Mexican dude heard the note of Senor Ramirez. It was as if some ghost were whispering each person's name from a land beyond and the ghost had something to tell them that would alter all the windings of their lives. It was as if this ghostly voice were the key to all they did not know nor would ever again have the opportunity to discover. And Senor Ramirez held that note, a midrange G, the note gently and slowly swelling louder and more full, more resonant and no vibrato but merely a flat tone as if he were warming up. But it was not warm-up, because the note kept swelling, and the volume increased, and soon the note was so loud that I could feel the trumpet in my own hands vibrating, and it was vibrating to that note, singing out its own G, but not its own, Senor

Ramirez's instead, and bottles rattled on the shelves behind the bar and gold fillings buzzed G's and ice danced in the glasses, when finally he glissed slow and deliberate upward, the note ascending through the quarter tones and the half tones and all the tones between and upward, the sallow and nasal tone of the gliss unaccountably clear and brassy still, and upward the gliss rose until he opened his valves roosted on a note—not even a note but a scream, a wail, an angel's cry—that had never before been played and never since tried.

I looked at Senor Ramirez then, and I saw him from behind, his immense torso, the veins in his neck bulging purple and black, his tuxedo coat stretched taut and near to breaking across his back, and that note he held and held, and yet it began to sound not like a note at all. It sounded like all notes, every note he'd ever played in his life and everywhere he'd ever played and everyone for whom he'd ever played. From the midrange G to the unutterable cry above he now held, that note was, somehow, his summary, his resume, his testament to sound and music and life and death. His back swelled in spasms and then slowly subsided beneath his jacket as he circle-breathed the note, holding it now minutes and beyond not only expectation but past comprehension, holding that cry as if he were never again going to be allowed another.

I closed my eyes and bowed my head.

Even though I hadn't wanted my girlfriend to come on tour with me, in a way I was glad she'd come. It meant that she'd be staying the night with me, and that was a first. How she got her father the banker to agree to let her come, I'll never know. She must have lied to him, the sin of lying, in her thinking, less frightful than the thought of me out of town alone. Since it was understood that she'd be sharing a motel room with me, I even shaved and brought some of Pop's cologne.

But when Senor Ramirez finished his solo, and it was my

turn, I opened my eyes and looked out into the crowd and I didn't see my girlfriend, at first. I started playing my riffs while the crowd was still going gaga about Senor Ramirez's cut, and since no one was paying attention to me anyway, I looked around the bar until I found her. She was heading out the door with the guy she'd been dancing with, his arm around her waist, her hand in the back pocket of his tight black slacks.

That's the way it had always been for me anyway. I was the guy all the girls could trust, and so I never got any nookie. I'd be their best goddamn friend, and they'd tell me about the men they had crushes on, and I'd say, "Resist!" since I wanted them for myself. And then some greaseball who drove a low-rider or played guitar or dealt smoke would get the reward of their pent-up naughtiness. Even my buddy Rich Gonzalez had stolen one of my girlfriends. But when I saw her walking out the door, my chest went empty and my eyes lost focus. She was the first girl I'd been around who wasn't on the hunt for someone else.

Senor Ramirez stood alongside me and rocked back and forth, heel to toe, to the band and to my solo, and for some reason, instead of playing schlock, running through the major and dominant scales I usually spun out by rote, bored with the two-change chords of typical Mexican tunes, I went nuts. It wasn't a crazy and haphazard kind of nuts, but an I-don't-give-a-shit kind of nuts. I felt like I'd been released from all responsibility and all expectation, even though I'd never had either in the first place. I felt like no one was listening and no one ever would, and it wouldn't ever matter if anyone ever heard another note I played.

So instead of playing my usual robot lines, instead of thinking about the chord progression and the rhythm of the drum set and the register and the 1-3 accents of the bored-numb bassist, I forgot without knowing I was forgetting, I felt the music instead of hearing it, I played without knowing I was playing, and the notes came not from my fingers and my lips and my lungs and diaphragm, but instead from my whole body, as if my body itself were playing the trumpet instead of my body's parts. To be honest, I don't remember what the hell I played. I could give you some highfalutin bullshit about boning the muse, but the truth is it's all a blur, because I wasn't thinking anything at all, not even thinking about my girlfriend. While I was playing I knew I must have been doing something good, though, because the people in the bar stopped looking at Senor Ramirez and they started looking at me. And while they looked at me I looked at them, not as individual people—I can't remember a single face—but as a crowd, a group of melded humanity, people moving to a sound that wasn't coming from the band and that wasn't coming from me but was instead *just there*, just there as if it always had been, as if it were not being played but were instead issuing from not only the band and not only the dancers and not only the bar, the town, the people and the race but from the combination of all of us and everything together, this moment of music in flux and rippling across the surface of time.

When I finished, we kicked back in with the head, Senor Ramirez and I doing our sixteenth-note duet with a precision and somehow instinctive knowledge of the significance of each other, our harmonies not the sound of two trumpets playing lines but instead of one musical unit, and not even that: of one musician playing one song and that song a song we'd created instead of played. And after the song, he leaned over to me during the applause and said, "You played well."

The night wasn't over, though. We took a break, and during the break, the guys of the band went out back for a second helping of their mamasita. Senor Ramirez and I walked toward a booth, and the people in the booth gathered up their drinks and cigarette packs and they stood up, inviting us to sit down. One of the men, a short fat man, well-dressed and with a waxed mustache that was stark and clean and beautiful, asked Senor

Ramirez what he would like to drink. "El Presidente," Senor Ramirez said, and the group started off to buy him the drink.

"Can you bring me one?" I said. I took a fiver from my wallet. "Scotch?"

I held the bill toward the mustached man. "I apologize," he said, and he waved my bill away and started toward the bar.

To Senor Ramirez I said, "Thank you."

"For nothing," he said. "You played well." He took a deep breath, and he looked at me. "Why?" he said.

"What do you mean?"

He cut me a look. "Why did you play well," he said, and this time his question wasn't a question. The way he said it this time let me know that he didn't want an answer.

I looked toward the bar. The mustached man had already got the drinks, and he was coming toward us. He set them on the table and said something in Spanish to Senor Ramirez. "Gracias," Senor Ramirez said, and he lifted his glass in toast.

The bar went silent. Everyone was watching us. When we clinked our glasses together, all you could hear was the sound of ice against glass.

Senor Ramirez popped his drink down, and then he slouched back in the red leather diamond-tucked cushions of the booth and closed his eyes and sighed a feathered sigh, a sigh of utter contentment and relief and satisfaction. I let him sit there awhile, let him enjoy that sigh and that satisfaction, let him bask in the heat of his shot of El Presidente.

I didn't know he was dead until the band came back and took the stand and Claudio motioned for us to come up to the stage. I nudged Senor Ramirez, and he didn't move. His eyes were sagging and drunken, tired, and it was so dark I couldn't tell whether or not his skin had changed colors. I don't know how I could have missed his death dance, but when I nudged him, I smelled the foulness of his clothes, and I knew that at last his great body was emptied of its spirit. He was trading eights with those among whom he belonged.

***

At the motel that night I put on Pop's cologne and took a shower and waited for my girlfriend. But she didn't show up. I spent the night tugging on a bottle of scotch I'd bought from the bartender and listening for the rattle of her keys. Some of the other guys in the band had the room next to mine, and they'd brought a girl back with them. I didn't know if my girlfriend had been killed or had abandoned me. I didn't know if I should call the cops, call her parents, or just wait.

In the morning I wandered Modesto, walking through junkyards looking for chrome moldings and bulb-domes and armrests for my station wagon. I found three armrests, and even though I only needed two, I bought all three. I went to a movie. I ate sausage and drank coffee at the diner. I yukked it up at the Main Street bar with the locals. I took a swim in the motel pool. I watched some television. A horse whinnied outside my motel window. The sunset was purple.

On my way to the bar, I stopped at a pawn shop, and the window display was almost entirely musical instruments. I asked the man behind the counter to show me his trumpets.

"You're in luck," he said. "I got five in today."

I closed my eyes and shook my head. "Shit," I said.

He cut me a look, and then he led me through a pile of drums and toolboxes and fishing tackle. He pointed to the wall.

"How much for all of them?" I said.

"A thousand."

"For one?"

"Two hundred fifty."

I ended up paying him $125 for Senor Ramirez's flugelhorn, a Bach with a gold plated bell that sounded like something angels played in heaven, soft and buttery and distant like the sound of a ship's horn five miles out to sea. That night, I was going to play a solo on that horn for Senor Ramirez. I was going to use all the money I made in Modesto to buy the trumpets for myself.

I got to the bar early, and from the parking lot I heard the band rehearsing, running through the horn parts again and again until the two trumpets got it right. Together they sounded very good. When I walked through the door, the guys in the band acted like they didn't even know me. I asked the bartender for a scotch, and he shook his head and said, "May I see your ID?"

"I'm with the band," I said.

"I can not serve minors," he said.

I unpacked my trumpet and walked toward the bandstand. The two trumpeters were young guys, Mexicans, and one of them was better than me, the other worse. Claudio raised his hand and cut off the band.

"We don't need you anymore," Claudio said.

"But I'm in the band," I said. "I know the parts."

"I am sorry, T-Bird," Claudio said.

"Just like that?"

He looked down at his keyboard. I looked at the other guys. None of them would look at me. Claudio said, "From the top," and the drummer kicked up the tune, and the band played.

I packed up my trumpet and went outside to my car and sat there, watching the lot fill up, watching the nicely dressed couples and groups of friends walk into the bar. The band began their first set, and I sat in my car listening, thinking about my girlfriend, about Senor Ramirez, about the girl who'd put her hand on my knee.

And then, I don't know why, I combed my hair and took a deep breath and got out of my car and walked right on into that bar.

"Scotch," I told the bartender.

"ID?" he said.

"No," I said. "Scotch."

And he smiled at me big, and he poured me a drink.

"This one," he said, "is from me."

I nodded thanks and turned around and leaned against the

bar, watching the dancers. It was still early, and the floor was not yet crowded. Los Asesinos was playing a cumbia, and the couples were paired off and dancing, the men in suits leading their partners around the floor, the women's dresses lifting to their thighs as they spun, gold jewelry flashing blue and red in the bar light, cigarette smoke swirling in the air above.

And I downed my scotch and took a step forward, and the next thing I knew, I was on the dance floor and dancing, not with any partner but alone, my arms curled in front of my chest as if I did have a partner. But I didn't, and I didn't care, and I was dancing. The crowd on the floor made space for me, and some of the people pointed, but no one stopped dancing and the band played well.

I closed my eyes, and I listened to the music, and I danced.

CHAPTER ELEVEN

Trading Eights

Pop kept getting worse. Everyone in town was glad he killed the Jarimallos and the Alvarezes, and he was a kind of hero around our part of Oakland. But instead of strutting around like the badass everyone thought he was, Pop seemed to shrink. He walked differently, his shoulders hunched, his eyes glazed and always looking at the ground. He didn't joke around much anymore. After work, instead of coming inside the trailer and watching television and eating hot fudge sundaes from Loard's Ice Creamery, he'd sit outside on a tire smoking cigars and looking out at the Nimitz Freeway. When the Raiders would beat the Kansas City Chiefs, he didn't care. When the A's took the World Series, he acted like nothing had happened at all. Jim Otto, the center for the Raiders, came into the station and bought a gas filter for his pickup truck, and while everyone else got his autograph, Pop installed the filter and wrote up the bill and sent Otto on his way. One time a funnel cloud formed right above the Mohawk station and our trailer, and while Clyde and I ducked for cover in the station, Pop sat there outside on his tire, smoking.

I wanted to tell him to blow, to howl like he did before he married Mom, to quit work at the Mohawk station, skate on the bills and hit the road, the clubs, the bars, play for pay, play for free. I wanted to shake him and put his horn back in his hands and watch him kick in the television screen, pack a duffel bag and walk back out into the streets of Oakland and San Francisco and smell that air, the night air, to look at the lights of the great cities, to smell the smoke of something other than his own cigars, to play jazz. But even if he could have found somewhere to blow, he wouldn't have gone.

"Jazz isn't a job," Pop said.

After the Oakland High graduation ceremony, Pop threw me a surprise party in the lube bays of the Mohawk station.

He lifted the rolling glass bay doors and the men inside the shop yelled, "Surprise, motherfucker!" and they threw sandwich-sized loaves of French bread at me.

Graduation was the day you moved out and found yourself a job. I didn't know what I was going to do for a living, but I'd saved up two hundred bucks, and that would go a long way. I could buy a lot of gas for two hundred bucks. I could eat for months. Two hundred bucks would buy a lot of junkyard parts for my station wagon if it broke down. I was set up pretty damn good, for a graduate.

Links of linguisca bubbled in vats of homemade Portuguese burgundy. The alignment rack was raised and draped with red-and-white-checkered tablecloths, and the concrete floor was slick with solvent.

I walked into the bays and shook hands with the men, and they hugged me and slapped my back. They poured beers down my throat. They wore grease-stained blue shirts with red-and-white name-patches. If I ever ended up in jail, these men would bail me out without asking what I'd done. Pop had even called Hiro and Rich, and they both handed me beers.

A Honda 750 pulled up at the ethyl pump, and on the back of the motorcycle was my mother.

"I'm in love," Rich Kuam said.

"Hubba fucking hubba," Joe Clausi said.

"Bitch," Pop said.

I hadn't seen her in eight years, though she'd always called on birthdays and Christmas. And she always called when she got a new husband. Including Pop, she'd married two air force pilots, a biker, a truck driver, and a traveling salesman. She'd marry anyone she hoped would take her out of Oakland.

She sat behind a tall skinny guy. I couldn't see the guy's face through the tinted plastic of his helmet's visor.

Pop grabbed a copy of *Tire Monthly* from the workbench and took the rest-room key and disappeared around the side of the station.

My mother stepped off the motorcycle, lifted the visor of the skinny guy's helmet and kissed him. He dropped his visor back down and sat there.

"Is that really you, T-Bird?" my mother called from the island. "My darling little boy all grown up into a hunk of a man. Come give Mommy a hug."

She walked into the lube bay. She wore hot-pants with stockings and a tube top and knee-high black leather boots. She'd gotten a boob job, and her breasts rode on her chest like Little Annie Fannie's cartoon boobies in *Playboy*.

She hugged me, both arms wrapped around my back, her body crushed into me. Her tits felt like basketballs shoved against my chest.

"Aren't you surprised to see me?" she asked. "Aren't you glad? Didn't you miss me?"

"I graduated today," I said.

"T-Bird dear, I've finally found the right one," my mother said. "John's simply wonderful. He's my new husband. *Your new father*. He works for Southern Pacific and we just go everywhere, riding around on trains, riding and riding and riding. Run run run, busy busy. You know how it is."

"Sure."

"John and me have a layover in Oakland tonight. You're still a virgin, aren't you? John and I ride in the caboose. I want you to play me a song on your trumpet. One you wrote *just for me.*"

I didn't say anything. She finally let me go. I stepped back.

"I have to tell you something." She leaned toward me. She lowered her voice. "John is *very* young," she said. "But he's every bit a *man.*" She smiled. "He just turned seventeen," she said. "Even though the railroad people think he's eighteen."

Before she left, she told me to meet her at the Union Pacific switching yard where their caboose was moored for the night.

How will I know which caboose?" I asked.

"You'll know," she said.

Some of the men cheered when my mother lifted her leg and straddled the seat of the motorcycle.

Pop lit a Roi-Tan and grabbed two beers and opened them and chugged from each in turn.

He wiped beer from his beard with his forearm. "The boy needs his goods."

He tugged a table cloth and beneath was a stack of Pennzoil boxes. The boxes were gift-wrapped with duct tape.

Joe Clausi of Clausi Carpets gave me carpet samples to use as floor mats for my navy-surplus station wagon. Steve Ballero of Concrete Wall Sawing gave me an acetylene torch welding/cutting kit. Ken Medeiros of Markstein Beverage gave me a case of Budweiser. Mike Santos of Santos Automotive and Kitchen Supply gave me a new rebuilt carburetor. George Webb of Webb's Body Shop gave me a can of Bondo. Rich Kuam of Kuam's Liquors gave me a box of Trojans. Everyone got a kick out of that one.

Hiro gave me a baseball card, a 1952 Willie Mays that I'd neglected to steal from him.

Rich gave me a bottle of tequila, the same brand I'd drunk in Reno when I fucked up the concert for Jack London Junior High.

Pop gave me a sleeping bag, a metal Coleman ice-chest, a laborers union card, and the family trumpet.

He handed the trumpet case to me and he said, "I made a living on this." He looked at me. "In the days when white men played trumpet."

He opened the case. The silver plating was tarnished black. The purple velvet was stained by slide grease and valve oil.

"You're not a musician until you make a living at it," Pop said. He handed me the horn. "And playing jazz with the niggers doesn't count. You know what classical players call mistakes?"

"What's that, Pop?"

"Jazz," Pop said.

He looked at the front door.

"You're eighteen," he said. "And a graduate. It's time for you to go away."

"Damn right!" Joe Clausi said.

"Make a living!" Pop said.

The men cheered. They cheered and they clapped and I loaded the gifts into the back of my station wagon and the men were still cheering and clapping as I drove away.

The first place I went was Archibald's Playhouse, a gray shack in West Oakland, a block from the Union Pacific switching yard. People lived upstairs, but downstairs men drank and played jazz. From the parking lot you could hear the trains clunk and squeal.

Mr. Beasley leaned against the bar at Archibald's and puffed away on a cigar. He clenched the cigar between his teeth and he reached out his hand to shake. He worked for Oakland Demolition, and his fingers had been whacked off in an accident. The thick brown stubs looked like cigar butts. He wore a straw hat over his white knotted hair.

"Amateur night," he said.

The rhythm section kicked off a B-flat blues, and an old white dude honked on a tenor, playing the head to "Kansas City."

"A month now he been coming," Mr. Beasley said. "Every week. Same tune every time. He's a retired man now and always wanted to play the saxophone and so he takes lessons at the *junior* college. All they taught him so far be 'Kansas City Here I Come.'"

Mr. Beasley shook his head, and then he smiled. "That boy got the blues but for serious."

One of the gin drinkers said, "Send that old white boy a drink!" and he held up a five-spot and people laughed.

The rhythm section kicked off "Cherokee." A tall thin black kid, clean shaven and wearing a white shirt and tie and glasses, stood on the plywood stage, his alto slung across his chest.

He let the band cut four choruses, the drummer riding the high hat and the bass plucking so fast the pianist could only play one chord per measure to keep tempo.

Then the kid altoman played the half-note/whole-note melody, each tone punching a chord change, clear and precise and not a note bent or scooped, no vibrato, each note pregnant, and the old gin drinkers looked at each other as if each were the father of this boy blowing the head of "Cherokee."

The altoman stood erect and tall, his eyes closed, his fingers the only moving sight in the bar, everyone watching those fingers now, waiting for them to stretch out, for the kid to solo. When the band snapped off for the solo break the kid waited, a pause that seemed to stop all time in Oakland in a grand caesura.

Ice clinked in glasses and you could hear the wheezing of the smokers.

And finally the altoman played. I ordered a Schlitz and a gin and leaned against the bar, and I drank.

I moved my trumpet case under the bar where no one could see it.

The kid altoman played more and I ordered another round

of drinks and then another, and even though I didn't smoke I bought a pack of Salems. The altoman floated through the changes, and the changes weren't Clifford Brown's anymore.

"That boy," Mr. Beasley said.

Mr. Beasley looked at me.

"Your turn now."

"Not tonight," I said. "I got to find a job."

"Only job you be finding tonight be up on that there stage," Mr. Beasley said.

"I need a *real* job," I said.

"You come by my work tomorrow, I'll get you one them *real* jobs."

I drove around the corner to the switching yard to meet my mother and my new stepfather. It had rained earlier in the day, and now it was clear, the air cold and iced as if with shards of glass, the pavement sparkling with the blue-green dew of shattered windshields.

A wind gusted through the alleys of train cars whipping up leaves of cellophane cigarette wrappers.

I walked along tracks, between trains, thousands of flatcars and boxcars and locomotives and an occasional caboose. Rusted Amtrak passenger cars, immense iron tombstones with nicotine windows and sun-scorched shades spread over the gravel and rail and broken wine bottles and splintered pallets. My feet slipped on the rain-wet stones that had been packed into soft bayside mud.

A train pulled slowly in, no blast of its whistle and no squeal of metal, no passengers unloading and no one to greet them if there had been, only a lone conductor coming to a gentle stop then stepping out as if he'd parked a precious antique car. He walked slowly down the rails and turned and he was gone.

A pair of stockings fluttered above the porch of a caboose.

John opened the caboose door when I knocked. He wore

tight jeans and a plaid shirt, a large silver belt-buckle the shape of Texas.

"T-Bird?" he said.

I nodded.

"Come on in," he said. "My place is yours." And the way he said it made me ashamed of myself, older than him and my first day no longer living at home, never having had a full-time job, a kid.

My mother was wearing a flimsy nightie, red and lacy, low cut.

The inside of the caboose looked like our trailer next to the Mohawk station, except bigger and older. The sink was filled with empty wine bottles. On the counter were three jugs of Spanada and a bottle of Cabin Still whiskey and a twelve-rack of Olympia.

"We went shopping!" my mother said. "We'll have so much fun. The last time I saw you, you were too young to drink. Now we can be a *family*."

"I'll have a whiskey and a beer," I said.

"There they are!" my mother said.

I poured a whiskey into a plastic cup and cracked a beer.

"Look at that," my mother said. "My little boy pours drinks just like a man."

I shot the cup of whiskey and guzzled the beer and then refilled and drank and refilled again. They kept pace with me, and soon we'd finished off the beer and the whiskey and we'd started on the wine.

I looked at John. Even though he was younger than me, he looked very old, his thin German face tanned and weathered like an old truck tire, eyes gray and cold as train rail. His hands were large and muscular like the hands of old workers.

We drank and talked and my mother laughed and outside the cranes dropped containers onto flatcars and cables whined as they rolled and unrolled on iron spools.

Then she talked about my father, how he used to play his

trumpet for her, how he serenaded her with the trumpet and how much I looked like him, how he looked when she married him, hairy and broad-shouldered and thick-necked and eyes gray as rain clouds and dry as plaster, just like mine.

But Pop's eyes were brown.

We ran out of liquor and my mother told me to take John for a booze run.

"Did you bring your trumpet?" my mother said.

"No."

"What?" she yelled. "I *told you* I want you to play a song for me," she yelled. "One you wrote *just for me*."

"I didn't bring it."

"Bring it."

John and I walked down the tracks away from the caboose.

"Wilma's a really great lady," John said.

I didn't say anything.

"You sure are lucky to have a mom like Wilma," John said.

I looked back toward the caboose. My mother stood on the porch, waving slow and smiling. She looked like she was posing for a dirty magazine. She looked like she'd never get old.

Fog had rolled in while we were drinking in the caboose, the sky now dropped onto us, a mist that revealed only one warehouse at a time as we walked. A dog slinked between two delivery trucks.

"You know where you're going?" I asked.

"Never been lost yet."

Ahead was a bar called The Mediterranean, a neon martini glass blinking red and the walls sided with rusted corrugated tin.

"Here," John said.

"But we need to find a store."

"Here."

"Have you ever seen her mad?"

"Yes," John said.

Inside The Mediterranean old black-haired Greeks wore hard hats and baseball caps with the names of local companies patched above the bills. The walls and ceiling were decorated with fishing gear: nets, tackle, stuffed fish, pictures of the Greek Isles, anchors and driftwood, rudders, ropes, harpoon guns.

Above our table was a stuffed swordfish, lacquered gray skin, glassy eye bulging out, staring.

"We need beers," John said.

"A little young, aren't you guys?" the old bartender said.

"Old enough for Southern Pacific," John said. He pulled out his wallet and flashed his union card.

The old bartender got us two beers, Budweiser. "Union beer for union men," he said.

"Union boys," I said.

John looked at me.

The old bartender walked away.

John kept staring at me.

"You got a problem?" I said.

"I know I'm younger than you," he said. "But Wilma's my wife, and she's your mother. That means I'm your father, and you're my son, so you'd better start acting like it."

"How's that?"

"By treating your mother with respect," John said. "Play your trumpet for her."

"You don't get it," I said. "Do you."

"Get what?"

I chugged my beer. "I'm not going to play for her."

John and I drank together. We drank a long time. We closed the place down.

Outside, the wind blew and fog billowed through the streets and you could hear the switching yard distant and muted and we stood there, John and I, and then we smiled, and I don't know who started first, but without deciding to I found myself running down the street, parting fog and hurdling fire hydrants and garbage cans and parking meters. And alongside me ran John, keeping step, and drunk and laughing we ran, flailing our arms and laughing and sometimes one of us would do a spin, twirling with arms outstretched like helicopter blades, and the other would pick up a rock and send it sailing over the roofs of warehouses. And we didn't stay to listen where it landed but ran, cutting the fog and leaving a double wake behind.

When we got to my car we stood laughing, leaned over and holding our sides and getting control of the laughter. And then one of us would giggle and the other would cough out a laugh, and then we'd both be laughing again, laughing so hard my stomach hurt and my eyes watered.

Finally I opened my car door, and John stood next to me, the trains backdropped behind him hazy and dark.

"I have to go," I said.

"So do I."

I got into my car and closed the door. "Take care of my mother," I said.

"I'll do that."

I watched him walk into the switching yard toward the caboose. I saw the shape of my mother standing in the open. When he got near her she yelled, "What do mean you don't have any booze?" and then John crouched beneath her swinging fists.

Her fists smacked his face and popped like distant gunshot.

The first job Oakland Demo sent Mr. Beasley and me on was a sewer tube, hammering out an old line that dead-ended near the wharves.

We duct-taped flashlights to our hard hats, and then we dropped down through the manhole, lowering the 90-pound jackhammers with the air hoses that trailed behind to the Ingersoll-Rand 250 compressor.

We stepped into black crusted tar up to our knees.

"It never dries up," Mr. Beasley said. He laughed. "Every time it rains it stinks all up again. I've worked sewers all over this Bay Area. Sometimes we lose men when their waders gets leaky. Eats clean through they legs."

He looked at me, the flashlight taped to his hardhat blazing at my face like a spotlight.

"Now you got a *real* job," he said.

By lunchtime my hands were bruised black and numb, and my stomach was beaten purple. We had to hold the jackhammers horizontally to break the wall, so with one hand I held the yoke near the bit, with the other hand I held the handle, and I pushed with my stomach. Mr. Beasley built himself a network of ropes attached to the rebar hanging from the ceiling of the tunnel so he could use both hands instead of his stomach to push.

"You didn't bring no rope?" he said.

"No."

"Where's your gloves?"

"I don't need gloves."

"Do it the easy way, it's easier."

After work, Mr. Beasley stood at the Cyclone gate waiting for me to finish packing away my tools so he could lock the gate.

"I'll stay here," I said.

"You need to go home," he said. "You got to be tired. You one dirty, smelly son bitch."

"I think I'll be staying here."

He looked at me, and he shook his head, and he said, "You needing anything?"

"No."

When he left, I took out the trumpet and played. The air was cold and the mouthpiece against my lips felt like dry ice, burning and sticking to the skin. The valves were slow and soft because of the cold.

The sewer lingered in my mouth.

Dogs barked and weeds rustled. A ship in the harbor sounded its horn, low and heavy through the fog, bumping in waves over soft crests of water. Someone popped off a few rounds in the distance. Then it was quiet again. I blew until the taste of the day's work went away.

I blew a long time.

The next day after work Mr. Beasley and I stood next to his camper and smoked and drank gin. A cold bay breeze blew.

"I heard you blowing horn," Mr. Beasley said. "Last night."

He looked at me. His eyes were very old. He tugged on the gin bottle and he brought up his other hand and pointed his finger stubs at me. The scarred ends were pink.

"I knew a man one time who played horn," Mr. Beasley said. "Baritone saxophone," he said. "He quit."

He lit a cigarette.

"He been sorry about that," he said.

"My father played trumpet," I said.

"Tomorrow we'll be done busting through that concrete," Mr. Beasley said. "That's your business, demo-man."

He handed me the bottle.

We finished the sewer job, and Oakland Demo sent us to the North-Side Neighborhood job.

The night before the wrecking crews began work, Mr. Beasley gave me a tour of the neighborhood.

We stood on the street, sidewalk expansion joints split with weeds and the hulks of stripped-down abandoned cars rusting on foxtail lawns, broken windows spanned with spider webs.

Mr. Beasley walked down the street.

He stopped in front of a sagging two-story Victorian.

"See that house," he said. "Time that house the pride of this neighborhood. Every room bright and lit up."

I looked down the street and tried to imagine a neighborhood, children and lovers and working men, cocktails in heirloom crystal snifters, roses and morning-dewed lawns and the smell of freshly painted wood.

A helicopter circled above for a moment, centered its spotlight on us for an instant, then dove into another part of the city.

"A man played bari lived here," Mr. Beasley said. "Wrote his own songs. Every time he played for the people he played a new song he wrote his ownself. Wasn't nobody playing jazz he didn't trade eights with."

He pointed across the street to a sagging barn-like church, the once white paint peeling and tattooed with graffiti, indecipherable like the kanji store-signs of Chinatown. We walked across the street. The needle of a syringe sparkled in the gutter. Mr. Beasley stood before the door of the church for an instant, then pushed it open and stepped in.

The concrete floor was coated with fine dust so soft underfoot that the floor seemed like the ancient surface of a moon.

Mr. Beasley gathered cardboard boxes and old newspapers and splintered boards and lit a fire in the center of the dark.

The fire rose and shadows stretched black and twisted and the smell of dust and dry and musted smoke powdered the air. The ceiling vaulted above and the walls were lined with broken pews. Mice scattered beneath.

He walked to where the altar would have been.

"Nighttime," Mr. Beasley said, "nighttime when the day work done this was the place men played."

He picked up a slat of wood from the floor and tossed it into the fire. Ashes and sparks rose and snapped in the air.

"One by one those jazzmen, they quit," Mr. Beasley said.

* * *

Mr. Beasley and I smoked cigarettes while dozers drove through the old houses and shops. By noon they'd cleared two blocks, the old houses and the shops and the jazzman church now leveled. In the distance men on porches drank and fanned themselves with fishing hats and rocked slow in wooden chairs.

We started working when the dozers were done, and I'd never seen Mr. Beasley work so hard, sweat pooled in the crevices of his face, the veins of his neck like piano wires, dust rising around him as if he'd hammered a hole into the fires of hell.

"Slow down," I said. "Let's take a break."

He kept hammering.

"You're going to kill yourself for a check," I said.

But he kept hammering and breaking foundations and the compressor whined in high gear. I stood in front of him and yelled, "Stop!" and he wouldn't look up at me. I crouched so I could see his eyes and "Stop!" I yelled, and he hammered and broke and rocked and hammered still, plates of concrete and rebar lifting with wedges of the hammer, and coveralled and hard-hatted Mr. Beasley worked.

And then I saw his tears. And when I saw those tears leaking out of his eyes like motor oil I understood what this neighborhood had once been, and I looked at his cigar-stub fingers, and I looked at this man demolishing already rubbled rock and sweating over the chugging jackhammer.

And I knew then that each time he listened to the jazzmen at Archibald's Playhouse, just listening—just being there, standing there with the men smoking—just listening and standing there with his glass of gin in his hand was an act of courage and shame.

I drove along the perimeters of parks where no children played. I drove along the shore of the bay, brine-reddened air salted and musty and dry, the shores foamed and dark.

I stopped across the street from Mohawk service station where Pop worked and saw him standing on the lot breaking down a truck tire, swinging his five-pound sledge against a split-rim 10:00 X-20, the canopy fluorescence lighting his hulk in spot, sparks of metal on metal popping into the night and the lead hammer flashing, the sound ringing across the asphalt. I wanted to honk my car horn and let him know I was there, but I didn't. I sat in my car, the family trumpet on the bench seat to my side, and watched the old man work, watched him swing his hammer and break down the tire, crowbar the split-ring and pull the flap and mount the recap, watched him stand over his work broad chested and washed in the light of his work.

I drove through warehouse-lined streets, and in the yard of each warehouse there was a man working, forklifting a pallet or dollying crates or push-brooming garbage.

I drank a six-pack of Schlitz and a half bottle of Gilbey's gin and I drove, until finally I parked in the dirt lot across from Archibald's Playhouse. The exhaust fan chugged the smoke of cigars and cigarettes to the rhythm of bass and drum and piano-chord blues. The music bobbed across tables and through windows and it pumped between the blades of the exhaust fan and into the parking lot where I sat on the seat of my navy-surplus station wagon liquored-up and bloodshot and my head against the steering wheel. I was feeling pretty Oakland.

The beat of bass and ride of cymbal cut into the lot. Lights beamed from everywhere, from parking-lot lamps, from yellow-bulbed foglights, from the windows of neighborhood homes, spiraled from the beacons of incoming trains, the spotlights of switching-yard towers.

I drove. I heard car horns and sirens and slamming wooden doors and the gab of folk.

Streetlight switchboxes clicked, directing deserted intersections.

There were places in the city I hadn't been.

* * *

I drove back to the Mohawk station. I walked around the side to the Airstream and knocked on the door. Pop didn't answer so I let myself in.

Pop sat on his bed in the dark smoking a cigar.

"Working?" Pop said.

I nodded.

"Tires on the car?"

"Fine," I said.

"You visit with your mother?"

I nodded.

"And?"

"Wanted me to play her a song."

Pop stared at me.

"I didn't do it."

He took a long drag and blew smoke rings. "The guy on the motorcycle?"

"Another stepfather."

Pop reached and took a Roi-Tan from the headboard. He handed it to me and gave me his Zippo. "I used to play for her," he said. "When we first met."

I lit my cigar.

"You know she'd never heard 'Carnival of Venice' before she met me?" he said. "Never even heard it. She'd never been to a concert. She didn't even know what a French horn was. She didn't know the difference between a trumpet and a cornet."

I nodded.

"I wouldn't have been happy if you'd have played for her," Pop said.

"You think I might have done it?"

"She can be very persuasive," Pop said.

CHAPTER TWELVE

Gunite Man

I got fired from my demo job when I refused to hang from a rope to jackhammer down a brick wall. I had a stash of money, though, enough so I didn't have to work for a few months. I got into my station wagon and drove, the car pointed north. Oakland boys don't dream of Los Angeles—we dream of Oregon and Washington, of Montana, of Jack London's Alaska. We dream of heading into the mountains and building cabins with trees we've chopped down with axes. We dream of living off a mythological frontier, the frontier our great-grandparents found when they came over Donner Pass in search of gold. We're cannibals all, and that we've built cities in California is our greatest mistake, because we've lost what makes us different from the slobs of the rest of the country. We've lost our fangs.

I didn't tell anyone I was leaving, where I was going, when I'd be back, because I didn't know. I didn't give a damn where I ended up, so long as it wasn't Oakland, and I saw the entire West through the windshield at seventy miles an hour, saw it bend past me and recede slowly in the rearview mirror, the misty coast all the way to Alaska, the volcanic Cascades, farm towns with new-and used-tractor lots instead of car lots, moose lumbering along like prehistoric and stupid monsters, sad old Indians selling goofy homemade jewelry on the side of the road near Alturas, sagging little valley-towns that had as many churches as houses and more trailer homes than either. I'd get adventurous and turn off the highway, and one time I found myself on a marijuana plantation in Humboldt County, old rusted tractors and trucks placed carefully to give the impression of a logging camp, the distant barking and yelping of hounds cutting between densely packed trees. I slept in the wheat fields of California's Central Valley, one time awakened by a combine that nearly mowed me down. I slept in apple orchards in Washington, I slept on the boiling rim of Mount Lassen, on a fishing boat bobbing at an abandoned dock in Juneau, along the banks of the Yukon. I drove the interstates, the crumbling county roads, every winding dike road in the Delta: as long as I was moving, everything was fine. As long as the scene changed, as long as the dashes on the road slipped beneath the left front tire, I was okay. But whenever I stopped, whether it was for food or gas, or whether it was at a dead-end dirt road in the farmlands, great fields of sunflowers bent toward the light or vegetables fanning out and disappearing into horizon—no matter where or when I turned off the key and listened to the engine diesel-knock a few times before coming to rest, it was always as if I had never been moving at all. Nothing had changed, nothing had gotten any better, and all I could think of was Oakland and the East Bay. I always feared that the car wouldn't start back up, that I'd be stuck wherever I was for the rest of my life, get murdered by some half-witted farm boy or lumberjack. I don't care what people say, you're safer in any city in the world than you are in America's "God's Country," in rural America where everyone who doesn't have a sister fucks their livestock, where retards sit on porches whittling and waiting for your car to break down so they can strip the skin from your body to use as binding for their Bibles. God's Country, my ass. You got a little buttshit town in the middle of nowhere, population one hundred, and no one's moved in or out since the town was founded. How many generations does it take before some toothless banjo-playing inbred hillbilly motherfucker, when he's finished with the horses, the goats, the sheep and the chickens, is screwing his sister, his retard aunt, his cousin, his nuclear waste-radiated one-eyed hermaphrodite little brother? The math ain't that fucking hard.

Rural America scares the shit out of me. I'd rather have my car break down in the deepest dungeons of darkie-town Chicago or Detroit or even Oakland, or in Mexican Los Angeles or El Paso or switchblade Tucson, than in hillbilly redneck Climax Springs, Missouri. At least I'd know the rules. When white people descend on your car like zombies from Vincent Price horror land—why are zombies always white?—you are fucked and fucked for good. Give me a ghetto where I can just buy the guys some Schlitz Malt Liquor-bull and drink it with them and trade stories into the fog of the Oakland night, all of us drunk and telling tales of woe about how we've been fucked over by women—the one thing we've all got in common—but don't strand me in God's Country. Those crackers scare the shit out of me. They make me long for Oakland. Fucking please, God, please don't ever strand me with those mutants.

The car usually did start, though, and I always got moving again, faster and faster, as if I were escaping from some invisible demon that always knew where I was heading and would be waiting for me when I got there.

Eventually, I went back to Oakland. It wasn't as if I missed the ghettos, the constant race war, my family. It seemed like I had to be there, like it was where I belonged, whether I liked it or not. I got a room in a run-down Victorian on a dead-end street. A flashing yellow light was attached to the Dead End sign, and drunks smashed into the pole every other week or so, drawn to the blinking light like bugs.

One night, my brother Clyde came over to visit and we got drunk on scotch. We decided we were going to throw a party for Pop. Pop had just gotten married to some fat little barmaid, but he was still feeling low. We were going to invite all the customers. We were going to cook linguisca. We were going to get a stripper with really big titties even if it cost a hundred bucks. Pop was worth it. When Clyde left, he went the wrong way down the street and drove into the pole. I didn't even find out that he'd died until the next night because I was so hungover I slept the day away. When I finally answered the phone, it was Pop.

"Clyde's dead," he said.

I didn't say anything.

"I said, Clyde's dead. Are you listening?"

"I'm listening, Pop. What happened?"

"You should know," Pop said. "He died at the end of your street. He drove into that pole."

"We were going to throw you a party, Pop."

"Well thanks for the party."

The city removed the blinking light. Wrecks became less frequent, but more severe.

I got a new job by selling dope to my landlord, Bob. He was tall, big and blond, and wore a mustache. He was tanned and always wore mirror sunglasses. He looked like a surfer bum. He was a foreman for a gunite company, and after I sold him a few bags of weed, he decided to give me a job. He needed me around.

Gunite is the air placement of concrete. It's how they make ditches and silos and vertical walls without using forms. Concrete is blasted through a high-pressure hose, and it's shot through that hose so hard it sticks to anything. You can shoot gunite on the ceiling of a sewer tube and it will just hang there like concrete glue. The Matterhorn at Disneyland is made of gunite. The giant concrete dinosaurs on I-10 are made of gunite. Guniters travel a lot, and the first job I got sent on was in Bishop, California, on the edge of the Mojave Desert. We were supposed to leave at five in the morning so we could make it through the Sierra Nevadas before dark. The crew was to meet at Bob's place.

"I like gunite," he said while we watched the sun start to peek over the foothills. "The Mexicans should be here any minute. They're always early. Rex'll be late. Rex'll be hungover if he's not drunk."

He lit a joint.

"I like marijuana," he said.

His mustache was so long and bushy he had to lift it up to get the joint into his mouth. He held in the smoke as long as he could, then coughed. He pushed the joint toward me.

I was hitting on the joint when I heard a car coming, rattling toward us. It was an old puke-green Plymouth, and the muffler bounced on the ground and made sparks.

"Rex," Bob said. "Every time he shows up for a job he's driving a different car. Always shitbuckets. He buys heaps of junk and drives them until they die—leaves them scattered all over the country." He took the joint from me. "I like marijuana a lot," he said.

The Plymouth rattled to a stop behind the rig truck.

I picked up my trumpet case and my suitcase and started for the back of the truck. It was a white Ford one-ton with a Koenig toolbox kit behind the cab, dual rear wheels, the boxes as high as my head on either side of the truck. The puke-green Plymouth was parked behind the truck. I didn't try to see what Rex looked like, but I knew he was watching me.

The back of the truck was filled with fiberglass poles, ropes, metal clamps, five-gallon gas cans, oil, grease, concrete tools—floats, trowels, water brushes, plastic buckets, fresnoes—and in the front, up by the cab, were four fifty-five-gallon steel drums. It smelled like dust, diesel, and gasoline. I tossed my suitcase on top of the heap and decided to bring my horn with me inside the cab.

"I like out-of-town jobs," Bob said.

He dug around in the ashtray, picked out a roach, and

smoked it down as we started off, followed by the puke-green Plymouth and a Chevy Impala full of Mexicans.

"Gunite is the perfect job," Bob said. "Can you roll?" He popped open a concrete-dusted briefcase and tossed me a baggie. "You'll really like gunite," he said.

By the time we got out onto the interstate, Bob had acquired two women's phone numbers. He would pull alongside and smile through his big blond mustache, and if the girl smiled back, he'd reach beside the seat and pull out a sign that read "PHONE #?" The girl would laugh. Then he would reach beside the seat and pull out a box of kids' flash cards and start going through the digits one at a time. He made me write down the numbers as the girl, giggling, nodded. After two or three numbers, the girl would give up and hold up her fingers for the remaining digits. When he got all seven numbers, he would pick the cards from his lap and flash them back, with me reading him the number.

"It never fails," he said. "I like flash cards."

About forty miles out of town, we spotted a car on fire on the other side of the road, across the median. When Bob saw the flames, he downshifted and put his foot down hard on the accelerator, starting across the median.

"You're going off the road," I said.

He plowed the big white Ford through the golden grass and weeds, trailer and all, into the oncoming traffic, skidded to a stop in front of the burning car, grabbed the fire extinguisher from behind the seat, opened it up on the engine of the brown Toyota Celica, put out the fire, nodded to the woman from behind his sunglasses, got back into the truck, drove back into the oncoming traffic, back across the weeds and grass in the median, and he drove ninety miles an hour until he caught back up with the spark-throwing puke-green Plymouth and the Chevy Impala full of Mexicans.

"You do that often?"

"Yes," he said. "I like putting out fires."

One of the Mexicans was watching us out the back of the Chevy, pounding his chest like Tarzan, curling his arms like a bodybuilder, gesturing at Bob.

After that, everyone called him Super-Bob.

Super-Bob looked over and blew marijuana smoke at me.

"You play sports?" he said. "I like sports."

"I used to play sports."

"How about now?"

"A little."

"Anytime you want to play sports, let me know," Super-Bob said. "Any sport, you name it."

I didn't say anything.

"Any sport," he said. "I'll beat you at any of them."

"Do you play chess?" I said.

"Chess isn't a sport," he said.

"We aren't supposed to go through Yosemite, Bob. Didn't you see the sign? 'No Commercial Vehicles in National Park.'"

"I can read," he said.

He drove for a while, then looked at me.

"If we get to the entrance before eight, they won't catch us," he said. "That's a direct order."

We got to the entrance at eight. An old man with a potbelly ran out of a cabin. He was in gray long underwear and he shook his fist in the air.

"Home free," Super-Bob said.

We were going downhill when the tire came off the pump trailer. It passed us and went careening over the side of the cliff, down into a valley.

"That tire was from the pump, Bob," I said. I looked in the rearview mirror. The trailer's axle was digging a furrow in the asphalt road.

"We can make it," he said.

We rounded a bend and Super-Bob said, "Damn."

He stopped the truck because two Park Service patrol cars blocked the road ahead. Behind the two patrol cars were four forest rangers. They had shotguns, and the shotguns were aimed at us. After we stopped one of the rangers put down his shotgun and picked up a bullhorn.

We were given an armed escort out of the park, dragging the trailer along by its frame. The axle had twisted off.

"If we had been just a little earlier," Super-Bob said, "we could have made it."

The job in Bishop was a sewage reservoir. It was as big as two football fields end to end, and we were shooting concrete on the dirt slopes and floor. The slopes were so steep that we had to use ropes to lower ourselves down every morning. It was butted up against the Nevada side of the Sierras, northwest of Death Valley.

It seemed to take hours for the sun to come up over the great desert, a bloodred line stretching across the far-off peaks of the Rockies, tracing the summits for hundreds of miles to the north and south. The sky turned purple and you could see the shapes of the mountains stretch into the sky, orange pyramids poking out into the purple of the morning, reaching into the black of the receding night. I stood on the rim of the pond, gnats in my face and the rustling of jackrabbits in the fields and that double image of the mountains, the red line and the orange negative image, like trees reflecting off a calm lake in the mountains.

My job was pretty easy. All I had to do was help a fat guy, Don Gordo, drag the hose around behind the nozzleman. The nozzleman was the guy who held the end of the hose. His was the hard job. If the hose kinked, he'd get blasted about fifty feet into the air. If the hose got loose, it was liable to whip around and knock his brains out.

I was minding my own business, pulling the hose, when Rex started giving me shit.

"Go ahead and hit me, kid," Rex said. It was 110 degrees.

"Go ahead," Super-Bob said. "Hit the old man."

Don Gordo laughed. The Mexicans laughed. Everyone was laughing.

Rex was old. His gray hair was wiry and tight. He had round glasses dotted with spots of concrete. One lens was cracked. He wore a beat-up fedora instead of a hard hat.

"Go ahead and hit me," Rex said.

He pushed me. The Mexicans were cooking burritos they'd tie-wired to the manifold of the air compressor. He pushed me again.

"What the fuck's wrong with you?" Rex said. "Hit me, you little pussy."

I took a swing, but Rex's fist shot out and he clocked me before my punch had a chance to land. I ended up facedown in the concrete.

"If there's one thing you need to know," Rex said, "it's don't ever fuck with Rex."

We'd been working twelve hours a day for two weeks straight, and at one o'clock in the afternoon one day Don Gordo's eyes glazed and he broke into a sheet of sweat and he passed out. Super-Bob walked to the orange Gott watercooler, unscrewed the white cap, carried it over to the fallen body of Don Gordo, and emptied the water on his chest and face. The water beaded on his skin as if on oil. Don Gordo spasmed and jerked awake.

"You claim six dependents on your W-4," Super-Bob said. "Unless you want them to starve, get back to work and behave like a gunite man."

Super-Bob found things for Don Gordo to do. Straighten the ground wires, boy. Refinish this panel of slope. Reset the jiffy jacks. Stack the planks so the site looks organized. Rake the rebound into the dirt. Get another barrel of Huntz curing compound and load it onto the truck.

Don Gordo ran in a constant panic, rushing back and forth across the pit, Super-Bob never letting him finish one chore before assigning him another, Don Gordo running faster and faster, and days passed, and unfinished chores stacked up, and Super-Bob watched with his arms crossed over his chest, a crass smile creased across his face, blond mustache stretched across his lip, Don Gordo passing out in the dust or in the concrete, and each time he passed out, Super-Bob stood over him with the water jug of rust-spackled water from the tanks of the mud trucks, splashing gray and red water over Don Gordo's groin, then over his chest, over the folds of his neck and over his face, and Don Gordo's eyes would pop open and he'd scramble to his feet and resume the chore he'd been attending to.

When Don Gordo died, I stared, watched his face turn white, the blood seeping from his forehead from where he'd split his head on a spike of #10 rebar driven into the dirt as a stake to keep the mesh from sliding down the slope. I watched Don Gordo's face turn blue, and I watched as the spurting blood stopped and Don Gordo's body began to twitch.

"Breaktime," Rex said.

Rex lit a cigarette.

"He pissed his pants," Rex said. "You know they're dead when they piss and shit their pants. It ain't like the movies where some dude carries the dead beauty in his arms. In real life he'd puke from the stench. That's Don Gordo's soul oozing out of him."

Don Gordo's body twitched and flopped and convulsed in seizures that reminded me of drunks I'd seen have fits in the streets of the city. I looked at Don Gordo's crotch, watched the stain spread, the blood from his head seep instead of spurt, and somehow it didn't seem real. Somehow it seemed cartoon.

Super-Bob tried mouth to mouth resuscitation. Blood seeped out of Don Gordo's ears as if Super-Bob blew too hard.

Rex uncapped his pint and drank.

When Super-Bob finished bending over Don Gordo, he looked back up at us.

"He's dead," Super-Bob said. "There's nothing more we can do. Get back to work."

We tried to carry Don Gordo up the slope and out of the hole, but we kept falling down, Don Gordo's body rolling on top of us.

"How are we supposed to get him up the slope?" I said. "He's pretty big."

"You have a point there," Super-Bob said.

Super-Bob thought about it.

"I have an idea," Super-Bob said.

"Sure those ropes are tight?"

"They're tight," I said.

"Then stand back," Super-Bob said. "Wouldn't want it to come loose and injure any of you. We're a man short as it is, now."

We climbed back down the slope and stood in the pit. Don Gordo was harnessed in a web of ropes cinched so tight that he hardly looked human, more like a huge walrus bound in fishing line. Super-Bob climbed into his foreman's truck and put it into granny gear and began pulling, the rope tied around the trailer clamp on his back bumper, Don Gordo beginning to slide up the slope, over the mesh, getting caught on rebar stakes, then tearing loose, strips of flesh dangling from his sides and slabs of viscera drooped over spikes of rebar like rough-hewn butcher cuts.

We shot concrete right on over the guts.

After work, Super-Bob called a safety meeting.

"Gentlemen, what happened today was unfortunate. But Don Gordo died doing something very important. He was the best hose-puller on the crew, and he will be missed."

He paused, and he looked around at us. "I want you all to remember," Super-Bob said, lifting his hard hat from his head and tucking it under his arm, then bowing his head a little, "that you are working for the biggest and best gunite company in the entire East Bay. Only fifty-three people in the world can say that. And you're each one of them."

When Super-Bob finished his speech, Rex walked to his car and pulled his union book out of his suitcase and started reading aloud to the crew.

"If you get a finger chopped off, it's worth five hundred," Rex said. "A hand or foot, a thousand. So that's five thousand one finger at a time, plus four thousand for the hands and feet. Nine thousand one part at a time. Don Gordo's wife'll get five thousand, since he died intact. He'd have been a lot better off dying one part at a time."

I had been working for Concrete-West Gunite Company for six months, and it was the rainy season. We were working a job in Foster City, a suburb twenty miles south of San Francisco, lining the slopes of a sewage canal with concrete. Foster City was an array of condos and shopping malls built on top of the old garbage dumps. It had been storming for two weeks, and the bottom of the ditch was filled with three feet of water, chemicals, tampons, black toilet-paper sludge, and other nasty things I didn't spend time identifying. The black sludge smelled like wet turds and rotten eggs. It had the sulfur smell of geysers or bubbling vats of mud at the base of a volcano.

We'd been running low on men lately. They kept quitting or dying on us. Super-Bob called the union hall. They sent us a black dude. "Ain't no way I be going down there in that shit," he said when he looked down into the open sewage canal. "We was slaves a hundred years ago, ain't no slave today."

We went through seven of them before the union agent sent us Fish.

"I don't care how bad it smells," Fish said. "For fifteen dollars a hour, I'll shovel this shit with a coke spoon."

"I like Fish," Super-Bob said.

The Mexicans didn't like Fish. They were afraid of him. Fish was six-foot-ten, 260 pounds. All muscle. His veins popped from beneath his skin. His head was the size of a watermelon, and his skin the blackish purple of real Africans. He could lift two 90-pound bags of cement at once, one in each hand. When Super-Bob hired Fish, he got to fire two of the Mexicans.

"How'd you get so strong, Fish?" I asked.

"All I ever did was work out," he said. "You got to, else you don't stand a nigger's chance."

"I don't work out."

"You ain't been to Quentin," Fish said. "I spent the last eleven years there, since I was a raw youngster."

We lost three Mexicans on the Foster City job. They refused to wear waders, and the sludge filled their rubber boots. Two got poisoned by the turds. The other one came to work one day and he started screaming after an hour in the hole. He climbed up the slope and stripped off his pants. His legs were red, as if he'd been sunburned. You could see his veins pulse and twitch.

He lost the legs.

Rex lit a cigarette. "Two thousand bucks for Miguel," Rex said. "Appendages."

On out-of-town jobs I roomed with Fish and Rex.

When the Mexicans noticed that I was spending a lot of time with Rex, they warned me.

"You want to watch the nasty gringo," they said. "Too much borracho. No good for you."

Rex warned me about the Mexicans.

"You got to be careful around wetbacks," Rex said. "They're a crew of goddamn liars, right down to the last greasy little taco."

After the Foster City job, Concrete-West sent us to Clearlake, in the wine country. We were shooting a little canal next to a walnut grove. After work, we would empty out our plastic work buckets, dump the trowels and floats and hammers and rolls of wire, and we'd fill our buckets with walnuts.

We stayed at a hotel on the shore of the lake. When we had all showered, Fish stood in the middle of the room in only his towel and he looked at me with weird eyes.

"Where you be coming from, the head or the hips?" he said.

Rex laughed and looked at me.

"The head," Fish said, "or the hips? Head or the hips?"

"I don't follow you, Fish."

Fish curled his arms in front of his hips and humped the air between them a couple of times. "I be coming strictly from the hips," he said.

Days, Fish and I took turns mixing the concrete behind the pump. One of us worked the sand scoop, the other busted sacks. Keebler ran the pump and yelled, "More material! More material!"

"He a raw youngster," Fish said.

I was busting sacks. I'd grab one cement sack from the pallet, carry it over to the gunite rig, and set it on top of the hopper. Then I'd cut the sack open with a shovel, letting the cement fall into the mix.

"Stand back, dude," Keebler said. "I'll show you how we do things in Utah!"

Keebler was the only other gunite man as young as me. We were both eighteen, but Keebler had been out of school four years already.

I used to tell Keebler about the great jazz clubs in San Francisco, how you'd pay four or five bucks and the jazzmen would play until three or four in the morning.

"What about the cunts? Are there lots of cunts?" he asked.

"You're lucky if there's a female bartender," I said.

"Cunts don't like me, anyway," Keebler said. "They all think they're too good for me. But they haven't seen me run the gunite pump. If they ever came to work and saw me working the pots, then they'd be singing a different song, tell you what."

He'd been in the gunite business since he was a baby, Keebler. His father was a gunite foreman for a scab outfit in Provo. Keebler knew gunite, he was raised in it. He knew how things were done.

He walked over to the pallet. He bent over, wrapped his arms around *two* bags, and lifted. His face turned red. He hobbled over to the hopper and pushed the two bags on top. Then he flailed at the bags with his fists. After a while, they broke open, and then he looked up at Fish and me.

"That's how we do things in Utah," he said.

After work, I'd go out to the end of the fishing dock with my trumpet and play. There'd always be a boat or two out on the lake, and I'd show off for them, hoping one loaded with girls would change its course and come over to me and invite me aboard.

I'd imagine the notes pushing across the water, across the lake, rolls of flowing black cloth easing into the dark and making ripples of sound in the glasslike surface that would roll to the opposite shore and then beyond and disappear into eternity.

One night, Fish came out to listen. When I heard him coming, I put the horn in my lap. He sat down next to me on the bobbing dock. It was foggy, and there was no breeze, so quiet you could hear the little waves slapping against the floats of the docks.

"Why you be doing this shit?" Fish said. "You should be playing that thing for a living."

He sat with his legs crossed Indian-style, his hands on his knees. He looked a thousand years old.

"Because I'm not a bum. What do you think?"

"Why don't you play that trumpet for your check? You don't need to be doing this shit."

"My father used to play trumpet," I said. "Before he married my mother. He played in the Oakland symphony. His father played in the Oakland symphony. But my father married my mother, and he quit playing his trumpet to make a living and support my mother and Kent and then me and Clyde, and then my mother got him thrown in jail because he caught her screwing the Angels. When he got out of jail, he ended up a grease monkey at a gas station, no cash, no credit, no education, bankrupt. My father, Pop, my father who could play 'Carnival of Venice' and who could triple-tongue scales in every key and four octaves—my father ended up pumping gas at a Mohawk station, checking people's oil, stooping over and putting air in their tires, thanking them when they gave him a quarter or fifty cents for a tip. He killed people too," I said. "Revenge. And now both my brothers are dead, and Pop works in a gas station, and he's got nothing. Not a fucking thing."

Fish didn't say anything. He stared out over the water. I heard something splash near the shore.

"So, me?" I said. "Me, I'm not going to make my father's mistake. First of all, no women fucking up my life. Second, dreams are for people who have a safety cushion, something to fall back on. If you want to chase dreams, you'd better have a trust fund, you'd better have some rich goddamn family behind you to catch you when you fall on your ass. You got to have plenty of ducats if you want to spend your life fucking around having fun. Meanwhile, the rest of us must work."

"You a raw youngster," Fish said.

"Not that raw," I said.

"Raw," Fish said.

In the dark over the lake I saw a white flash dropping from the sky. It hit the water, and then there was splashing. I heard the beat of wings, and the bird lifted itself up and away.

"Fish?"

"Yeah?"

"What did you go to San Quentin for?"

"I shot a man when I was robbing a liquor store," Fish said. "I was a raw youngster, eighteen. Bitch told the cops."

When I went back to the hotel, Rex had taken a hit of Orange Sunshine, and he was frying seriously. He told Fish and me about what it was like for him to be fifteen. That's how old Rex was wen he burned the cop's house down and moved out West. He had told O'Reilly the cop not to cut his hair when O'Reilly and two of his mick cop buddies tackled Rex in the Jersey City alley and took out their shears. Rex told him not to cut his hair or he would burn O'Reilly's fucking house down. But the cop wouldn't listen, and he cut Rex's hair off. And not only that, but the mick cop O'Reilly ripped Rex's earring out of his ear. Rex took out his golden mushroom earring and showed Fish and me the scar.

The next night, after Rex doused the outside of O'Reilly's house with gasoline, he knocked on the front door and told

O'Reilly he'd better get his mick family out, because he was going to burn his fucking house down. O'Reilly stared at Rex with a dumb mick look.

Rex dropped the match and ran.

Rex had been married once, to some uptown broad he didn't know how the hell he got mixed up with in the first place. And when he left The Bitch, he left the gunite business right on her goddamn lawn. The Bitch had wanted him to make more money, to stop working for everybody in town and start his own fucking business.

He called his company Uptown Gunite.

The Bitch liked the name. It showed respectability.

Before Uptown Gunite, all The Bitch ever did was whine because Rex didn't make enough money. So when the company started turning huge profits, he bought her a goddamn fur coat, a goddamn new car, and a goddamn new house, uptown. Then all she ever did was whine because he was never home.

Rex got up to get a beer. Fish got up and put out the light. We pretended we were asleep.

Rex clicked on the light and cracked his beer.

"Look at this." Rex pulled up his shirt. A purple scar ran the length of his back. "When I told The Bitch that I wanted a divorce, she said that she wanted the fucking business. I told her to fuck off, and she came after me with a knife. I'd had enough of her shit. I said, 'You got it, bitch,' and I left the goddamn gunite rig right on the front lawn. Then I called the quarry and ordered 200-ton of sand and had them dump it on the lawn. Got the batch plant to spread 30-ton of cement over the sand."

Rex light a cigarette and smiled. I'd never seen him so happy.

"It rained that night," Rex said. "Ha."

Rex laughed again. "Ha," he said. "There's the goddamn business!"

The sun was due up soon. Birds squawked and made horrible winter-bird noises.

"Get me to work," Rex said. "Get me to work fast. I think

I'm going to pass out, and if I do, I want to be where I'll get paid for it."

When we got back to San Francisco after the Clearlake job, Rex offered to give me a tour of the city. He had a Volkswagen he wanted to sell me for five hundred bucks, which sounded like a good deal to me, and after I took a look at the car, he'd show me around town.

"I've seen the city," I said. "The Legion of Honor, Fisherman's Wharf, Columbus and Broadway, Chinatown, Union Square."

"You haven't seen shit, Oakland boy," Rex said. "Come with me. *I'll* show you some city."

I met Rex at his place. He lived beneath a wooden house, in the garage. Tacked to the Sheetrock wall was a faded black-and-white picture. The man in wore a baggy pea coat. He stood beside a ship's gangplank.

The Volkswagen was parked at the back of the garage, and next to it was a mattress with a sleeping bag.

"The Bug wouldn't start today," Rex said. "Here's the keys. You can pick it up this weekend, get it towed. It's still worth the five bills, though. Got the cash?"

"Got the pink slip?"

"No pink slip. Never had one. You want the fucking car or not?"

I gave him the cash.

"The first round's on me," Rex said.

It was raining, and we were walking down the street when an old hag stepped off a MUNI bus, opened her umbrella without even watching what she was doing, and poked Rex in the face.

"Gunite lesson number one," Rex said. "Don't ever fuck with Rex."

He ripped the umbrella from her hand, threw it on the sidewalk, jumped up and down on it for a while, and then picked it up and handed the wreckage back to the old lady. The old lady was crying.

Rex turned to me.

"You want to get by in this world?" Rex said. "Don't ever let anyone fuck with you. End of lesson."

We walked from his place in the Potrero district into the Mission district. The doorways were lined with hobos and their boxes and blankets. A lady hobo stood between two cars and lifted her dresses and sprayed piss all over herself like a skunk. A person with a raisin-shriveled face stood on the corner shaking. I couldn't tell if it was a man or a woman, but it didn't have a nose, just two holes in the front of its face like a pig snout. An old Negro lady emerged from an alley. Her face looked like roofing tar. "Every goddamn day the same motherfucker shit," she said. "I get up, I sits my fat black ass down on this here porch, and then I just sits here! All day every goddamn day the same motherfucker shit. Day in day out. I just sits here." A businessman bumped into a black woman carrying a baby, and the baby dropped to the sidewalk. The black woman chased after the businessman, screaming, "Look what you did, whitey. Look at my baby. Look what you did." And the businessman kept walking. The baby lay silent and motionless on the sidewalk, and people stepped around it. The black woman walked back to the baby and picked it up and walked toward another businessman, and again the baby ended up silent and still on the sidewalk. "Look what you did, whitey," she called. Everyone's face leaked something. It was raining, and the streets made gravy.

We stopped at a bar next to the Greyhound station on Seventh Street. Inside, on the walls, were old yellow pictures of the 1906 earthquake. Attached to the stools were old drunks. The bar smelled like wet dog.

At one table sat young men with short hair and mustaches.

"What do you mean, three-fifty for the drinks?" Rex

screamed at the fat barmaid. Even her fingers were fat. I bet she had fat on her ears.

"Three-fifty for the drinks," she said.

The men at the table stopped talking. They stopped drinking. They put out their cigarettes. They looked at Rex.

"I don't have to pay for the drinks," Rex said. "I've been drinking here for years, and Skipper, your boss, Fatso, never makes me pay. I supply him. Give me my goddamn drinks, Porky."

One of the young men with short hair and mustaches stood up. "Who in the hell do you think you are?" he asked.

"I'm Rex," Rex said. "Faggot."

The man shoved Rex. Rex smiled. "I'll meet you in the alley," Rex said.

They squared off and Rex kicked him in the nuts, then kicked his face, and the man with short hair and a mustache was on the ground, out cold. Rex took his wallet, and we got right on out of there.

We headed back into the warehouse district south of Mission, and we stopped and Rex checked the wallet.

"Shit," Rex said.

"No cash?"

"Cop," Rex said, and he showed me the badge.

Our job in San Francisco was to shoot concrete onto the old rotting wooden pylons that held up what was left of Pier 70. We worked with the tides, shoving off at high tide from the shore, working through low tide, then returning at high tide. We'd weave our way around beneath the piers, blasting concrete through the air and onto mesh we had wrapped around the splintering wood.

"I ain't never seen no shit like this before," Fish said.

* * *

Keebler showed us how they climbed from rafts to the tops of piers in Utah. In Utah, instead of using the ladder that drops down into the water, they climb thin nylon ropes like monkeys.

Fish didn't like water. "I ain't going out there on them flimsy little rafts ain't got no life jacket," he said.

Super-Bob gave him an orange life jacket. It looked like a baby-bib on Fish and didn't even reach down past his ribs. Fish stared at it, then out at the bobbing rafts waiting for us beneath Pier 70.

"Sorry, Fish," Super-Bob said. "They only make one size."

At high tide, the deck of the raft would be only two feet from the underside of the pier. We had to lie down on our bellies like reptiles on the wet rafts. The rafts were slimed with muck from the bay—seaweed and oil and diesel and garbage—and wet concrete oozed from the hose.

Rex didn't care about getting slammed against the underside of the piers by the wakes of passing Coast Guard cutters. He laughed and giggled and talked about the pretty colors, the webs of light, the shimmering flashes on the rippling water, the faraway sounds of sails fluttering on the bay.

We were going around in circles on the raft because none of us knew the Spanish words for "If you point the goddamn hose to the rear of the raft, it's easier to move the fucking raft forward."

"We already shoot it there," Samuel said. "No waste the concrete."

He didn't want to waste that concrete, so he was trying to shoot the pylons thirty feet in front of the raft. He had never learned about Sir Isaac Newton's Third Law of Motion, which states that for every action there is a reaction that is equal and opposite in direction.

"We can't go that way with you shooting in the same direction, Sam," I said.

"We already shoot it there," Samuel said.

Rex had had enough.

He marched across the raft. Samuel kept trying to shoot the distant pylons while Rex tried to wrench the hose away from him.

"Nozzle not you job," Samuel said. "Esta *my* job. You no nozzleman! Not you job."

Jalisco nodded in agreement with Samuel.

It was them against us.

Rex and me gave up. We were on the clock. We weren't getting paid for how many pylons we shot—we were getting paid by the hour.

It was high tide and we were weaving through the pylon catacombs and making our way back to shore. Fish barely fit between the raft and the underside of the pier, and he was getting cut up by the nails and pieces of rebar that stuck through the wooden planks of the pier above like hundreds of bayonets.

"How much further is it to shore?" Fish said.

"Here it comes, Fish," Rex said. "Here it comes. Look!"

When Fish looked, he saw a fucking tidal wave coming, and it was coming for him. It rolled humpbacked against the underside of the pier, and Fish started screaming.

"We going under," he screamed. "We going under." His eyes bugged out like eggs. "Man, we be going down."

"What's the matter, Fish can't swim?" Keebler said.

We went under.

First we were slapped up against the pier, the bay swallowing us. We held our breaths and waited for the raft to drop back down. Then we dropped, but the next wave came and slapped us against the pier again, against the nails, the rebar, the wires.

When the waves were past, Fish was in the water. He bobbed and thrashed, the orange lifejacket popping up from beneath the green froth, his giant head jerking around like a hooked swordfish fighting for its life.

"I'm going to die! Man, I'm going to die!"

Fish didn't die, but Keebler was still hanging from the underside of the pier. His chest was flat against the pier, and a spike of rebar stuck through his back, and he dangled there like a rag. Keebler's insides were sliding along the iron rebar and dripping onto the raft. Keebler was stone dead.

Rex and Jalisco peeled Keebler off the underside of the pier while Samuel and I fished Fish out of the water and onto the raft.

When we reached shore, we lay Fish and Keebler side by side on a slab of concrete. Fish breathed with his mouth open wide, gasping, his arms and legs quaking with spasms.

"You disobeyed a direct order," Super-Bob said. "And you're going to pay for it."

"What?" I said.

The ambulance was already on its way. Everyone was looking. Even Fish had gotten up from the slab of concrete and walked over to see what was happening. He still had his little orange life jacket on.

Keebler was oozing.

"Whatever happened to you, anyway?" Super-Bob asked me. "When you first started with us, out in Bishop, I really liked you. You were a good kid, then. You used to do as you were told. Now you do whatever you think is right. I don't like that. I don't like you anymore."

"I didn't disobey a direct order."

"You did too. I told you to get fuel for the truck last night."

"I put fuel in the truck."

"But you did it this morning. I saw you at the Union 76 station. I told you to get fuel *last night*. You, therefore, disobeyed a direct order."

He had me. His argument was flawless. There was nothing I

could do.

Rex looked at me in disgust. "Haven't you had enough of his shit?" Rex said. "Hit him. Hit the fuck. Go ahead and hit him, you pussy."

"Don't do it," Fish said. "This shit ain't nothing. It ain't that bad."

Fish was taking off his life jacket.

"I quit," I said.

"Good," Super-Bob said. "You'll never work for Concrete-West again."

"And I'm never coming back," I said.

"You'll be back," Rex said. "No one escapes."

A couple of days after I quit I went over to Rex's place to get the Volkswagen. I figured that Rex would be at work, so I lifted the garage door. The car wasn't there. The picture of the old man standing beside the ship was gone. The dark wall was lighter in color where the picture had been.

I went upstairs and knocked on the door of the old Victorian house. A fat man in a white T-shirt and suspenders answered.

"What?" he said.

"You know where Rex is?"

"Never heard of anyone named Rex."

"Lived in the garage beneath you."

"No one ever lived in there," he said. "And I never heard of anyone named Rex."

He shut the door.

CHAPTER THIRTEEN

Noches de los Muertos

As a guniter, I saw seven men killed. I saw three men lose their legs, one lose his fingers, and another a lung. The lime in the concrete chewed up lungs like a meat grinder turns steak into burger.

I was promoted from hose-puller to finisher, which meant an extra thirty cents per hour. I was a lousy finisher, but I kept my ass alive and intact. Once, when we were working a high-rise in San Francisco, the foreman, Garrick, told me to haul the concrete hose up to the top of some scaffolding. "Nope," I said. "That scaffolding's not tied to the wall. It'll tip over. I'm not killing myself for a check."

He didn't fire me—he made one of the Mexicans lug that hose up the tiers of scaffolding. The Mexican construction workers in California will do anything they're told because most of them are illegal and need the cash to send home to their families south of the border. When the guy reached the sixth tier, the scaffold tipped backward and he got splattered on the street like a pumpkin, guts everywhere, pedestrians screaming and dudes in fancy cars cursing at us for messing up their windshields.

The eighth death was a Cuban named Fernandez. No splattered guts, no spikes through the chest, no plumes of blood shooting into the air and making patterns on the wet concrete, no severed limbs. What happened was this: the nozzleman lost control of the concrete hose, and the hose whipped around like a huge snake having an epileptic fit. It conked Fernandez in the back of the head, and Fernandez died. Bonk—that was all she wrote. We lost our best finisher. That sucked.

The union hall sent us about a dozen men, and none of them made it more than a couple hours before quitting. Eventually word got out at the hall and no one would even come to the job site—a ditch we were lining with gunite.

Finally, the home office in Oakland sent us their top finisher, a Mexican named Romero who was a gunite legend. Rumor had it that he could cut a ditch slope so precisely that no forms or ground wires were needed.

"Romero's the best finisher in the business," Garrick said. He looked at me. "T-Bird, you do whatever Romero says."

We blew a couple nine-yard cement trucks, and then Romero threw his tools down in the wet concrete, crossed his arms and stared at me, his heavy eyelids drooping over his dark brown eyes, exhaling a sigh so loud that I could hear it over the noise of all the equipment.

"What's wrong with you?" I said.

"No hablo ingles," he said.

"You don't like my work?" I said. "What's wrong with my work? Tell me what the hell's wrong with my work."

Romero didn't say anything. He took my fresnoe and my trowel and reworked the section of concrete I'd just finished.

Later that day, I asked him to let me borrow his wood float.

"No comprendo," Romero said.

We were out of town in Oakdale, a rotten little cowboy town in the Central Valley. The locals wore cowboy hats and drove pickup trucks and all their shirts were plaid. The liquor store sold only beer and whiskey. Tractors and combines waited at the stoplight and parked in front of the diner.

Now that my roommate, Fernandez, was dead, I had to room with the legendary Romero. After work, he lay back on the dusty motel bed and turned on the news.

"If you buy a steak I'll barbecue it for you," I said. "I've got a barbecue pit in my car."

"No comprendo," Romero said.

I set up my barbecue pit by the motel pool, a grimy little kidney-shaped jobber with water-skeeters zipping over a cruddy surface I could have walked across. Then I took out my trumpet and oiled the valves and played. I played the Mexican songs I'd learned when I was working with Los Asesinos: cumbias, rancheras, some salsas, a couple of mariachi tunes we'd played at cheesy weddings.

Romero came out of the room and walked through the parking lot and crossed the highway. He went into the market. I kept playing. Romero walked out of the market with a twelve-pack of Budweiser and a plastic bag.

He stood on the other side of the pool for a moment, then pulled up a rubber-strapped folding lounge chair next to me. He took a steak out of the plastic bag and put it on the barbecue pit. He opened a beer and held it out to me. I kept playing. He set the beer down on the concrete next to me and opened one for himself. I finished the song I'd been playing, "San Fernando," a cumbia.

Romero nodded and pointed at the open can of Bud. "Una cerveza for you."

I looked at him. "No comprendo," I said. I played another song.

When I finished, Romero said, "Have the beer. From me."

I looked at him, then at the beer. I took a swig.

"You make pretty good for trompeta."

"For a gringo?"

Romero held up his beer to click against mine. I tapped my can against his.

"For the gringo," he said. He smiled.

* * *

The last day of the Oakdale ditch job, Romero showed me the trick to cutting a straight ditch slope. We didn't use screeds to cut the concrete like flat-workers do. We used fresnoes—wide flat trowels on the ends of fiberglass poles. After the nozzleman blasted concrete on the dirt and wire-mesh reinforcement, Romero placed his fresnoe at the uppermost part of the ditch, then in one long smooth motion pulled it down over the concrete, cutting away the excess mud and leaving a perfect, straight wall. When the ditch we were lining was full, the sewage would rise evenly on both slopes. My job was to slick the wet concrete out after Romero cut it.

When I tried to cut the slope, Romero called the nozzleman back and made him shoot more concrete over my work.

"You make the watermelons," Romero said, and he made a shape with his hand like the hump of a camel.

Romero waited until the nozzleman finished reshooting the slope then he turned to me. "You savvy tractor?" he said. He put his forearm in front of himself at a diagonal angle. "Tractor no push. The tractor cut, no push."

He moved his arm forward like the blade of a grader, then used his fresnoe on the slope, cutting, as always, a perfectly flat wall. For the first time, I noticed that he pulled the fresnoe down at a slight angle, whereas I always pulled it straight down.

"Comprende? Cut, no push," he said.

I nodded.

"I comprende," I said.

He pointed his finger at me. "No tell nobody," he said. "Keep it for you self."

We had been back in Oakland for a month, guniting the inner walls of the Oakland jail. That was a fun job, the Oakland jail. Sometimes we'd run loads of pure sand from the hopper and into the rig, which then sent the sand straight to the nozzle and into the walls. Hey, we wanted to give the future inmates a chance to dig themselves out, and a wall of pure sand with a sheen of concrete over it at least gave them a fighting chance. Most people who end up in the Oakland jail are only there because some shithead or woman ratted them out when they really weren't doing anything very wrong.

It's easy to live without a home, and it's even easier getting a job. Whenever I didn't have work between gunite jobs, I'd wait around at a job site for a few days until someone didn't show up, and then I'd get at least a day's work. I got jobs doing all kinds of things I didn't know how to do: welding, bricklaying, sheet-rocking, carpet-laying, plumbing. It always took the foreman at least half the day to figure out I didn't know what the hell I was doing, and then I'd have half a day's wages. After work I showered at whatever college campus was around, walked right in like I was a student. The colleges even supplied towels. Nights I slept in my station wagon.

One day Romero wanted to take me out to dinner so I could meet his family. He gave me instructions on how to get to the restaurant and told me to meet him there at seven-thirty.

I drove through the Alameda Tube, beneath the channel, and came up on the island. Navy reconnaissance planes flew over the enlisted men's shacks to the right at Alameda Naval Air Station, and ahead, beyond the cargo cranes and radio towers, the sky turned from light gray to dark gray. Neon lights on the boulevard flickered and the fog lamps lining the streets drew orange clouds of mosquitoes and moths.

Romero stood outside Casa Carlita wearing a suit and tie, black shined shoes, his gray-streaked hair greased and parted on the side.

"Wait aqui for un momento," Romero said.

He disappeared between two Dumpsters while I waited for him in the gravel parking lot. When he came back, he had a teenager with him. Romero pointed at my station wagon. "Ese carro," he said.

The boy didn't say anything. He looked at Romero and tipped his head sideways.

Romero reached into his coat pocket and pulled out his wallet. A cloud of concrete dust puffed into the air when he opened it and gave the boy a bill. The boy walked over to my station wagon and leaned against it, lighting a cigarette and blowing smoke rings.

Romero led me through the back door. A mural of a bullfight was painted on the wall, the background red and orange and yellow, and standing over the dead bull was a naked woman with a superhumanly abundant bosom, bull's blood streaming down her thighs.

"Nice chi-chis," Romero said, and he put his fingers beneath one of the giant nipples and brushed the wall as if tickling the underside of a baby's chin. "You like?"

In the kitchen two Mexican boys loaded dishes into trays and onto a conveyor belt that led to the dishwashing machine. They sang Beatles songs in Spanish.

The cooks grinned and said hello to Romero, and one of the waitresses, dressed in a red, Spanish-style skirt with white lace, came over to him and pinched his belly through his suit.

Romero's wife and daughter sat at a large table in the corner farthest from the kitchen. His wife wore a flower-print dress, and his daughter, three or four years old, wore a light purple dress. I was ashamed of myself. Romero in his suit, the women in dresses, and me in jeans and a dirty T-shirt.

"Mi amigo, T-Bird," Romero said.

The women smiled.

"You need drink," Romero said. "Dos tequilas," he told the waitress.

Romero's daughter looked at her mother. Then she looked at Romero. She said something in Spanish.

"Callate," Romero said. Then he smiled, and in a soft fatherly voice, said, "Callate, por favor."

The girl was quiet.

The waitress brought the drinks and the menus. Romero downed his tequila in a gulp and looked over at me, and I downed my drink too. Romero raised his hand and called for the waitress to bring another round.

"Esta noche, we make a happy, mi amigo," he said.

We drank, and at the end of the evening, Romero looked at me and smiled. "You liking mi familia?"

"Yes," I said. "Very much."

"We no like you living in the car."

"I'm trying to save money," I said. "It's not that bad."

"Maybe you come live in mi casa."

"I don't want to pay rent, Romero. That's the point."

Romero looked offended. "No pay the rent for amigos," he said. "You teach my wife and my daughter the ingles, you no pay the rent."

I called the Mohawk station to tell Pop my phone number and give him my address.

"T-Bird," Pop's wife said. "No matter what, remember we love you."

"What are you talking about?"

"You need to come right over," she said. "You need to talk to your father."

I drove to the Mohawk station. Before I could even knock on the trailer door, Pop's wife opened it.

"No matter what," she said. "Remember, T-Bird, we all love you."

"What's the deal?"

"Your father's in the back."

The room was dark, no buzzing neon bar-signs, no flickering television screens, no lamp spotlit over his checkbook. Pop sat on his bed and stared at the floor.

"Hey-hey," I said.

He glanced at me, then looked back down. "You've lost weight," he said.

"Work," I said.

"I'm not your father," he said.

"What?"

"I'm sorry for the way I've treated you," Pop said.

It was the first time Pop had ever apologized to me for anything. Stones of dread bagged in my gut.

"Don't apologize to me," I said.

"You were born before I married your mother," he said.

He didn't look up at me.

"Why are you telling me this?"

"Your mother called," Pop said. "The bitch says she's going to tell you."

"You raised me," I said.

"You'd be crying and she didn't know what to do," Pop said. "So I'd lay you on my chest and talk to you. You'd stop crying. You'd go to sleep. I married her. I never meant to treat you different than your brothers."

The room was so dark that I couldn't see his eyes.

"I never wanted you to know," he said. "We falsified your birth certificate so you wouldn't find out."

"It doesn't matter," I said.

"I'm sorry," Pop said. "And I took Kent from you."

"How were you to know they'd kill him?"

"I grew up here," Pop said. "I should have known."

"I got Clyde drunk the night he died."

"Not your fault."

"Not your fault."

We sat quiet a long time.

"Don't you want to know who your father is?"

"I know who my father is," I said.

I turned and looked back as I walked out of the room. Pop's glasses reflected like two Moon hubcaps, but I couldn't tell where the light came from.

* * *

When I got back to Romero's house I went into the bathroom and shaved off my beard.

For the first time in my life I didn't look like Pop.

And I thought about it: neither did Clyde or Kent.

No one looked like Pop.

Every night when Romero and I got home, his wife had dinner ready for us, tortillas and jalapenos and refried beans and rice and sometimes she cooked chickens, one for Romero and one for me.

The house had two bedrooms and one bathroom, the tub old-fashioned with claw feet and a rubber plug attached to a metal chain, paint chipping like scales from the windowsill. Outside the blackberry bushes climbed the fence and in the mornings the blossoms smelled like fancy shampoo.

The front room, where I slept, was like a museum, the walls lined with faded daguerreotypes and pictures of Mexican families, Romero's ancestors and those of his wife, and in the pictures the people wore suits and wide-collared dresses. They stared out with frozen eyes as if they could see right through my skin to my soul. In one picture they stood in the snow, probably the only time it had snowed in their lives, their polished dress shoes dusted with ash-like flakes. A poster-size picture, old and yellowed, of Pancho Villa, belts of bullets crisscrossing his chest, was tacked to the wall over the couch.

Nights I taught his wife and child how to read and speak English. I used flash cards and children's books I bought at a used-book store in Berkeley. After the lessons, Romero and I drank brandy, the room dark and the streets outside quiet. We never talked much, just sat and drank and sometimes we smoked his Mexican cigars. Each night before he went to bed he gave me a pat on the back and then we took one last shot of brandy. And I'd sit there for a while in the dark, smelling the scent of food and smoking Salems, slightly drunk and belly full, legs and arms tired from the day's work, satisfied.

In late October the company sent us on a job in Seattle, working on the basement of the Columbia Center, guniting the walls of the hole that would become the underground parking lot.

I rode with Romero. We left before the sun rose and in the dark drove out of Oakland and across the Carquinez Strait over the great Sacramento River and into the Central Valley. It was fall, but I could still smell the crops, the onions and garlic and the sugared smell of fruit blossoms, apple and lemon and plum and apricot. When the sun came up over the Sierras I squinted in the brightness of the green valley fields, basketball-sized sunflowers craning toward the east, saw-toothed snowcaps rising orange above purple foothills.

"We're out of there," I said. "Adios Oakland."

"Is no vacation," Romero said. "We go for working."

"But we're working somewhere else."

"Everywhere you making work," Romero said, "the same. I no want to go for Seattle. I wanting to stay with my family for El Dia de los Muertos."

"What?"

"The night of the dead peoples," Romero said. "On this night all the blood of the family coming back for you."

At the Oregon border I took a deep breath and sucked in the air. It felt different, foreign, as if I'd crossed an international border. We drove over the hills, patches of trees between clear-cut sections on the slopes like the squares of a verdant checkerboard.

Romero and I drove all night instead of staying in Oregon with the rest of the crew in Portland.

At the motel, I laughed when Romero pulled a bottle of Korbel brandy out of his suitcase.

"Como?" Romero asked.

I opened up my bag and pulled out a bottle of Presidente brandy.

Romero shook his head. "I no like the Mexicano brandy."

"What?"

"In Mexico," Romero said, "the rich putos making dinero too much. The poor peoples making nada. You drinking the Mexicano brandy, you make the rich putos more richer. In Los Estados Unidos, you drinking gringo brandy, everybody making mas dinero."

Since we'd arrived a full day ahead of schedule, the next morning I woke up and said, "Let's go to Canada."

Romero crossed his arms over his chest and shook his head. "I no need to see the Canada. I tired. We work tomorrow."

"It's only a hundred miles, Romero. We might not get another chance to see it for years. Let's go."

We loaded the ice chest with beer, jalapenos, salami and cheese, and we started north on I-5. Romero drove while I drank off my hangover. It was misty out, and the trees and grass and bushes sparkled on the hillsides as we drove through canyons and moved into the northern- Washington dairylands.

"Dame una cerveza," Romero said, and he rolled down the window halfway and sucked in the rich moist air.

When we crossed the border, Romero turned to me.

"Canada no es Estados Unidos?" he said.

"What?"

"Canada no Estados Unidos?"

"No, Romero. It's another country. Canada and the United States are two different countries."

"No need pasaporte? No need green card?"

"Of course not," I said. "The U.S. and Canada are amigos."

Romero pulled over to the side of the road and told me to drive.

We passed through Vancouver, its white granite buildings against the bright green backdrop of mountains and hills, its orderly rows of neat businesses and shops, banks and travel agencies. We drove through Stanley Park and over a steep bridge, the water beneath a deep jade green, ferries and barges and a cruise liner slicing the soft green water. It was beautiful, like nothing I'd ever seen, strangely foreign though only twenty-five miles from the U.S. border.

When we got to Horseshoe Bay I asked Romero if he wanted me to take his picture. The ferry was loaded with cars and people, getting ready to leave for Vancouver Island, the propellers churning and frothing the green water beneath the vessel.

I held the camera up and Romero looked away.

"Come on, Romero," I said. "Smile."

He waved his hand and looked out at the water, his chest out and back straightened. As I looked at him through the viewfinder, and I wondered what it must have been like for him all these years in the States taking orders from mongrel-bred gringos.

I took the picture as the ferry plowed away, Romero facing out at the distant islands across the water.

On the way back, the traffic was jammed up at the border. We drank some beers while we crept forward. Pale green clouds hung low in the sky. It started to sprinkle.

On the Canadian side of the border, there is an imitation Roman arch. Its inscription reads: "May all who pass here find these gates open."

"You're okay," the officer at the port of entry said. "Is he a citizen?"

"I don't know."

The officer leaned into my window. "I need to see your green card."

"Como?" Romero said.

"Green card."

Romero pulled out his wallet. He emptied it on the seat. He looked at the Canadian border officer and shrugged. "I forget my green card."

"I need to see it," the officer said.

I handed the officer Romero's driver's license and his union card. "I've known him for four years, sir," I said. "He works for Concrete-West Gunite Company in Oakland, California. He has a house, a family. We only came here to see Canada. You let us through this morning. He's been in the United States for ten years."

"Then Mr. Uribe here should know better. Whoever let you in should have checked Mr. Uribe's green card."

The officer called to another officer, one wearing a gun and billy club. The officer with the gun asked Romero to get out of the car slowly, then produced handcuffs, which he snapped onto Romero's wrists before frisking him.

The first officer put his hand on my shoulder and said, "You'll have to pull over there and park your car."

The detention center was only about a mile from the checkpoint. Romero sat on a folding chair across the desk of the interrogating officer.

"No comprendo," Romero said.

"When did you enter the United States?"

"No comprendo."

"When did you first secure a visa?"

"No comprendo."

"What part of Mexico do you come from?"

"No comprendo."

"Did you enter illegally?"

"No comprendo, *senor.*"

A thin guard with a mustache that looked like a lady's eyebrow was taking Romero to his cell. Romero stopped in the corridor and looked at me.

"I'm sorry," I said.

"No problema," Romero said. "You call my wife?"

"Yes."

"Gracias," Romero said. He smiled. He turned and led the guard off to the waiting car.

I stopped Romero's Nova on the U.S. side of the border and looked back at the port of entry. I looked at the imitation Roman arch, the trees that hid the detention center from view, the distant Canadian Rockies, mossy green at their bases, gray rock and traces of snow at higher altitudes, poking up into the thick white clouds. I watched the steady flow of American cars crossing the border, going into Canada for a drive or a vacation, and the Canadian and U.S. plates on the cars driving past me on the highway.

I didn't go back to Seattle. Instead I drove nonstop back to Oakland. The sun had set and I heard the horn blast of a departing ship. Instead of walking right into Romero's house, I knocked on the door.

Romero's wife and daughter looked at me.

"No Romero," I said. "He's been deported. In Mexico now. Romero in jail in Mexico."

I didn't know what to do. They kept looking at me.

"No Romero?" his wife said. Then she started yelling at me in Spanish, stomping around the room. She went into the kitchen and started washing the dishes furiously, crashing them into the cupboards as she dried them.

"Federales," I said. "La migra."

"Como?" she said.

"La migra," I said. My eyes were watery.

She smiled and then she started laughing, a high-pitched laugh, and it occurred to me how odd it was that a Mexican laugh, a Negro laugh, a Japanese laugh, an English laugh, all sounded different. And she came to me and put her arms around me and patted my back as if I were a child and kept laughing.

"What's so funny?" I said. "What's so goddamn funny?" I said. "Romero's gone. He's been deported. He's probably in jail. No mas Romero!"

She kept laughing.

I turned and walked to my car. I didn't want to spend the night with a crazed grieving Mexican woman. God knows what she might do to herself, or to me. I looked for a place to sleep, and everywhere I stopped there were people, sometimes couples necking in steam-windowed cars, sometimes park rangers, hobos and stoners and sometimes even though I couldn't hear anyone, people seemed to be watching me, people crouched in bushes or behind parked pickup trucks or looking through the blinds of darkened office windows. I stopped at the Mohawk station and shut off the engine of my station wagon and the shop dog started barking and the lights of Pop's trailer came on and I started my car and drove with the headlights off until I hit the freeway on-ramp. I took the San Mateo Bridge and slept on the beach at Pescadero, south of Half Moon Bay.

I woke up when it got light, and it was so foggy I couldn't see anything and I didn't want to drive and even if I did drive I didn't have anywhere I wanted to go. I sat on the beach and played my trumpet into the fog, the surf so loud and fog so dense the sound of the trumpet seemed not to come out of the horn but instead hummed only in my ears.

After dark I drove back to Alameda, to Romero's house. The windows danced yellow with candlelight. Muffled classical music, choral, came from inside. Great, I thought, she's playing death music. She's lost it.

I knocked.

Romero answered the door. He wore his black suit, and his hair was slicked and his shoes polished and shining.

I started laughing.

"How did you get out of jail? How did you get home so fast? Are you all right?"

Romero laughed and opened the door wide, and inside candles lined the tables and in the center of the room stood his wife and daughter and they wore black dresses and silver jewelry. The classical music was Verdi's *Requiem Mass.*

"El Dia de los Muertos," Romero said. "Tonight is the very especial night. Tonight we talking with all family, forever back."

On the coffee table in the middle of the room were bottles of Korbel brandy and Budweiser and a platter of rice and beans and four roasted chickens, candles flickering across the glass bottles, papier-mâché skulls placed between each of the dishes.

"The Canada policia sending me to Mexico City," Romero said. "Give me the first class. Wine, brandy, food very bueno. And give me one hundred dollars for spending."

He smiled and patted my back.

"But how'd you get back?"

He pulled an envelope from the mantel and handed it to me. Inside was a Mexican passport and other papers.

"My brother's," Romero said. "I mail it for him tomorrow. No problema."

We sat around the table, candlelight making our faces dance orange and red and shadowed.

"El dia de los muertos," Romero said. "On this night all the family come back. You pray to the dead family, they coming back for you this night. They giving you, how you say—" he tapped his forehead, "—the history."

I kneeled at the coffee-table altar with Romero and his family, and Romero said a prayer in Spanish. When he finished everyone looked at me.

"Comprendes?" Romero said.

I didn't understand the words, but I nodded, and I said, "Yo comprendo."

CHAPTER FOURTEEN

First and Last Chance

I'd lost track of Rich Gonzalez, but one night, when I was hammered and drinking hard still, I got a phone call from him. His father had died, and the funeral was the next day. He wanted me to come, and I did.

There were only five people at the funeral—Rich's mother, his sisters, Rich, and me. The eulogy was in Spanish, and it was brief. Nobody thought she'd do it, but Mrs. Gonzalez cried. She cried hard. After everybody else left the grave she stood there crying. You could hear her even with the windows of your car rolled up.

I knew the graveyard pretty damned well. Mr. Gonzalez was buried in the same graveyard as Grandfather Murphy, the same graveyard as both my brothers.

After the funeral, Rich and I went to Heinold's First and Last Chance Saloon in Jack London Square. It's almost impossible to avoid Jack London if you live in Oakland—Jack London Square, Jack London Park, posters and pictures of Jack London in the bookstores and museums, the books by London you read in elementary school, junior high, high school, and in the offices of doctors and gas stations. And even if there's no physical evidence of London, people tell stories about him as if they know him personally, as if the night before they'd gotten hammered with him and stormed the town. He seems to loom over everyone like an accusation. If you're an Oakland loser, don't blame Oakland—it's your own damn fault.

Mr. Gonzalez used to invite us to meet him at the First and Last Chance, and when we showed up to drink with him, there was always a pitcher of Budweiser and a pair of whiskey-rocks waiting for us.

"Nobody I know ever saw him when he wasn't drunk," Rich said. He loosened his funeral tie. "He was a drunk. Lived a drunk, died of drink, and in hell he's at the bar with the other drunks."

A sign behind the bar read "No Profanity." Another sign said "No checks. No credit. No credit cards. No Cigars. No pipes. No brains, no drinks." Gimme-hats stained with grease and smoke dangled from the ceiling like mushrooms.

The First and Last Chance, one of the oldest buildings in Oakland, drooped out over the water of the San Francisco Bay. A sagging log-walled shack, it had survived every Bay Area earthquake of the last hundred years, but when you walked across the raked plank floor, you stepped lightly. It was Jack London's haunt in his pirate days. He got drunk there many times, and he listened to the stories of the other sailors and traded lies with them.

I ordered another round. The waitress was as old as the bar. She was still pretty, though, in an old sort of way. The drinks were good—the ice floated on the whiskey.

"You remember the time we broke down in the projects?" I said.

"I don't remember much," Rich said. "We were pretty damned drunk."

An oldster opened the door and a wash of gray light made the smoke in the bar look like stacked mattresses. He said, "Spark," and an old matted dog emerged from beneath a barstool and walked out the door.

"We'd be dead if your father hadn't come and gotten us."

"He missed work at the cannery the next day," Rich said. "Hungover."

"The next morning he made us drink beers to get rid of the hangovers." I finished off a beer. "Now that's a father."

We drank more, and I looked at the old pictures tacked to the log walls, pictures of faded black-and-white men wearing pea coats and knit caps.

I bought another round of drinks.

"At least you know for sure who your father is," I said. "At least he knows who you are," I said. "Knew, anyway."

When Rich's father died, I was working a job at the FMC plant in San Jose. It was an easy job, but not one I liked. At FMC they build tanks, little ones, high-speed jobbers that take corners like Ferraris, low to the ground and sleek and painted green or brown, depending on the batch. In the morning welding torches lit the windows of the factory buildings like sheet lightning, clicking and snapping and sometimes throwing showers of sparks into the air like fireworks. You could smell the dry carbon scent of ozone in the air.

Our job at FMC was to line an immense swimming tank with gunite. The swim tank stretched as wide as a football field and as long as three, and it was to be a practice pool for the amphibious tanks. All day long, as we worked laying 6x6x10 iron mesh on the dirt to reinforce the concrete we were to shoot, tanks sped around the circumference of the pool on a dirt racetrack. The only time they stopped was at eleven when the catering truck honked its "La Cucaracha." Then the test drivers pulled up alongside the catering truck and popped their hatches and, wearing their white lab clothes and baseball caps (A's and Giants), ordered breakfast burritos and Danishes and cups of coffee, then stood on the edge of the hole eating and watching us work.

"Doesn't this bother you, Romero?" I said.

He looked at me and knitted his brow. "What?"

"This," I said. "Helping to make tanks. Helping to kill people."

Romero shook his head slowly and smiled. "You thinking maybe some other trabajo you killing less peoples?"

"Sure," I said. "Maybe I should work in a paper mill."

"You make the paper, maybe somebody writing the letters for making la guerra," Romero said. "Every job you make kills people."

I stayed later than the other workers each day, getting paid time and a half to watch over the equipment because it needed to be guarded from the neighborhood kids. The FMC security system was made to keep out Russians and Chinese spies, not San Jose street kids. Before I was named company sentry, each morning when we got to the job site we'd find our tools missing, graffiti sprayed on the sides of the equipment trucks and compressors, wooden elevation stakes pulled out of the ground. One night they slashed all the tires and smeared K-Y jelly on the windows. Another time they cut all the motor belts.

Nights after work, I'd smoke cigarettes and drink beers and feel the sunset breeze blow across the sweat on my skin and dry it into cakes of salt. I'd never contacted the man from whose sperm I'd sprung, but I knew where he lived and knew his phone number because I'd called Sacramento information and there he was, living on Auburn Boulevard, right down the street from the hotel where he used to take my mother, and after Rich's father died I thought a lot about the son of a bitch. My mother had told me that he couldn't marry her because he was Catholic, and Catholics couldn't marry pregnant girls because it was against their religion. Her father, my grandfather on her side of the family, had never spoken to me, bastard that I was. My mother told me that I'd come from good blood, that I wasn't from the scum blood of the Irish Catholic Murphys, that I wasn't like my brothers because I was half blue-blood French Canadian stock. I thought about the shitty neighborhood I'd grown up in, being one of the only white kids in my school and getting the hell beat out of me often. I thought about the times my mother had taken off with the Angels on road trips and left me alone to fend for myself in the projects of Cypress Street, no food in the fridge and sometimes the power being shut off because she'd forgotten to pay the bills. I wanted to find this supposed father of mine and drive him to the corner of Cypress and 14th and kick him out of my navy-surplus station wagon and drive off, leaving him to fend for himself on the streets of my youth.

After work one day I found Rich at the First and Last Chance and he was already drunk as a lord, his head slung low from its own weight and the little wooden table dense with empties and waterlogged paper napkins, the ashtray full and beer-soaked butts piled up in the bottoms of drained bottles.

The old barmaid poured me a whiskey and a draft. It was a Saturday afternoon, and the only other person in the bar was an old-timer who might have been one of the sailor boys in the ancient photographs on the walls. He was toothless and his lips were wrinkled and sucked in, and when he drank he tipped his head back and poured from the bottle as if he were drinking from a garden hose.

"Rich," I said.

He said, "Go away."

"You look like shit," I said. "It's too early in the day to look like shit."

He rolled his head to the side, and then slowly turned it until it was cocked sideways and he could see me. His eyes looked somewhere past me and he said, "Mom read the will today."

I nodded and tossed back my whiskey and looked at the old barmaid and she poured me another.

"Go away," Rich said. He waved his arm across the table and knocked over some bottles.

"Sure," I said, and I drank some beer.

"He left me everything."

"Good," I said. "How much?"

"He left me all he ever had in the world that was his."

"Cash?"

"He left me his trailer and his furniture and he had photo albums and an old bottle of tequila he'd never opened but it was dated with a black marker in his handwriting, and he bought it the day I was born, and he never opened it."

I drank beer. My napkin stuck to the bottom of the mug, but I didn't pull it off. I noticed one of the business cards stapled to the walls and ceiling that read "Germar the Magician." Leaning in the corner next to the bar were an acetylene tank and a crow bar. An old menu behind the cash register read "Heinold's Menu. Beef Stew .45. Meat Balls & Spaghetti .45. Chile .50."

Rich's head dropped down again, and then he popped back up and looked at me like a sober person. "Well I opened it," he said. He stared at me, and suddenly he was not drunk. "I opened that damn bottle and I drank it down to the nasty sour worm."

"One time Jack London got stuck in Oakland for a month waiting for a boat to ship out on," I said. "And during that month he vowed to himself he'd stay sober and stay away from whores and tobacco and live the straight and narrow. You know what happened?" I said. "He fought every day, that's what happened. Every day he'd get up in the morning and his knuckles were ripped and shredded and scabbed from the fights, and his face was swollen with knots that looked like potatoes, and sometimes both of his eyes were so beaten up he couldn't see. He couldn't write because he couldn't hold a pencil, but he didn't care. He climbed down the fire escape in the morning and fought all day with anyone he could find, bums and cops and barkeeps and sailors, fought them all and sometimes won but often he didn't. He fought so much he felt like he was drunk even though he wasn't."

"That's it?"

"No," I said. "The more he got beat up, the more he wanted to ship out. But the more he wanted to ship out, the worse he looked, so no one would hire him. Got to where he couldn't control his bowels and shat himself and didn't have anywhere to bathe and so he walked around like that, smelling bad and looking like a demon and trying to fight people, looking so hideous that even when he tried to pick a fight he couldn't get anyone mad at him. Instead they laughed."

"Thanks for cheering me up," Rich said.

The barmaid brought another round of whiskeys and beers and handed them to us. There was no room on the table.

"So what happened?"

"I don't know," I said.

"What's the point, then?"

"The point is this," I said. Rich looked at me and his face was tight with hate. "No one laughed at your father."

I dialed the phone.

"John Poulin," the man said.

"Is this the same John Poulin that worked at McClellan Air Force Base?"

"Who is this?"

"T-Bird Murphy."

"I don't know any T-Bird Murphy."

"When my mother was pregnant, the guy who used to buy her cigarettes drove a T-Bird. When she was pregnant he told her he'd put an abortion pill under his foreskin so they could zap the little zygote if she'd just let him fuck her a few more times. She named me after his car," I said. "T-Bird. Her name was Wilma Ware. Word is she gives great head."

He didn't say anything, and I didn't say anything either. Then he said, "How'd you find me?"

"I called information."

"Information," he said. I heard him blow air through his nose, a nose-scoff.

"I don't want anything from you," I said. "I want to look at you. I'm not a bum."

"No," I said. "You're not a bum," I said. "You're a motherfucker. A fucker of my mother."

A woman's voice in the background asked him who he was talking to.

"Give me your number," he said. "I'll call you back."

I gave him my number. "Oakland?" he said. "Oakland," I said.

I hung up. I got really drunk.

In the morning I felt bad, and when I saw my telephone book open next to the phone, I felt worse. I hadn't slept, but I hadn't been awake either, just drunk awake, afraid I'd be late for work at the FMC plant. It was still dark outside. I knew I'd called people, but I didn't know who I'd called or what I'd said. Drinking and dialing—the only thing scarier than blacking out at a party.

The next morning at work cold white bacon grease hangover sweat leaked from my skin. We'd begun shooting the gunite on the dirt slopes of the pool. Once the mud comes out of the hose, you can't take a break, because if you do, it's hard when you go back to work—if you stop to eat or piss or take a breather, you're only making the day harder on yourself. And the gunite pump, the Thompson Sidewinder diesel hydraulic-piston "shotcrete" system, doesn't get tired like people do. At the end of the day it's still pumping out nine-yard concrete trucks in seventeen minutes just like it did in the morning. It is very unpleasant to be a hungover gunite man.

But you go to work anyway. If you call in sick, you lose your job, because unemployed men hang around the job sites a half hour before work starts, buzzards waiting for you to call in with some lame-ass excuse.

Romero laughed when he saw me at the water jug, and then he smiled a shit-eating grin and kept smiling. He jogged in place. With one hand he dragged the concrete hose along behind the nozzleman. With the other he finished the placed concrete with his fresnoe.

"This job too easy for me," Romero said. "No problema."

I turned to throw up, but held it down. My eyes watered. I looked at Romero.

"Too much tequila for el gringo poquito!"

Usually, when hungover, I'd laugh. But I didn't. I slung the concrete hose over my shoulder and went back to work.

Romero put his hand on my shoulder and turned me toward him. He wasn't smiling anymore. He tilted his head and looked at my eyes. "You okay?" he said. "I'm always okay," I said.

Every day after work I'd go to the First and Last Chance and tank up, spending the money I'd intended to save for college by sucking down Dewar's and J & B, and sometimes, when the bar was empty, I'd drink the fancy single malts. I'd drink there until last call, not even talking to any of the regulars or the old barmaid, looking through my cigarette smoke at the dusty bottles lining the blackened wooden shelf behind the bar. Days at work I felt like shit at first, but gradually I didn't feel bad at all. I felt like I imagined everyone else felt when they heard the concrete pump fire up—spent and numb and just senseless enough to make it through the day shooting mud on the slopes and floor of the massive swimming pool for amphibious tanks.

One day—it was early spring and the pollen was so thick the tables were pale green with dusty scum from blooming flowers—I was sitting at the First and Last Chance and the barmaid shoved a scotch in front of me even though the one I was working on was still full. I gave her the questioning look.

"The guy at the table sent it," she said.

A fag, I thought.

But when I turned around I saw that it was Pop. He was wearing his blue work coveralls, his name, Bud, stitched in red on a white oval patch on one side of his chest, Joe's Tire Service embroidered in thick white letters on the other side. His beard was thatched with grease and his forehead beaded with black oil. His hand was so big I couldn't see the glass he held. A seagull walked in through the open door, then hopped back outside. Somewhere a foghorn sounded, and I heard the warning beeper of a truck backing into place.

He came to the bar and sat next to me.

"Heard you've been spending some time here," he said.

I ordered him a drink. The barmaid poured him a vodka. I hadn't seen Pop drink hard liquor in many years.

"I used to come here sometimes," Pop said. "Not often, but sometimes." He pulled on his drink and knocked back half of it. "Got in a fight with your mother at that table over there." He pointed. "She won."

"It's quiet," I said. "And nobody knows me here."

"You weren't that hard to find," Pop said.

"No one is," I said.

He finished his drink and wagged his heavy finger at the barmaid, and she poured him another.

"I was looking at the chalkboard in the shop and you haven't been in for an oil change in a long time," Pop said. "Air filter's due, need to check the tranny fluid, and your tires need to be rotated."

We sat quiet for a long time. We drank some rounds, and each time when the barmaid brought the rounds and I put my money on the bar, Pop pushed my cash away and shoved his forward. Cool bay air blew in through the door. The floor of the First and Last Chance was made of the waterlogged boards of a whaling ship, and the wind came up from beneath the building, came up off the water and shot right up your pant legs. Sometimes the wind whipped up just right and the bar moaned like the open pipes and conduits of a construction site, a moan that sounded like a thousand laborers stretching their bones in the morning before work.

"Jack London used to come here," I said.

"Jack London Square," Pop said.

"This was his port," I said. "From here he used to ship out. He spent more time at sea than he did here, but this was the place he came back to. He sat at this bar and you know what he did?"

"I'd imagine he drank."

"He drank," I said. "He drank and he chased women and sometimes he caught them. He caught them and he slept with them, and one year when he couldn't get a ship he fostered four children and was in port long enough to see them, each of them, born. And you know what he did? He didn't stick around to be their fathers. What he did was when he started making money as a writer, fifteen years later, he bought each of them a boat big enough to call home and seaworthy enough to remain home. No one knows what happened to those kids, no one knows whether they were boys or girls, and no one even knows their names—hell, Jack London might have made the whole thing up—but I like to think of those kids grown into adults and those adults grown into sailors, and I like to think of them on the water and the winds filling their sails. Sunsets and sunrises and foreign ports and rum and all the spices that go with these things. I like to think of them that way."

Pop nodded. It was late and I was drunk, and the next day was a workday but I knew I wouldn't sleep, not this night and maybe never again. My ears hummed with booze.

"Got a late night call from you about a month ago," Pop said.

I nodded but didn't look at him. I drank. I waved my hand at the barmaid for another drink, and she brought it. I looked at Pop. "What did I say?"

He looked down at his drink, and he said, "I've heard some

Jack London stories at this bar."

He was looking at himself in the tarred mirror behind the bar, and I wondered what he saw, if he saw the man I did, or if he saw someone else. His face was dark with grease from work and I noticed that his hair was not yet gray, but black as oil. "When your mother and I first started dating I used to come here before I went to see her. I'd come here and drink in some courage. Never drank in enough, though. Instead of breaking up with her, I married the bitch."

"Why did you do it?"

"You know, that Jack London," Pop said, "he used to play cards here. Poker, and he always won, or so the story goes. I was sitting here one night, drunk, and this old-timer comes up to me and he says, 'He was my grandfather, you know.' I say, 'Who's that, old-timer?' And he says, 'Mr. London. My grandfather. These are his cards,' the old-timer says, and he pulls a deck of old playing cards from his pocket and shuffles them on the table, riffles them back together and taps them on the table to get them neat again. 'My grandfather,' he says, and I nod. 'He always won when he played cards,' he says. 'Always won because he always told the truth, and no one believed him. When he had a full house or a straight, he told the other players, and they would think he was bluffing, so they'd meet his raises and raise him back. But he never bluffed, that granddad of mine. He never bluffed and he always won. The cards don't lie if the player don't lie.' That's what that old-timer told me about Jack London. I bought him a drink."

Pop had been looking at the mirror the whole time he'd been telling me the story as if he'd been telling it to himself, as if he'd never told it before and wanted to make sure he'd gotten it right.

"You know," Pop said, and he took a deep breath. "Get-back isn't all it's cracked up to be. Sometimes you have to suck it up and be pleasant. Sometimes get-back doesn't pay. Sometimes," he said, "sometimes you regret get-back for the rest of your life."

He drank up, and he left.
But I kept right on a-drinking.

In the morning I called work collect, because that's the way you have to call people from jail.

I called work and told the foreman I couldn't come in because I was locked up on a drunk-and-disorderly charge, that I'd be in the next day, after I made bail. The foreman laughed at me and said, "Welcome to the *real world,* boy. Was a time when you was the only one wasn't a jailbird. Not no more, boy. See you tomorrow!"

I opened a beer and my phone book and I drank and dialed.

"John Poulin."

"It's time you met me."

"Hold on while I switch phones," he said.

I finished my beer and cracked another.

"You there?" he said.

"I'm here."

"It's a little early," he said.

"This afternoon," I said. "At the First and Last Chance Saloon. You know where it is?"

"I know where it is. What time?"

"This afternoon," I said.

"This afternoon?"

"After noon, I'll be there," I said.

"How will I know you?" he said.

"I'll know *you.*"

Before I went into the First and Last Chance Saloon I drove around and looked at the neighborhood. At sunrise I stopped in front of Pete Wang's Market, where I used to steal comic books and baseball cards and candy bars and porno magazines, and I saw Pete standing behind the counter and heard him talking

Chinese with old ladies, and they all laughed as Pete took hanging ducks from the window and chopped off their heads. I parked at the Berkeley Pier next to the great sundial, a gift from Japan after World War II, and I looked over and saw San Francisco rise in black blocks above the shimmer of the orange sunrise skin of the bay, and I remembered when one of my mother's Hell's Angel friends, Fat Fred, gave me a ride out to the end of the pier on his Harley chopper, and we drank Olympia beers together.

One time I got a date with a girl from Piedmont, the rich neighborhood of Oakland, and picked her up at her house and took her to see *Measure for Measure* at the American Conservatory Theater on Geary Street in San Francisco, and we made out on Union Square beneath Christmas-lit trees, and she agreed to come home with me to Oakland to listen to my record collection, and when she saw the trailer next to the Mohawk gas station, she demanded I take her back home. "No one is home," I said. "They're all out of town." We sat in my car next to the fence Pop had made out of 10.00 X-20 retreads. "Take me home," she said. So I took her home. And this morning, with the sun now up, I sat in the same car in front of her house, the house of her family. Someone was stirring behind the pale gauzy curtains.

When I pulled up to the First and Last Chance, the barmaid was nudging the sleepers in the doorway, and when they woke she stretched her arm down toward them and helped them to their feet. She brushed the sawdust off a man's pants, and she straightened another's hair, poking him in the belly and saying something he thought was funny. She opened up and they all went inside.

Inside the bar I watched the flames of the gaslights wobble in their glass chimneys. The stuffed deer's head over the bar was black with soot and cigarette smoke, and its hair had fallen out in patches. Next to the stove in the corner was a clock that hadn't worked since the 1906 earthquake. Someone spilled a drink across the bar, and the old barmaid threw him a rag.

A few hours later Poulin walked in. I'd expected some kind of rush of feelings—hatred, contempt, spite—but instead all that happened was I noticed he looked like me except older and shorter. He stood in the narrow doorway for a moment looking around.

I downed my drink and looked at the barmaid. "Two whiskeys and two beers," I said. She opened the beers and looked at the man coming toward me as she poured the whiskeys. She set the drinks on the bar.

"*Your* two are on me," she said.

Poulin sat on the stool next to mine.

The barmaid pointed at his drinks. "Five bucks," she said.

He paid. He knocked back his whiskey. He looked at me. He said, "Unbelievable."

I nodded, and I lit a cigarette. "I'm supposed to be at work," I said.

"I have a job," he said. "I'm not a bum."

The barmaid brought another round of whiskeys. My eyes were dried up from booze and smoke.

"What kind of work do you do?" he said.

"Gunite," I said. "Concrete."

"Swimming pools?"

"Ditches, mostly," I said. "You?"

"Chrome plating machines," he said. "I repair them." He looked at the old oxygen tank at the end of the bar. "This was Jack London's old joint," he said. He stared at me for an instant. He shook his head. "Unbelievable," he said.

"What's so unbelievable?"

"This," he said.

One of the other drinkers fell off his stool. The other men helped him up, and someone bought him a drink.

"How's your mother?"

"Let's get out of here," I said.

* * *

He followed me to the graveyard in Piedmont, in the hills east of town, where the rich folks lived in fancy houses and Oakland's dead lay buried.

I parked my car in front of the chapel and walked through the wrought-iron gates and up the hill, and I heard Poulin's footsteps crunch in the gravel as he followed me. The sun had begun to sink low over the bay, but the tombstones and sepulchers and vaults as big as trailer homes cast no shadows in the suffused and fog-refracted light. The oncoming night breeze had begun. There were no leaves in the trees to shake.

Low on the second slope of the hilly graveyard, next to the old crypts, I stopped and waited for Poulin. I lit a cigarette. He walked up next to me and stopped, and he lit one too. I pointed down at two markers, flat brick-sized plates of granite. "The great-grandparents Murphy," I said.

I started again up the hill, walking over graves and markers and I noticed how soft the sod was beneath my feet, how it gave beneath each step as if all the caskets had rotted away. I stopped again, this time high on the hill with the new graves, shiny ones without marble angels and nowhere a stone or monument larger than a gasoline pump.

I pointed at the ground again. "Grandfather and Grandmother Murphy," I said. "And their stillborn son. And my brothers, Kent and Clyde. And Mr. Chin. The extra space is for my father," I said, "Pop," I said, "the man who brought me up. He buried Mr. Chin, Grandfather Murphy's Siamese cat, between the markers. He did it late at night when the watchmen weren't looking. Buried Mr. Chin in a Hefty garbage bag."

I lit another cigarette and looked beyond the trees and over the bay. San Francisco had disappeared behind the canopy of fog, and I could see the fog coming across the water, coming on wide and thorough and complete, graying the water beneath and spreading wider as it came. Soon it would reach the First and Last Chance, and then it would smother the city of Oakland and all the people who lived and worked there. And after that it would come upon us, Poulin and me, and it would come upon too all the corpses who lay stone dead and rotted in the graveyard beneath our feet. It was a fog that came every day this time of year, and there was nothing special about it, or about the people who lived and died beneath it. It was as common as East Bay grease.

Before Mr. Gonzalez died, he told a Jack London story.

He told it one night after work, Rich not yet changed out of his Caterpillar coveralls, and me dusty with concrete. Mr. Gonzalez was still in his Del Monte greens, and he was red and brown with tomato paste. We were all pretty hammered, and for some reason the old barmaid had done up her hair in a ragged gray bun. She wore a pencil over one ear and a cigarette over the other. Mr. Gonzalez was mescal-stoned, his eyes dilated, his hands steady.

"My grandfather," he said, and then he looked at Rich, "your great-grandfather, Ricardo, worked for Senor Jack. Worked as a butcher on El Rancho Bonito, Jack London's 'Beautiful Ranch.' Grandfather Gonzalez one time drank tequila with Senor Jack in the kitchen. He was slick with the blood of a hog, a fat one that had been hanging upside down by its tied hooves and curing for two days in the barn, blood draining into a tin bucket on the ground—blood is good for many things, and not to be wasted—Grandfather Gonzalez's apron stiff and brown and barnyard hay-dust clinging. He used to tell the story of Jack London drinking tequila every Cinco de Mayo."

"I never met the man," Rich said.

"He died very young," Mr. Gonzalez said. "He had no joy in his life."

"What did he say about Jack London?" I said.

"He had no joy in his life, but Cinco de Mayo he would tell the story of Senor Jack," Mr. Gonzalez said. "'Senor Jack was not the good man for tequila, Senor Jack,' he would say. He'd be saying this with a bottle in his hand, and then he'd tip that bottle and drink, and you could see the bubbles pop inside the bottle as the tequila went down. 'No, Senor Jack and tequila were not friendly brothers. Because although liquor is a serum of truth, there are different truths. Sometimes liquor frees the truth of good thinking, and sometimes it lets unloosed the truth of bad thinking. For Senor London, tequila unloosed very bad truth.'"

Mr. Gonzalez pulled his flask of mescal from his pocket and refilled his drink, and he drank. His eyes shone with memory. He might have been faking it, but his voice sounded different. It sounded older. It sounded more Mexican.

"Senor Jack said, and he's looking at my clothes and pointing with his finger, 'Bring me the blood.' 'The blood?' I say. 'The blood of the pig,' he say. 'For what?' I tell him. 'For me,' he say. 'It's mine.' So I bring him the blood. And when I bring the blood, he picks up the pail and the pail is not nice and the blood is not like blood but like wet earth soaked with blood, brown like beans and curdled like the butter. 'Tequila,' says Senor Jack. 'All the tequila we've got, the cabron!' So I bring the tequila, and six bottles I bring. 'Pour!' he says, and so I pour, and when I pour Senor Jack mixes with the wood spoon. He's making the drink of the devil, and I'm pouring the devil's tequila."

Mr. Gonzalez looked at us. He smiled. Rich tossed back his drink. Someone walked into the bar, and I noticed that the old wooden door did not creak.

"The drink is splashing," Mr. Gonzalez said, and he kept smiling. "The drink is splashing so hard he is mixing, splashing on our clothes and shoes and sometimes on our faces too. Our hands are red with tequila and the blood of pig. I know what is coming next, and when it comes, I drink. I drink for my soul, I drink for my pleasure, I drink because I am alive and the hog is not. Senor Jack drinks from the pail and it runs down his chin like the food of a baby. But the blood and tequila do not run down my chin and neck. I spill no blood when I drink."

***

In my station wagon I drove toward the Mohawk station where I knew I'd find Pop still working even though the sun had gone down and he should have been already in his trailer next door drinking a day's end Budweiser and eating steak cooked medium rare. I'd shaken hands with Poulin when we said goodbye, and his hand, the hand of the man who'd fathered me, was the hand of a man I did not know, a doughy hand, weak and clean and alien. And when I got to the shop I did find Pop working, found him beating truck tires. Three Yandell Trucking rigs had pulled in and, all together, needed eight tires either patched or replaced.

"Need a hand?" I said.

"Make yourself useful," Pop said.

I pulled a crowbar and a hydraulic hand-jack and a 4x4 from the service truck and, on my back, crawled beneath one of the rigs. I set the jack on top of a 4-by and then screwed the head of the jack up against the A-frame. I tightened the wing nut at the base of the jack, and then slid the end of the crowbar into the sleeve of the jack, and I pumped the lever until the front end of the Peterbilt lifted off the ground. I snapped an air hammer onto a hose and rattled the lug nuts off the chrome wheel. After I jimmied the wheel off the lug nuts, I screwed the core out of the air valve and listened to the tube whistle down, shrinking and shriveling, the stale rubbered smell of tire air blowing into my face. When the air stopped, I got a ten-pound sledge from the service truck's side panel and stood atop the tire, straddling it, my feet on the rubber sidewalls, and I lifted the sledge over my shoulder and guided the head down onto the split-ring that held the rim in place. It took me four blows, and when the ring broke free from the rim, I used the crowbar as a wedge to pop the ring off and then set the ring, four feet wide, on the asphalt. Then I stood atop the tire again and again beat down with the sledgehammer, this time to break the rubber free from the rim. I swung down on the rubber just above the rim. Nothing—so I moved my feet to the right and lifted the hammer and swung down again, and I kept circling the tire, swinging down, moving, swinging down, until finally the seal between rubber and metal broke, and the tire broke down, and I hoisted it up against my thighs and chest and with the crowbar leaned over the tread and jimmied the immense rim out, working the bar between the iron and the rubber edge until the rim came loose, and I jumped backward so the iron would not break my shins or crush my feet. I pried the flap from inside the tire, then pulled out the deflated tube and aired it up to find the leak. It was a small hole, but it whistled loud enough that I didn't have to dunk the tube in the water tank. I marked the hole with a yellow grease-crayon.

I looked over at Pop. His back was to me, and his sledge hoisted over his shoulder. When he swung the hammer down, its arc flickered in the fluorescent lighting from the service-station canopy above.

I knew it was going to be a long night. There were still six more tires to bust. And then we'd have to hammer them all together again. But I also knew that when I got home—late—and to bed, I'd sleep well, knowing I'd done an honest day's work.

Photo credit: Turner Miles Anthony Williamson

Eric Miles Williamson was raised in Oakland, California, by Kent Williamson, who adopted him. He was a professional trumpet player, then became a construction worker, then went to college and became a writer. He is now raising his two sons in deep South Texas, ten miles from the Rio Grande River and the Border Wall. Down & Out Books will be publishing his extensive letters and journals.

On the following pages are a few more great titles from the Down & Out Books publishing family.

For a complete list of books and to sign up for our newsletter, go to DownAndOutBooks.com.

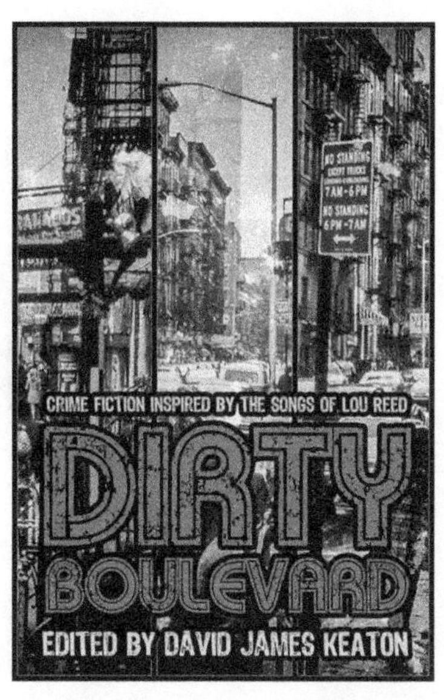

Dirty Boulevard
Crime Fiction Inspired by the Songs of Lou Reed
David James Keaton, Editor

Down & Out Books
September 2018
978-1-948235-49-5

Inspired by the outcasts, outlaws, and other outré inhabitants of rock legend Lou Reed's songbook, *Dirty Boulevard* traffics in crime fiction that's sometimes velvety and sometimes vicious, but always, absolutely, rock & roll.

Inside, you'll find stories from the fire escapes to the underground, stories filled with metal machine music, stories for gender-bending, rule-breaking, mind-blasting midnight revelries and drunken, dangerous, dark nights of the heart.

The One That Got Away
Joe Clifford

Down & Out Books
December 2018
978-1-948235-42-6

In the early 2000s, a string of abductions rocked the small upstate town of Reine, New York. Only one girl survived: Alex Salerno. The killer was sent away. Life returned to normal. No more girls would have to die.

Until another one did...

Welcome to Holyhell
Math Bird

All Due Respect, an imprint of
Down & Out Books
October 2018
978-1-948235-34-1

Finding that briefcase full of cash in the scorching summer of 1976 seemed the answer to all young Jay Ellis's prayers. But he didn't bargain for the harsh truths to follow: greed, cruelty, murder and deceit, the games people play, and how kindness lurks in the most unexpected places.

Set in the borderlands of northeast Wales, *Welcome to Holyhell* is a coming-of-age crime, noir novel.

A Brutal Bunch of Heartbroken Saps
A Love & Bullets Hookup
Nick Kolakowski

Shotgun Honey, an imprint of
Down & Out Books
978-1-943402-81-6

Bill is a hustler's hustler with a taste for the high life...who suddenly grows a conscience. However, living the clean life takes a whole lot of money, and so Bill decides to steal a fortune from his employer before skipping town.

Pursued by crooked cops, dimwitted bouncers, and a wisecracking assassin, Bill will need to be a quick study in the way of the gun if he wants to survive his own getaway. Who knew that an honest attempt at redemption could rack up a body count like this?